AND NOW THERE'S ZELDA...

CAROLYN CLARKE

Black Rose Writing | Texas

ISBN: 978-1-68513-411-2
PUBLISHED BY BLACK ROSE WRITING
www.blackrosewriting.com

Printed in the United States of America
Suggested Retail Price (SRP) $20.95

And Now There's Zelda is printed in Sabon Lt Std

*As a planet-friendly publisher, Black Rose Writing does its best to eliminate unnecessary waste to reduce paper usage and energy costs, while never compromising the reading experience. As a result, the final word count vs. page count may not meet common expectations.

To Tony and the girls.
As always, thank you for your patience, encouragement and support.

PRAISE FOR
AND NOW THERE'S ZELDA ...

'Fans of *Little Fires Everywhere* by Celeste Ng and *The Joy Luck Club* by Amy Tan will adore Clarke's novel. It is filled with heart and drama.'
- ***The Book Commentary***

'A funny, uplifting story about one woman's lesson in letting go- even though this means she has to make peace with her mother-in-law AND a potential daughter-in-law who just might be her sweet son's biggest mistake.'
-Maddie Dawson, Washington Post bestselling author of *Matchmaking for Beginners*

'A roller coaster ride of three generations finding their place in the world, laced with acute observations, great descriptions and a satisfying denouement.'
-Maddie Please, bestselling author of *The Old Ducks' Club*

'*And Now There's Zelda* is a funny and warm-hearted take on contemporary life for the contemporary woman.'
-Cary J Hansson, bestselling author of *The Midlife Trilogy*

'There were plenty of heart-warming scenes that made this a feel-good read.'
-***Readers' Favorite (5 star review)***

A special thank you to my dearest family, friends and colleagues who encouraged me to write this second book. I also owe an enormous debt of gratitude to those who gave me constructive comments and suggestions on one or more chapters including Anthony Teekasingh, Karen Samson, Marcella Corroeli Jager, Mihaela Axenti, Ana Perez, Peri Flores and Katharen Martin.

AND NOW
THERE'S
ZELDA...

1 – Sign of the Times

I'm not the type to have a *Life is Good* bumper sticker with a cheesy grin plastered on the back of my car, but I have to admit, life *is* pretty good. Even in the face of freezing temperatures, mild dehydration, and endless traffic on a Saturday afternoon, I felt optimistic.

I was bubbling with excitement after another successful client meeting. It'd been four and a half years, and the feeling of accomplishment from a business collaboration still rushes through me. Today was supposed to be an initial meeting, but unexpectedly, it transformed into a contract-signing bonanza. Instead of staging *one* house, we'd be staging a whopping *seven* that Better Homes Real Estate was putting on the market.

It's hard to believe that *I*, Allison Montgomery, went from being a bored and frustrated kindergarten teacher to a successful home staging business owner. It's even harder to believe that my mother-in-law, Margaret, the very person who'd been a major source of frustration for me and my marriage since the day we met, is the same person who provided the financial backing and the encouragement and the emotional support that allowed me to launch and grow my business. I couldn't wait to get home to tell her about this latest success. Bizarre would be an understatement.

Clearly, aside from Margaret, and me for toughening up and gaining clarity and confidence, my mother, Rosemary, deserves a share of the credit. She's been my guru when it comes to being a better person. She's been my guru to learning to 'read the signs' too. When George, my father-in-law, died five years ago, and all hell broke loose with Margaret, it was kindness and patience, and an openness to change that made the difference. Don't get me wrong. Life isn't perfect. Mean people still suck. Running a business is no cakewalk. And as for Margaret? Well, she can still be at times...*well*, Margaret. But things have gotten better. Next level, actually.

Traffic started moving again and the next song on my playlist, Taylor Swift's *Shake It Off*, started playing. I sang my Grammy worthy duet with her as loud as humanly possible, swaying side to side and tapping my thumbs on the steering wheel. In the car beside me, a little boy was pointing in my direction and laughing. I waved, then laughed right back.

Keeping my eyes on the road, I was suddenly brought back to reality. A big, orange, diamond-shaped sign that read **CAUTION: ROUGH ROAD AHEAD** jumped out at me. I'd seen this sign before. But this time, it sent a chill down my spine. Not because I was going faster than I should have been. And not because I had to grip the steering wheel tightly to maintain control of my speed. This time, it felt like this message or sign or whatever you want to call it, was meant for me.

The suspension groaned under the weight of the car. I could feel the wheels bouncing over every little bump and piece of loose rock. It was like driving on an old cobblestone street, except this one had no historic charm. *Pay attention to the signs the Universe sends you, Allie. They're important*, I heard my mother's voice echoing in my ears. I followed the cars ahead around the neon orange traffic cones. Moments later, I cleared the construction zone, returning to safer ground. *Shake it off, shake it off...* advised Taylor. When I reached Cherry Blossom Street, I picked up the pace. I passed by the Montessori school and my eyes were drawn to the sign out front. **IN A WORLD WHERE YOU CAN BE ANYTHING, BE**

KIND. I felt the shiver once more. But…*why?!* I *am* kind to everyone. To my husband, Hank. To the kids. To my mother *and* Hank's mother. To my friends, my team…*I even donate blood for God's sake!*

I pulled into our driveway, turned off the car, then took several deep breaths. *What the hell just happened?* I tried 'shaking off' the strangeness of the drive home. And it was *strange*. My life *is* good. And everything seems fine. So why did I have this ominous feeling inside me?

I stepped into our redecorated foyer and Bailey, our five-year-old monster labradoodle, greeted me with his slobbery kisses. He impressed me with his sixth sense. Somehow, he could tell we were almost home before we turned onto our street. I bent down carefully to avoid twisting my hip as he wiggled against my knees, looking for extra belly rubs. When I straightened to my full length, I detected the rich and savory smell of seared meat. *Strange.* This aroma of fresh thyme and savory garlic could only mean one thing. Margaret was making dinner. But Saturday night is pizza night. *Caution: Rough Road Ahead?*

Breathe, Allie. Breathe. Did I get the days mixed up? No. It was Saturday. But then again, maybe Margaret's the one who scrambled up the calendar. *Let it go, Allie. She lives in your basement—a luxurious one, granted, but it's still a basement.* I reminded myself to *be kind,* then gave myself a mental pat on the back for choosing the right path before shimmying off my heavy wool coat.

"You don't have to type in a passcode now. Just hold it up to your face and it'll unlock," I heard Hank say when I got into the kitchen. I couldn't hide my surprise at seeing him pointing what looked like a brand-new phone at Margaret's face.

I set my keys on the counter. "You bought your mom an iPhone?" I said, my brows raised high. She once referred to them as 'soul suckers', but now it seemed her Facebook addiction had brought her over to the dark side.

3

Margaret sniffed primly, adopting a look I doubt anyone could replicate as her facial unlock. "Cameron finally convinced me. He said *Sara*—"

"Siri," Hank corrected.

"*Siri* can help me with anything I don't know how to work," Margaret said, then positioned her face in front of her phone again.

"Mom, you don't have to move your head in circles every time…it can tell who you are if you just look at it normally."

I walked over to Hank, kissed the top of his growing bald spot, then eased around the table to sit across from Margaret, all while keeping one hand on Hank's shoulder. Letting out a deep breath, I relaxed into the chair.

It was around four and a half years ago that things shifted between Margaret and me. Good things can happen when you stop resisting and let go because you're 1) tired of fighting for control, 2) overwhelmed by fear and anxiety, and 3) out of options and have no other choice. That's what led to Margaret and me agreeing she would sell her condo, move into our basement, and finance my new start.

Of course, Margaret's financial backing came with strings attached, or more like a web I felt I'd walked into face-first. At the beginning of it all, I wasn't happy. But Margaret was because she was living with us. I wasn't happy in the months that followed either, but after crying and complaining about what a terrible mistake I might've made during several wine nights with my best friend and trouble-shooter, Val, we settled on what became the perfect role for Margaret in the business—her sharp tongue and Pitbull-like attitude come in handy when dealing with difficult clients and vendors. As for living with us, she has her own entrance to the basement and certain boundaries, like *not* coming upstairs to clean or make dinner unannounced, unless I needed help. Going from an active 'cold war' to what could almost be called a friendship seemed like nothing short of a miracle.

Margaret looked up from her phone while her index finger continued tapping on the screen. Before I could tell her the good news, she asked, "How did it go with Better Homes?"

"Good! They signed up today." I grinned, leaning forward on my elbows. "And with *seven* houses." I grinned again.

"*Oh*, Al, that's great!" Hank reached over and squeezed my hand.

Margaret smiled, putting down her phone. "I never had any doubt," she said. From there, she was all business, pushing for the particulars of the account. Who knew she'd be so good at this? Strictly from a business standpoint, it was nice having her invested in this as much as I was.

"They'll double check the dates for the first showings and get back to us," I assured her.

Looking satisfied, Margaret nodded and, with her unsteady hand, reached for her phone and began tapping away again. Without looking up, she asked, "Did you give them your personal number?"

I shook my head while holding up my hands, scrunching up my nose. "Yeah, *I know*. But I just can't have them go through Bea." Bea, who took the place of our daughter Samantha who was off gallivanting across Europe and quite possibly changing her entire life trajectory, was our office assistant. Although Bea is sweet, her constant mistakes and missed deadlines had caused a lot of aggravation.

"What's the point of paying her if you won't let her assist?" Margaret leveled me with her own look of impatience, but I just shrugged. I refused to concede her perfectly good point.

"She'll be fine," I said. *I'll do everything in my power to make it so.* Slumping back into my chair, I changed the subject. "I miss Samantha—"

"Oh, speaking of Sam," Hank interjected, bolting upright in his chair, "she called earlier and said she might not be back for Florida."

I bolted upright too. "*WHAT?!*"

Hank took a long, deep breath. "Apparently, she got a once-in-a-lifetime job opportunity and just can't say no. It sounds like it might be worthwhile—"

"But what about my mother's—"

"She said she called her and it's completely—"

"But it's her grandmother's seventy-fifth birthday *and* our family trip." I shook my head in disappointment. It was just like Samantha to be selfish in an unhealthy way.

Hank chuckled ahead of answering. "Allie, you know your mother would want her to grab onto any opportunity…and honestly, I can't say I disagree."

"I know, *I know*," I said.

Hank ran his hand through his hair, taking another deep breath. He looked over at Margaret, then back to me. Clearly, there was more bad news coming.

"What is it?" I asked, cautiously.

He was about to say something but closed his mouth. His hesitation was palpable, which made it hard for me to keep from narrowing my eyes at him. He took another deep breath, then cleared his throat. "Erm, it's looking less likely that I'm going to be able to make it too because of the merger," he said and then tacked on, "they'll need me here to finalize the deal, so…"

"Oh, Hank, *really?!*" I moved toward the refrigerator, my frustration rising. Bailey followed behind me, likely wanting dinner. I turned back from the fridge door, his eyes were wide and filled with hope. I inhaled deeply, suppressing my emotions, and trying to speak without bitterness. "I understand, but it's just… without Sam…without you—this whole trip feels like it's falling apart."

Margaret seemed to have lost all interest in her phone, looking over her glasses at us.

Hank walked over to me and gently said, "I *know*, Allie, but it's not set in stone yet."

I nodded, my gaze fixed blankly over his shoulder when he enveloped me in his arms. He smelled of Margaret's cooking. A thought then struck me. "Wait a minute. Why is the dining room table set for dinner?" I pulled back, casting a questioning look at Hank, and my attention shifted to the kitchen table, where Margaret's new phone box and the remnants of its wrapping were scattered.

"*Oh!*" Margaret declared, clapping her hands. "That's right, you don't know. Cam's back." She heaved herself to her feet, then bounced over to the stove. "I made his favorite dinner...with all the fixings," she added before smiling proudly.

With my disappointment temporarily swept away by a sudden rush of excitement, I joyfully protested, "Why didn't you tell me sooner...*oh*, I bet he brought a ton of dirty laundry with him." I rushed to the foot of the stairs and called up to him, "*CAM?!*"

"Sorry, Allie," I heard Margaret's voice behind me. "He's not here yet. But he is in town and it's almost dinner time. So, he should be here soon."

My head reared back slightly. "*Oh.*" I lifted my foot off the bottom stair and made my way back to the kitchen. I wrestled my phone out of my back pocket. "Let's check his ETA," I said, my grin still stretching from ear to ear. It'd been almost six weeks since I saw his face. And communicating through one-or two-line texts was getting tiring. Unlike his sister, Cameron wasn't into Zoom or much into FaceTime. It was like having someone just show up at your house totally unannounced, he'd say. *Well, too bad.*

Cameron answered after the first ring. "*Hey, Mom.*"

"Hey, sweetie," I responded, excitedly, too excitedly, pacing back and forth with a hungry Bailey trailing behind me. "Almost here?"

"*Um, no,*" he said slowly. "*I wasn't planning on coming home until later tonight—why?*"

I moved into the dining room and lowered my voice. "Oh, Cam. Your grandma made roast beef for you. Didn't you tell her you weren't coming for dinner?"

"*I'm sorry,*" he said. "*I told her I was coming home but I didn't say I'd be back for dinner.*"

"Is there any chance you can be here? She went through all this trouble," I said, holding my phone tighter up against my ear. I was fully aware that it wasn't an issue for Margaret. Cooking was one of her greatest hobbies. Without sounding too desperate, I added, "You could always go back out after..." Holding my breath, I waited for his response. *What can I say? I missed the kid!*

"*No...um...it's just that...maybe...,*" he paused, then I heard a brief scraping sound followed by his voice heavily muffled, as if he were speaking to someone else. "*Okay, yeah. Be there soon,*" he finally said.

One of the best things about having Cameron go off to college is seeing his sweet face when he comes home. Strutting back into the kitchen and smiling broadly, I announced, "Cam's on his way!"

After what seemed like an eternity, Bailey, now with a full belly, suddenly jumped out of his bed and raced to the front door. Several minutes and a substantial amount of enthusiastic whimpering later, Cameron finally called out from the foyer. "I'm home!"

"We're in the kitchen!" I called back, pushing myself away from the table and rushing to the door. A shooting pain went down my leg. "Dinner's running a bit—" The words died in my throat when I saw Cameron standing next to a strange looking girl as they took off their coats. Only, he did not look like my baby. He looked like an adult—clean-shaven with a fresh haircut, pressed pants, and a collared shirt. And who was this girl, looking equally adult-like in a black, skin-tight dress with a neon pink side braid in her dirty blond hair and several tattoos on her arm that looked like they'd been done by a six-year-old?

Cameron looked up just as Margaret and Hank arrived. He put his hand on the girl's shoulder, cleared his throat, and said with cautious excitement, "Mom, Dad, Grandma…this is Zelda…my fiancé!"

What the hell?!

I tried my best to keep my jaw from hitting the floor. My mother's warning to pay attention to the 'signs' echoed loudly in my head and the words from that gigantic, orange, diamond-shaped construction sign flashed before my eyes. **CAUTION: ROUGH ROAD AHEAD.**

2 – AND NOW THERE'S...*ZELDA?*

It was quiet. Quiet enough you could hear a pin drop. Well, you could have, if it weren't for the ridiculously loud ticking of Margaret's ugly old grandfather clock which had somehow ended up becoming a permanent fixture at the far side of our living room.

Tick.

Tick.

Tick.

Wait...did he say her name was Zelda?

I forced myself to breathe, looking at Cameron. He was beaming with nervous excitement. He searched our faces, reading our reactions with hope and anticipation. I couldn't think. All I could do was stand there, staring, in stunned silence.

Tick.

Tick.

Tick.

Zelda's gaze flitted from face to face. She had one hand held onto Cameron's arm and the other one clutched tightly onto her pink plaid coat. Margaret tilted her head, looking mildly confused. Zelda didn't have the same youthful, nervous energy that Cameron did. I certainly didn't know her, but she seemed tired and unphased by the fact she was meeting her potential 'in-laws' for the first time. She looked a bit dead inside and that expression remained in place as I tried, instinctively, to put on a welcoming smile, hoping Hank would break the silence soon. He couldn't possibly be expecting me to take the lead here.

Tick.

Tick.

Tick.

"Ah, wow! *Oh*, my God, Zelda, welcome!" Hank declared, breaking the awkward silence. He hurriedly moved forward to envelope her in a warm, welcoming embrace. He then turned to Cameron and gave him a big, back-slapping, bear hug. Sometimes, Hank's calm, cool, easy-going nature irritates me. But right now, it was a godsend.

Meanwhile, Margaret and I were left to gather our wits. Her eyes narrowed and then she gave me a deliberate and meaningful look. To my great surprise, she stepped forward. She switched spots with Hank, giving Zelda a hug. "Welcome, Zelda," she said with a great big smile, "it's so nice to meet you!" I almost laughed. That was not the greeting I got when Hank first brought me home to meet George and Margaret. But then again, this wasn't Margaret's first rodeo. The look she just gave me meant she had something more to say on the subject.

Having recovered somewhat, I moved forward and greeted Zelda with a big smile and friendly hug too. "Of course, Zelda, welcome!" I said, trying hard to mask my inner shock with a masterful display of warmth.

"Thank you, Mrs. Montgomery," she said, blushing visibly. "Cam has told me so much about you!"

I gave her the very best smile I could muster up, then turned my attention to Cameron. He kissed his grandmother, still beaming. It'd been a while since I'd seen him looking happy. Holding up my arms, I pulled him in for a hug, squeezing him hard.

"Mom—"

"It's so good to have you home," I said, pulling back and holding his shoulders in my hands. I scanned his face and squeezed his arms. I stepped further back to look fully at him. When I did, my stomach tightened with a thin thread of dread. My eyes caught sight of not only a skull tattoo on Zelda's wrist, but a shiny black ring on the fourth finger of her left hand.

This *cannot* be happening. Not again.

A rush of emotions filled me. Less than a year ago, Cameron's heart was shattered. He had been manipulated by a mean, selfish girl named Penny. The agony of that experience spiraled into a profound depression. It beat the spirits out of him so bad, it robbed him of his motivation to do anything after that, including school.

Cameron's brightness dimmed when he saw me staring blankly at him. It lasted only a moment, but his perceptive nature meant he must have sensed that this announcement would, at the very least, come as a surprise.

Breathe, Allie.

I smiled big and bright. "C'mon, let's get this dinner going." Stepping between him and Zelda, I gave him a slight shove toward the dining room. "Margaret?" I jerked my head toward the kitchen, thinking nothing of my hurried walk, after motioning for Hank to go with them.

"Hang up your coats, you two, and then go sit down," I heard Margaret say while she followed in my wake.

It took everything I had not to collapse in a heap right then and there. I barely managed to wait until they were out of earshot before I grabbed Margaret's arm and silently mouthed, "What the...?"

She gave me a patient shake of her head. "Easy...dinner first," she mouthed back, and then spun around to check on the roast.

Easy? How could she be so calm?

Margaret brought the food and warmed plates to the dining room table. I forced a smile and tried to sound happy, bringing out my favorite Chardonnay. Nothing like good wine to help stabilize the mood.

I smiled at Cameron, then leaned across the table to pour some for Zelda. However, before I could begin, she covered her glass with her hand, cleared her throat, and with an uncomfortable half-smile, she said, "None for me." There was a pause. "Thank you."

Unsure if it was my choice of wine, I looked at the bottle, then back at Zelda. "Oh, are you allergic?" I asked her, trying not to sound offended.

"No, no," she replied. She spoke quickly. "I'm just not much of a drinker."

"Oh?" I mumbled.

Okay, I get it, but unless you have allergies, or religious restrictions, or are in recovery, or have a medical condition, or... Who refuses a glass of wine? The very act of sitting down at a table and having a drink for the very first time with your fiancé's family is akin to declaring, *I'm someone you can trust.* But refusing, that's like showing up to a potluck without a dish—technically allowable, yes, but who would do that?

Wait, *a medical condition?* Like pregnancy?

Red flag no. 1!

Avoiding Cameron's hard stare, I poured wine into my glass—a heavy pour, yes, but I was going to need it to get through tonight—and sat down next to Hank, ignoring his questioning and slightly amused look.

When everyone had their food, Hank raised his glass, and with a big smile said, "Cam, it's good to have you home. Zelda, welcome, we're so glad to have you here with us. Allie, congrats on the new client and Mom, congrats on the new phone. Cheers, everyone!" We all raised our glasses, said 'cheers', and took a sip of wine. Except for Zelda, of course, who sipped on water. Didn't she know toasting with water meant you wished bad luck or even death on your host?

Everyone dug in except for me. I drank more of my wine and continued contemplating Zelda's refusal. *Health nut?* Maybe she's one of those self-righteous sorts, I convinced myself. Part of me plunged into the horrors of her possibly being pregnant.

"So, Zelda, huh?" Hank said. "I hope you don't mind my saying, but that's an interesting name."

"Yes, it's from the 'Legend of Zelda' video game. It's a popular series by Nintendo," she answered. "My father was a huge gamer." She glanced at Cameron and then back at Hank. "*Zelda* is my middle name but it's what I've always been called. I guess you could say I'm a living testament to the inherent risks associated with letting gamers name their children," she said, her face contorting.

Inherent risks associated with... Who even speaks like that? And yeah, we know about 'Legend of Zelda'. Cameron was obsessed with that game when he was younger. I vividly recall him sinking hours into that stupid fantasy world. He was completely enthralled by this 'Princess Zelda'. He said he liked her because she was smart, tough, and fearless. We poured a small fortune into these games over the years—birthdays, graduation, Christmas, you name it. Lo and behold, it seemed he'd walked in with his very own living, breathing 'Princess Zelda'.

"Oh, wow," Hank said. "I completely forgot about that game. Yeah, it was Cam's favorite."

I took another long sip and laughed politely. Okay, maybe it was a little *too* loud and sounded a little *too* forced, but enough of the small talk. I needed answers.

"So..." I said as everyone's forks clanked lightly against their plates, fully intending to break the tension—or add to it, depending on how this conversation was going to go, "how did the two of you meet?"

Cameron looked at Zelda with adoring, puppy dog eyes and then turned back to me saying proudly, "We met at a pub near school—"

"At a pub?" I interrupted. *She doesn't drink but hangs out in pubs?*

"Yeah," he said, "it was back in November. I was sitting at a table working on a paper, and Zelda came right over and just sat down and started talking to me," he boasted, affectionately leaning his head on her shoulder for a quick second before going on. "I wish I could say it's because she saw me from across the room and couldn't resist, but she was trying to get away from these old guys. Anyways—"

"Anyway," I said, absentmindedly topping up my wine glass.

Cameron gave me a confused look and I immediately regretted the grammar lesson. I was right, but it *is* a terrible habit.

"*Anyway*," he said, with a nod in my direction, "we just started talking and practically fell in love on the spot. I mean, it was like fate or something."

Zelda looked at Cameron and smiled, her face turning as pink as the braid in her hair.

I rubbed my lips together. So, I thought, *she* went after *him*.

Red flag no. 2.

"That's very sweet, my dear," Margaret said warmly while smiling at Cameron and picking up a tiny piece of potato that had the temerity to slip off her plate and land on the table.

Hank continued smiling, clearly trying to avoid what he seemed to think was becoming an awkward conversation. "So, what are you studying, Zelda?" he asked.

She took an extra long drink of water, prompting Cameron to quickly jump in. "Well, she was studying psychology, but is just taking a bit of a break," he said.

And now, a dropout?

Red flag no.3.

It was getting harder and harder for me to keep calm. My heart was breaking. A girlfriend was one thing, but a *fiancé*? Especially some girl who went hunting for guys in a college pub when she didn't even finish school herself?

"*Oh?*" Hank said between chews. His face was a mix of compassion and childlike wonder.

"So, are you working?" I asked pointedly, then turned my gaze back to Zelda.

Again, Cameron jumped in. "Yeah, she just needed some time off. It happens," he said with the tiniest little shrug. "She's working at the seniors' place over on Baxter during the day and then evenings and weekends at Harpers. It's kind of funny we met at school even though we both grew up here."

Funny? Not funny.

"Well, good for you," Margaret said with crinkled eyes and a genuine smile.

Good for you? My temperature started to rise, and I was this close to storming off upstairs. Okay, yeah, so she has a job. Well, okay, two. But what happened to the Margaret who made my life a living hell for decades? This girl is avoiding eye contact *and* making Cameron do all the talking. What *is* she trying to hide?

Red flags no.4 and 5, in my book.

I turned away from Cameron and looked directly at Zelda. "Well, that certainly is quite a coincidence. So, are you planning on going back to school?"

"Yes, eventually," she answered softly, shifting uncomfortably in her chair. She quickly added, "I'm just not sure when." And then she broke eye contact again.

I gave her a brittle smile, sticking my fork into a piece of beef with more force than needed. Clearly, this girl had no ambition of her own.

Red flag no. 6.

I downed the last of my wine and sat back with my arms folded tightly against my chest while taking a long, hard look at this 'Princess Zelda'. What exactly was it that I was supposed to like about this girl?

Reading my rapidly darkening mood, Hank cleared his throat and pulled everyone's attention to him. "Hey Cam, did you hear Sam's news?" he said, secretly shooting me a slightly disapproving look.

"Sort of," he answered. "She's going to be volunteering or something, right?"

"No, it's actually a job opportunity," Hank confirmed, "and it sounds like a good one. But it does mean she won't be coming to Florida with us."

"Oh, wow," Cameron said, "that's too bad. But I guess when something good comes along, you gotta grab it with both hands, right?"

"She's still young, Cam," I snapped. "It's not as if she'll never have another opportunity. There *is* something to be said for being selective, you know."

Either he didn't get my hint, or he decided to ignore it because he just leaned over to Zelda and said, "It's my grandma's 75th birthday and we're all supposed to be going down to Florida to help her celebrate."

Zelda nodded her head sympathetically and just as quietly said to Cameron, "It's really warm down there this time of the year, isn't it?"

"Still winter, but it's practically tropical compared to here," he answered while rubbing his hand over his head.

Just then, the shrill ring of Hank's phone cut in. He gave me a slightly concerned look and then excused himself to take the call in the kitchen.

Cameron and Zelda continued their private conversation while Margaret sat picking at her salad and watching them with a speculative look. I refilled my water glass and sat there, growing increasingly impatient while waiting for Hank to return.

"Have you ever been to Florida, Zelda?" I asked, doing my best to strike up a casual conversation. I suppose it was a step above discussing the weather, but right now, I was more interested in the look Hank had given me. It was impossible to decipher.

Zelda's dark-painted lips were about to part when Hank re-entered the room. "Sorry, that was Stan," he said, initially avoiding eye contact with me before sitting down. He knew how I felt about his skewed work-life balance, and it looked like he was about to drop a bombshell. *This was not going to be good.* He took off his silver-rimmed glasses and rubbed his eyes. When he finally looked at me after putting them back on, he said, "It's confirmed. I can't make the trip either."

Boom!

Flooded with disappointment, I took another big gulp of water and then tried my best not to set the glass down too hard against the table.

"We're right in the middle of this merger, and if it goes well, I could end up running the whole division. I need to handle this stage personally," he explained to Cameron, apologetically but also with a certain sense of pride. He reached over and put his hand on mine. "I'm sorry, Al. I know you were looking forward to this being a family trip."

Margaret sighed a heavy sigh for all of us to hear. "Oh, Henry. You need to give yourself a good week off, don't you think?"

Hank nodded in agreement, but I knew he was looking forward to the prospect of moving up the company ladder. Still, he needed the downtime. We all did. I tried to keep the wobble out of my voice as adrenaline coursed through my veins. "I'm not the only one looking forward to it, Hank. You know my mother is, too. We've already paid for everything, and now you and Sam are having to bail—"

"I'm not bailing—"

"Zelda can come!" Cameron jumped in.

Again, there was that gigantic, orange, diamond-shaped construction sign flashing before my eyes. **CAUTION: ROUGH ROAD AHEAD.**

All thoughts of the lecture I was about to give Hank on the importance of work-life balance and being there for his family flew out of my mind. I whipped my head toward Cameron, then back at Zelda, holding my breath. *No. You can't. Absolutely not. Say no!*

"I…" She hesitated, looking at Cameron's encouraging and hopeful face. "I don't want to impose, and I'd need to check with work." Her glance at me was quick.

That wasn't a *no*. I took a breath, fully prepared to be as *dis*couraging as necessary.

"I'll go, too!" Margaret said, dabbing the corners of her mouth with her napkin.

God, almighty. First Zelda, now Margaret.

"That's a great idea, Cam. You, too, Mom," Hank said before looking at me expectantly. "What do you think about that, Al? Looks like it's going to be a family vacation after all!"

"Yeah," I said, still in shock and reeling from the whiplash of what had just happened. "Yeah…no—it'll be…great," I said, adding an Oscar worthy smile.

I looked at Margaret and could see her drafting everyone's itinerary in her head.

Great. *Fabulous.*

Well, Margaret would be a better buffer than Hank. Because clearly, in his mind, Cameron and Zelda were already a thing.

Time to get back to business. Even putting aside this whole fiancé thing for a moment, if she was going to be joining our family vacation, I needed to know more, now.

"So, what does your family do, Zelda?"

She shifted in her chair and immediately seemed uncomfortable. "Ah, nothing special, really," she said, looking down. "It's just my mom and me, and she's more or less retired."

That's vague. 'More or less retired' from what? And no mention of her father, the gamer? What is she trying to hide? I nodded along, but still.

Red flag no. 7.

"Oh," I said, "Retired? So early? That must be nice."

Suddenly, Zelda's phone vibrated on the table beside her plate. She grabbed it immediately and brought it down to her lap. "Ah, yeah...she...*um*...opted for early retirement," she said while typing on her phone.

I forced a smile when she finally looked up. Her face was flushed, and she looked even more uncomfortable. *Rude and clearly evasive.*

Red flag no. 8!

"*OK* then," I said, making it very clear she hadn't provided anything close to a satisfactory explanation. I decided to switch gears and followed up with, "So...Cam said you guys fell in love right away. Is that how you'd describe it?"

For a few seconds, Zelda thought deeply, staring heavenward. She moved her hand under the table to hold Cameron's, I assumed. "Oh, I definitely felt something right away," she said. "I mean, he's very sweet and genuine—which is far less common than you'd think. But he's also very smart and very perceptive—and it turns out he's brilliant at what he does. I think he's got a bright future ahead of him. So, yeah, I'd say it was pretty clear right away that he's a keeper."

A keeper, huh?

Her phone went off again, and once more, she ignored us while she responded to whoever it was that was so much more important than her 'fiancé and future in-laws'.

I waited for her to look up. "…Well, he certainly is very special," I said, casting a loving glance at Cameron. He seemed so happy. But he'd been happy with Penny, too, and we all know how that turned out. Smelling blood in the water, I pressed on. "But, of course, you've only known him for a couple of months, and he's still in school. So, why the engagement?" I asked. He did seem…better. Really better, actually. But the second I thought about Penny and all that she did to Cameron, the more my chest tightened. I tried to focus on the feeling of my feet on the floor.

Tick.

Tick.

Tick.

"Well, uh…," she started. Zelda looked at Cameron and then looked back to me. "I guess it's like Cam said, when something good comes along, you've got to grab it with both hands, right?"

But before I could respond, Hank quickly stood up and declared a little too loudly, "Well, speaking of something good coming along, let's have some dessert!"

Margaret and I both gave him a hard look before getting up to collect the dishes.

When Cameron and Zelda got up, Hank smiled. "No, you two sit tight. We'll handle the dishes and get dessert ready."

Margaret and I followed Hank into the kitchen. After we put the dishes down, I pulled Margaret aside. "Can you believe this girl, no school, no real job… she barely looked up from her plate or her phone and when she did, she called Cam 'a keeper'?" I said in one big breath.

For a few seconds, Margaret said nothing. "Zelda *is* rather quiet," she eventually whispered.

"And what's with the 'no wine' thing?" I said, rubbing my upper arm with the palm of my hand. "I mean, not even a sip to be polite? And why so vague about her family? Something's just not right here, Margaret. Cam can't go through another Penny situation, and neither can I."

Margaret chewed her lower lip for a second and then said, as if suddenly catching up, "Yes, well, we're definitely going to need to find out what's really going on here."

Hank practically stepped in between us with a tub of frozen yogurt in one hand, and a plate of Margaret's home-made peanut butter cookies in the other. "How about we get through dessert first," he said with a raised eyebrow and half a grin.

I shot him a dirty look but then followed him back to the dining room.

At the table, Margaret pushed the plate closer to Zelda with a smile. "They're peanut butter cookies, dear. Cam's favorite," she said proudly. Meanwhile, I motioned Zelda to pass me her coffee cup.

"Ah, no. Actually, I don't eat sweets or drink coffee, either. Sorry," she said in a terribly apologetic way. "But I'm sure they're wonderful," she added quickly.

I smiled sharply, brushing a stray strand of hair from my face. "Well, I guess that explains why you're so skinny."

Cameron gave me an irritated look. I clenched my jaw to keep from saying anything more before he stood up. "We really should be going," he announced.

"So soon?" Margaret asked as he swooped down to give her a kiss on the cheek.

He moved back to his father for a quick hug. "Yeah. Sorry, Grandma. We just came for a quick bite," he said, coming over and giving me a light hug.

I watched Hank hug Zelda before she skirted to the door, placing Cameron between the two of us. Well, at least she had some sense. She pulled on her coat. "Thank you so much for having me," she said quickly. "Dinner was lovely, and it was such a pleasure meeting you all."

Cameron moved over and helped her with her zipper, mumbling, "Yeah, it was great. I'll see you all later." He flashed a brief smile and, just like that, they were out the door.

I stood there for a moment feeling exhausted, frustrated and, well...angry. Angry and sad. With just...everything. And what mother wouldn't want to protect their child from a devastating heartbreak? Especially when it's happened before. Oh, my poor Cameron. First there was Penny, and *now* there's Zelda!

3 – A Penny for Your Thoughts

I felt just as stunned as when they'd arrived. I mean, really, what just happened? It was like a hurricane had come out of nowhere, turned our lives upside down, and then disappeared.

I whipped around to Hank and Margaret after I locked the front door behind Cameron and Zelda. "What the *hell* was that?" I said sharply. "And where the *hell* were the two of you when…*oh*, just forget it." Cameron was still *my* son, *my* child, *my* baby. I wanted to cry. But I wasn't about to lose it and start blubbering like a baby. I felt like I was about to be crushed by a tidal wave of emotions and needed a convenient 'escape'. "I need to go to the bathroom," I said, then hurried upstairs and shut the bedroom door behind me.

Needing to recalibrate, I crawled onto our bed and closed my eyes. I imagined a warm tropical breeze that smelled of sweet coconuts blowing over me. When Cameron left, I had such a strong urge to tell him to zip up his coat, put on his hat and watch out for bad drivers or weird people. But I didn't. He probably would have turned a few shades of red, rolled his eyes and said something about not being a kid any more before rushing off with Hurricane Zelda. Suddenly, the warm breeze blowing over me that I'd been imagining, turned into a howling gale that smelled of seaweed and dead fish. Okay, not helpful. I took a long, deep breath and tried to focus on pleasant thoughts. Instead, all I could hear was the rattling of dishes from the kitchen and the relentless *tick, tick, ticking* of

Margaret's grandfather clock. Restless, I rolled over, grabbed my iPad off the bedside table and with a tap, I opened up Google to get some advice from today's version of Dear Abby.

[search] why is it hard to let go of your adult son

Hundreds and hundreds of results came up. Clearly, I'm not the only woman in this world faced with the challenge of trying to protect her son, even against his will, from all the evils of the world. We mothers simply cannot just get over it like that and be expected to go on with our lives. Frowning, I chewed on one of my ragged fingernails and read Google's first response.

The average young adult male (ages 18 - 24) is often foolish and, if in college, frequently drunk. In most cases, and places, while considered an adult, they have yet to fully develop. They are often still very emotional, tend to have a more childlike way of looking at life and are prone to throwing temper tantrums. Young adult males may still need help from a more mature adult, like a parent, to handle complex situations and to validate their decisions before they act - particularly when setting boundaries in unhealthy romantic situations. Increasingly, adult males will live in their parents' house until the parents either sell the house or are dead.

Exactly. See!

No wonder I felt the way I did after Cameron drove off in his car, well, Samantha's car, with 'Princess Zelda' sitting next to him in the front seat. And no wonder I felt such a strong need to protect him. He's not ready to face the world, and he's certainly not ready for a younger and probably even more manipulative version of Penny. If I let this Zelda do to him what Penny did, Cameron may never be able to face the world. Sitting hunched over my iPad, I furiously tapped my fingers as I typed in another burning question for Google.

[search] what to do when you hate your son's new girlfriend

Milliseconds after I hit 'enter', a flood of results popped up on the screen. There were millions of websites full of articles and discussion groups on the subject. Clearly, another hot topic in this world. I clicked on a random link but soon felt all jittery after I read the first paragraph. Somehow, I ended up watching cute and funny cat videos. That did the trick. Twenty minutes later, I headed back downstairs.

"Oh, *there you are*," Margaret said matter-of-factly from the kitchen table. "Feeling better?" she asked, folding her arms, and staring at me. "You know," she went on, picking up her phone, "I was just telling Henry that all your long bathroom breaks might be a sign of constipation. I found this very interesting article right on my phone. Listen to this. One orange has *four* grams of fiber. I didn't know that. And boiled green beans, one cup, has *nine* grams of fiber. I did not know that either." She smiled behind her glasses. "It might be time to update your diet, Allison," she added. "I can certainly see why they call these things smartphones…" she trailed off, apparently lost in the depths of another Google search.

I stared at her for a second, shaking my head. "That's great, Margaret," I said, raising my eyebrows appreciatively. They say that television is a plug-in drug, but smartphones are like an IV full of crack. And Margaret was hooked. At least it helped her with respecting the boundaries around here. She was sitting down instead of being underfoot and directing traffic while Hank and I cleaned up.

I followed Hank to the dining room and watched him put the rustic wooden tray back in the middle of the table. Another wave of sadness crashed in. "He brought home a girl, Hank," I said, steadying myself with the back of a chair. "And not just a *girl…a fiancé*." That part sliced right through me.

Hank gave me one of his infuriating 'patient' smiles. "Yeah, I know. It was definitely an interesting dinner," he said, putting his hand on my arm briefly before moving back into the kitchen.

I followed close behind him. "Interesting? That's all you have to say about it?"

"Well, whatever else she may be, she certainly is pretty," Margaret chimed in.

"*Pretty?* Pretty manipulative if you ask me. Did you see her give him the old *let's get the hell out of here* nod? And did you see how quickly he obeyed her?" I countered.

"I saw she was slightly distracted, and yes, she did give him a nudge," Hank said, caressing my lower back.

"She didn't even offer to help with the dishes." I turned to face him, regretting giving up the back rubs.

"Well, I did tell them to sit and relax, so that probably had something to do with it," he responded, again with that same patient, understanding, loving and, at the moment, still incredibly infuriating smile of his.

Margaret's eyes narrowed. "Wasn't Zelda a little taller than Cam? Half an inch? Or maybe he was slouching." She then made a frustrated noise. "Hank, I can't get this stupid thing to Facebook."

I exhaled loudly and shook my head in frustration. "Who doesn't like wine, coffee *and* dessert?" I muttered under my breath.

"*Aha*, got it!" Margaret exclaimed.

"Got what?" I asked, momentarily confused.

"*Facebook*," she replied. "What's her last name?"

I hurried to the table and sat down. Margaret slowly typed Zelda's name in the search bar. They'd heard and knew everything I did about this girl, which was pretty much nothing. "She didn't say," I gritted out between my teeth.

Margaret looked up for a second, as if lost in thought. "Oh, I can check Cameron's profile. They're probably Facebook friends."

Hank joined us as the page loaded. I was skeptical about Cameron using Facebook. He claimed it was dead with millennials and younger people because their parents and grandparents, like Margaret, were now using it.

As expected, Cameron's profile looked like it hadn't been touched in a while. The most recent posts were strange and dark and didn't make any sense. Before all that depressing stuff, there were posts of Cameron and Penny. One post depicted them having dinner at an expensive restaurant, another showcased them indulging in a shopping spree for jewelry, and a third captured Penny's gaze directed toward some other guy while Cameron took a selfie with her. There was nothing about Zelda.

I looked over at Hank, then Margaret. Neither of them seemed as upset as I was. It wasn't like he had scraped his knee and we'd made it all better with a simple kiss and a band-aid. It was sheer torture listening to him sobbing on the phone, and in his room for weeks on end after what that traveling con artist did to him. His whole world had come completely crashing down and we'd all spent countless hours, including Samantha, 'talking him off the ledge' and then helping him pick up the pieces of his shattered confidence and self-esteem.

"Cam can't go through this again. And he's too young to have a fiancé," I finally said.

"I hear you, Allie," Hank said. "Maybe he is too young to get married. But one thing's for sure, he's definitely too young to give up on relationships. Remember, getting engaged is not the same as getting married. And, in fairness, we don't even know Zelda. First meetings are always the hardest and they're often awkward. Who knows, she might be the best thing that's ever happened to him. I know the girl I brought home to meet my folks certainly was." He gave me a slight wink and then said, "Look, all I know is that we can't protect him from the world."

I offered him a brittle smile, chanting my inner mantra of *be a kinder, gentler you* while my sciatica sent an unexpected searing bolt of pain down my leg, making it hard to breathe. Hank sounded an awful lot like his late father, George. I loved George. And I love Hank, dearly. But Cameron possessed a greater sensitivity and fragility than Hank ever truly grasped.

Margaret's finger suddenly stopped swiping. She took off her glasses and looked over at me. "Since I'm going to Florida, I should really start planning, shouldn't I?"

"Ah…"

"Let's seeeee…WHAT'S. THE. CURRENT. WEATHER. IN. FLO-RI-DA," she said in slow motion as she typed out each word. "What do you think I should bring?"

"Well, you—"

"What's the name of the hotel?"

It was absurd. Margaret, of all people, didn't seem particularly concerned about Zelda. I closed my eyes tightly before looking at her again. Twenty-seven years ago, she was the one who was hell-bent on protecting her son from his fiancé. I posed no threat and had, in fact, gone out of my way to leave a favorable impression.

"It'll be okay. You'll see. Just keep breathing," Hank whispered sweetly. I nodded and then told myself to try and keep an open mind as he slipped upstairs to Samantha's room, which was partially now his office. I missed Samantha. She would have been a great ally tonight.

I pictured next week's trip to Florida and shuddered. I'd been looking forward to getting away for one last fun-filled, family vacation in the sun to connect and create memories. One last time, before the kids got too busy with their own lives or before significant others got thrown into the mix. Now, instead of Hank and Samantha, there would be Margaret and maybe even Zelda. Margaret was set in her ways, and I couldn't begin to imagine her and my mother together. It's like trying to balance out a bitter vinegar with an unusual oil.

Bailey's piercing bark snapped me back to the present as he bolted to the front door. Moments later, I heard the front door opening. *So soon?* Cameron didn't bother taking off his coat. By the time I got to the stairs, he was already halfway up, laughing with his phone pressed to his ear.

Seriously? Not even a *hi, I'm back?*

Honestly, I wasn't trying to eavesdrop with heavy breaths outside of Cameron's bedroom while I waited patiently for his laughter to trail off. Peeking through the slightly opened door, I could see his winter coat hung neatly on the back of his chair and next to it on the floor, his gray duffle bag filled with folded clothes. That was new.

The floorboards creaked when I shifted my weight from one foot to the other after another sharp pain in my hip. "Hey, let me call you back," I heard him say.

I waited until he put his phone down before opening the door fully and leaning against the door jamb. Despite my sadness, I smiled. "Welcome home, by the way." I wanted to talk about Zelda and what happened at dinner. But I decided to ease into the whole 'Penny' conversation, and not dive-in headfirst.

A heavy sigh left his thin lips. "Thanks," he said, already sounding bored and irritated as he looked up at me from his bed with those deep brown eyes of his.

I took a quick breath and pushed on. "I know you're on break next week, but did you clear the following week with your professors?"

"Yeah," he mumbled, his eyes back on me, "it's fine."

I considered pressing further, but then thought it might be wiser to simply have faith in his ability to achieve good grades. Unlike Samantha, we never had to bribe or reward him for making an effort. He's a smart kid who swims effortlessly in a sea of A's. Well, at least when he's not, you know, getting his heart broken by some con artist. Penny made Cameron fall head over heels in love with her and had him spend all the money he'd saved working summers on her. When that was gone, she drained the money we gave him for tuition and living expenses. When that was gone, so was she. She even took the gift basket I sent to him for Easter too. It had been a bitter, *bitter* experience. He cried and cried. Now, here was this

Zelda person leading him around by the nose. I was starting to think he'd forgotten what Penny had done to him. Well, *I* certainly hadn't.

Entering further into his room, I noticed a little heart-shaped red pillow on the bed beside him. I gave him a bright smile and remarked, "That's a cute pillow."

All I received in response was a faint, half-hearted half-smile.

Think, think, think. I sat down with a focused determination of keeping the conversation simple at first, but instead blurted out, "Cam, you're too *young.*" *Welp, there's no time like the present.*

Cameron deflated, not responding. He grabbed the little heart-shaped pillow and squeezed it.

Silence.

"I don't want to see you get hurt again, Cam," I said softly. "Not like the way you did with Penny. I—*we* were so worried about you."

His mouth fell open slightly. "Mom, I'm fine now. And Zelda's different, believe me."

"How can you be so sure?" I said, looking him in the eyes. After all the red flags her behavior raised during dinner, I had a strong feeling that this relationship was going to be scarier and uglier for Cameron, and more worrisome for me. "I mean, she obviously didn't want to be here and couldn't wait to take you away," I added.

There was a very long pause.

"Mom, you don't even know her and that's not what happened!" he said, now standing and looking down at me. To which I had to take a deep, energizing breath before lifting myself up off the bed.

"I'm sorry but…it really didn't seem like she wanted to be here. She kept looking at her phone and made you answer questions for her," I stammered, growing increasingly uncomfortable. I hate confrontation. It makes me all hot and shaky. So, I sat back down, twisting my hands together anxiously.

Cameron was standing stiffly and now had his hand on the doorknob, as if desperately wanting me to leave. Instead of opening the door further and ushering me out, he slammed it shut and turned back to me. "Zelda is…*amazing*," he began, "and she believes in me, she supports me and makes me laugh. Plus, she's very smart, very caring, and very loyal."

His words created a kind of pressure on my chest. "Okay, well…what did you think of Penny when you met her?" I said.

We both wore frowns now and all I could envision was Zelda, standing there, with that stupid pink braid in her hair, poised to sink her claws into my innocent, kind-hearted, sensitive son.

He looked down at the floor and shook his head. After taking a deep breath of his own, he licked his lips. "Mom, Zelda is *not* Penny. I don't know how to convince you of that beyond telling you that she's amazing. She has two jobs and works hard… that's why she looked so tired tonight. Plus, her mother—"

"Sweetie," I started, standing up again as a bead of sweat rolled down my spine, "it's been less than a year since Penny ripped your heart out." I was ready to wrap my arms around him, but I could tell he was tense like me. Instead, I reached over and switched on the ceiling fan. He switched it off immediately. I took a step back. "Look, you found Zelda, or *she* found *you*, and that's great, but you're not thinking straight. You're rebounding, mesmerized by a girl who you think genuinely loves you. And even if she does, you're both *too young* to get married." *No one under thirty should ever get married, and I can give a hundred good reasons why.* I ignored Cameron's eye roll. "Your education…it should be your priority," I finally said as I leaned against his desk for support, stewing silently.

"You're not even listening, Mom…" he said but then trailed off when the floorboards creaked outside the door. He opened the door abruptly.

There was Margaret, sticking her head inside and shouting happily, "Oh good, you're back!"

Without a word to her, Cameron stormed out of the room and down the stairs with Margaret chasing after him and asking if he wanted more cookies.

Breathe Allie, breathe.

In the kitchen, I busied myself with adding various appointments and events to the calendar on the fridge. A mix of anger, anxiety, and a whole lot of impatience coursed through me as I watched Margaret settle next to Cameron with a plate full of cookies.

She gave him a moment and spoke cautiously. "I noticed the black ring on Zelda's finger… and didn't want to ask in front of her—is that *really* what engagement rings look like these days?"

I kept my eyes on the calendar, bobbing my head up and down in agreement with Margaret's question.

"Yeah, a lot of people are going with black rings now, Grandma. But it's not a real one. That'll probably have to wait until after I graduate. Zelda says she loves this ring, but she deserves more, and I want to get that for her."

Darn, darn, darn. I wasn't in the mood to listen to one more minute of this utterly unrealistic conversation. Oddly, I wasn't inclined to indulge in heaps of wine with Val either.

I went back upstairs, and Bailey followed me with an extra bounce in his step. My brain was struggling to behave normally. I was jealous. I should have had an extra bounce in my step too. *I signed a huge new client today.* But all I felt was antsy.

It was still early and despite the cold, I wanted ice cream. Not frozen yogurt. Ice cream. Creamy, decadent ice cream. And I didn't *want* it, I *deserved* it. Two, *no*, three scoops.

One scoop for Hank and Samantha bailing.

One scoop for Margaret and Zelda crashing our family vacation.

And one scoop for Cameron possibly getting his heart smashed into a million little pieces.

I lightly knocked on Hank's office door and peeked inside. He swiveled around in his new chair. "Up for a walk?" I asked him.

We walked arm in arm to the new ice cream shop three blocks away. Bathed in warm, dim lighting and adorned with black chalkboard walls, it was already one of my favorite places. Once we settled into the corner booth, situated under a green wall sconce and in front of an oversized bowl of French vanilla, pecan caramel, and classic chocolate ice cream, we clinked our spoons together, just as we always did when we were feeling fun and spontaneous. *"Ice Cream Cheers,"* we chimed in unison.

I smiled at him and opened my eyes wide as that heavenly mix of flavors and creamy and crunchy textures hit my taste buds. Leaning forward for another scoop, Hank looked up, like he was inspecting the dark pine covered ceiling, and then seemed almost nervous when he looked back at me. "He's growing up, Allie," he said. "I know he went through a lot, and I know you did, too," he took a deep breath, gathering himself, "but I've got to tell you, he looks happy to me." He paused. "Happier than he's been in a very long time. And he actually brought her home to meet us…"

I held up my hand to stop him. "He wasn't going to, Hank," I said. "Not until I called."

"Well, maybe not today, but he just got back," he countered. "Maybe he wanted to get settled in first."

I held my hands up to stop him right there. "Didn't you see how many 'red flags' there were at dinner? She's clearly manipulating him, just like Penny did."

Hank was about to protest but I pushed on.

"I don't like her. Plus, she has a terrifying skull tattoo with large gaping eye sockets on her arm," I said. "Jeez, what *is* it with these millennials and their tattoo obsessions?" I took a long deep breath. And then another large spoonful of ice cream.

Hank squinted his eyes, contemplating my words.

All I wanted was for Cameron to be happy. I'd love nothing more than for Zelda to be as wonderful as he believed her to be. However, a nagging sensation deep inside was causing my stomach to churn. I mean, why didn't Cameron tell me about Zelda? Why spring her on us by coming in and announcing her as his fiancé? They say *love is blind* but sometimes it's deaf and a little dumb too.

"Allie, we just met her," Hank said. "You gotta give this a chance. Let's try to get to know her. I promise, it'll be better for you and Cameron." He squeezed my arm gently. "And about the trip. I know how much you were looking forward to having everyone together. But I promise, I'll make it up to you…maybe you and I can do something special."

"Just the two of us?" I tried to think back to the last time we took a vacation together.

"Mmhm," he nodded. "Picture this. No snow—"

"My bags are already packed," I said. It wasn't the whole family vacation I was hoping for, but spending time alone with Hank would be something special.

He waved his free hand around in front of him, painting an imaginary picture. "Summertime, vineyards, Italy…"

"*Seriously?* You mean it?" That was it, the trip of a lifetime, the one we'd always talked about but never did. My heart skipped a beat, and I had to blink rapidly to clear my eyes.

"It'll be a celebration of all we've accomplished over the last few years, your successful career change and, hopefully, my promotion. What do you say?" he asked, with a gleam in his eyes.

"Yes, absolutely. A thousand times, yes. Let's do it!"

When we got back home, I started feeling antsy again. Maybe it was my sciatica acting up, or maybe it was Margaret's TV blasting downstairs. Nothing would fix how I felt right now about Cameron and Zelda, but the thought of going to Italy might quiet whatever was simmering inside me. At least for now, I thought, limping past the sounds of laughter coming from behind Cameron's bedroom door.

4 – The Breakfast of Champions

Are you there, George? It's me, Allie.

I know that parents and kids don't always get along. Lord knows that Samantha and I have had our battles over some of her 'more questionable' choices—remember Keith? How he took her, and Margaret, for a big ride. I get why Samantha's had her share of heartbreaks. With this thing she's had for 'bad boys', well, let's just say it doesn't take a genius to see it coming. But I never thought I'd have to worry about Cameron ruining his life with some girl, especially after what happened with Penny.

But now there's Zelda. And get this, George, she isn't just his girlfriend, she's his fiancé. God, even saying that makes me queasy. He's only twenty-two, for crying out loud! And yet, after only knowing this girl for a few months, he wants to marry her! He hasn't graduated from college yet, and this Zelda is a dropout who went after him in some bar and thinks of him as a 'keeper'—like he's some kind of meal ticket or passport to a better life. How can I possibly stand by and let her just use him up and toss him away when she's done with him—just like Penny did. I mean, what kind of mother would I be if I did that?

I tried to talk to him about it, to show him he's making a huge mistake, but I think it just made things worse. Obviously, I don't want to upset him, but his judgement is clouded by love.

On a happier note, you'd be so proud of Hank. He may be getting a huge promotion. And we're finally going to Italy—just the two of us! You raised a good man, George. Speaking of vacations, we're taking Margaret to Florida with us. I admit, I'm a little nervous about it, especially given how opinionated she and my mother are. Hopefully, it won't be too bad. Right?

As always, I miss you something fierce.

Allie xoxo

They say the way to a man's heart is through his stomach. I think it works with boys too. Food can be a useful tool for saying sorry, re-visiting a conversation and, hopefully, even helping a love-sick twenty-two-year-old come to his senses. Regardless, I couldn't resist adding more chocolate chips to the pancake batter and more bacon slices to the pan. It was a small gesture, but it made me feel better.

From time to time, I know I tend to bulldoze my way through things, which isn't always my intention. I upset Cameron last night, and although I can sometimes be a bull in a China shop, I also possess an insatiable desire to mend things. *Ugh*, enough with the clichés. I genuinely dislike having someone I care about angry with me.

"Whoa, what's all this, Mom?" Cameron said, his voice still groggy.

I turned around and met his eyes with a wide grin. "It's been so long since you've been home, and so long since we've enjoyed some pancakes and bacon together. So, I figured I'd whip some up for us, in honor of your first day back," I said. "Go ahead, grab a seat. It's almost ready."

I could see the excitement and anticipation cutting through the early morning fog in his eyes. My plan was already starting to work. He sat down in his unofficial but beloved spot at the kitchen table, his corner chair. We all had a favorite spot. It was the hub of our family's existence—it's where we did most of our laughing, fighting, and sharing of stories.

"Can we talk about the trip?" I said gently while handing him a large mug of hot cocoa.

"Ahh…sure…" he said cautiously.

I walked to the stove and then turned back around. "I know that inviting Zelda to Florida was a knee-jerk reaction to hearing that your dad and Sam aren't coming, but I wish we could have talked about it first," I said, holding my breath and bracing for his reaction. When he didn't make a face and instead just took a big gulp of cocoa, I felt encouraged. I turned around, flipped another pancake, and continued. "You have to consider that—"

"My goodness, Allison, that *awful* smell is going to be the death of me," I heard Margaret's voice even before the basement door opened.

I turned slightly to see her wearing what looked like my old straw hat. When she saw the mess I'd made on the counter and on the stove, she twisted her face into a look of pure disgust. *Oh*, if only I had a picture of her with that look and that old, ragged, misshapen hat. It would be a tremendous source of laughter and an antidote for even the gloomiest of days.

"You better not be feeding Henry any of that bacon." Her warning was gravely serious.

I was about to say something, but my mouth clamped closed. While Margaret was not one to hold back on giving 'advice' when it came to me and my relationship with her son—though she's gotten better over the past five years—this one was legit. After Hank had a mild heart attack shortly after George passed, we had to make changes to his diet. Bacon was strictly off limits. I just… "Oh, don't worry, Margaret. This is not for him," I assured her finally. And firmly.

"Anyway, Cam," I said, adding another pancake to the stack and bringing the conversation back to Zelda, "this was supposed to be a family trip and we don't even know her. Besides, with your father and sister not coming, this is a perfect opportunity for you and me to spend some quality—"

"Oh, speaking of the trip," Margaret exclaimed, excitedly clapping her hands together, "I found my old sun hat, down in the basement. She took it off her head, admiring the somewhat tattered blue ribbon and wide but fraying brim. This will be great for that Florida sun. You know me and the sun…"

Oh, for the love of… I gripped the spatula tightly and was grateful that she couldn't see the irritation that must have been written all over my face. Apparently, Margaret had been digging through the boxes in the storage room again because 'her' hat was definitely 'my' hat…from many Halloweens ago.

"It's got a real Florida vibe, Grandma," Cameron said supportively while shooting me a secret smile.

Suddenly, Zoom chimed from my iPad—which meant my conversation with Cameron was going to have to be put on hold, at least for now anyway.

I quickly placed the bacon on a paper towel lined plate while Margaret watched carefully, like I was handling some kind of hazardous material. "I'm going to see what else I can find for the trip," she announced, giving the plate one last warning look before turning on her heels and marching back downstairs. I closed my eyes for a second. *Give me strength.*

Zoom chimed again. "Okay, Cam, it's Zoom time with Sam. Take over, will you?" I said, extending the spatula toward him.

"*Hang on*, Sam," I called out, as Cameron and I switched places.

I sat down at the table, adjusting the brightness on the screen.

"Hi, Mom," Samantha said with a smile. "Hey, what's that all over your shirt?"

I glanced down at the flour before dusting it off. "Oh, we're making pancakes."

"With bacon?"

"Of course."

"Grandma can't be too happy about that." My shoulders stiffened.

"No, but it's for your brother, not your father—"

"Hi, Sammy!" Cameron shouted over his shoulder, sounding for an instant like the playful and innocent boy I remembered.

"Hi, Cammy!" Samantha shouted back.

"Listen, Mom…I'm not going to be home on Thursday like we planned." There was a long pause and then, "I've got a really great job opportunity so I'm going to be staying here for a while," she said. I could tell she was nervous about telling me by the way she was fidgeting with her hands. "But I already talked to Grandma," she added quickly, "and she's totally okay with it."

Samantha waited anxiously while I pushed down my rising disappointment. "Yeah, I heard. Your father told me already," I breathed out and widened my eyes. "I hear it's got real potential." I gave her my best smile and saw her visibly relax.

"Yeah, it really is," she said. "And I'm really sorry about missing the trip. I know you were looking forward to us all being together."

I was about to tell her exactly how the trip had changed, but with Cameron still poking holes in the pancakes on the stove, I decided against it. Instead, I smiled even more broadly and said, "So…tell me about Paris!"

Samantha's face lit up as she talked about her newfound love for Europe—the sights, the sounds, the art, the food, the people. She went on and on, with a spark in her eyes. As I got more comfortable in my seat, I couldn't help but wonder about her future. *Was it really going to be in the home staging business with me?* I rested my arms on the table and when she finished telling me about the ornate interiors and the towering spires of the cathedrals, I tried to mirror her excitement. "*Well, well, well.* It certainly sounds like you've been having quite the experience," I said, smiling of course. "With an exciting new job, do you think you'll ever want to come back?"

"Mom, I…" She hesitated, "maybe we should talk more after Florida."

Nodding, I peeked over the top of my readers to see Cameron loading his plate. He silently informed me that he was heading up to his room. As soon as I heard the faint creak of the top stair, I immediately shifted my attention back to Samantha. "You're not going to believe this…Cam's *engaged*. And to some girl named *Zelda*," I whispered into the camera. "I didn't even know he was dating again. He just brought her to dinner last night and dropped the bomb on us."

Samantha's face looked suspiciously blank. "Wow, I knew he was seeing someone," she said, "but I didn't know anything about an engagement."

I slumped back into my chair. Well, I guess it made sense she knew he was dating. Cameron and Samantha talk. "Isn't *Zelda* an unusual name?" I gave off a quick high-pitched chuckle. "Do you know her?" I asked, feeling a little hurt at being left out of the loop.

She shook her head, looking intently at me. "I know we went to high school together and I remember hearing her name, but I don't think I actually ever met her," she said. "All I know is what Cam's been telling me. She sounds nice enough. How'd the dinner go?"

My throat constricted. "*Terrible*," I said, "I think she might be another Penny."

As I told her about the dinner and then more about Zelda, and how Zelda seemed to have Cameron wrapped around her little finger, a thought finally hit me. "Hey, you're good at finding things on social media, right? Do you think you could dig up anything on her?"

Samantha shifted in her seat and then glanced at her phone, nodding. "Sure…I'll see what I can find. But I have to get going—"

"Okay, thanks. It was so good to—" *ah, what the hell?* I tapped the power button vigorously after the screen went blank, then rubbed my face in frustration, realizing I had forgotten to charge my iPad last night.

"See if you can *dig up* anything on her?!" Cameron's voice sounded from the kitchen threshold. I turned immediately and swallowed the lump in my throat. He leveled a piercing glare at me that could have shattered glass.

"Cameron, look…," I said, standing up quickly. Suddenly, the basement door banged open with a loud thud. Margaret made another grand entrance. Smiling, she raised her arms high in the air and threw them wide. She'd found another one of my old hats. When she finally noticed the tension between Cameron and me, she lowered her arms slowly.

"Allison," she said, walking right up to me with her hands now on her hips like she had something very serious and important to say, "what should I wear to your mother's party?"

"I…ahh…" My mind struggled to make the leap from dealing with Cameron's death glare to Margaret's fashion emergency. The right attire. For a birthday party. Being held at a retirement residence. "Maybe a nice sundress?" was all I could manage to say.

"A SUNDRESS?! With these old legs?!" she fired back, shaking her head in disbelief at my scandalous suggestion. "And don't say shorts either because it's basically the same thing. I need, *uh*, what are those things called? *Clam diggers?*"

I looked at her for a moment with a completely blank stare. What the hell were *clam diggers?* "Do you mean 'Capris'?" I said, feeling a little irritated at being interrupted for this.

"*Capris?*" she repeated, looking awfully confused. Seconds later, she asked, "And what are planes like these days? Still narrow, uncomfortable seats? That won't be much good for my old back, but if I can get an aisle seat, then I can stick my legs out."

I could see Cameron out of the corner of my eye. He was brooding darkly, waiting for his grandmother to go back downstairs. "Ahh…I think the seats are bigger now but, yeah, an aisle seat might not be a bad idea," I said, with a slightly louder sigh than I'd intended.

With a nod, she adjusted her hat. "You know, I read a news story once about an alligator that got into a hotel in Florida. Can you imagine?" she said, her voice filling the room.

Cameron and I responded in unison, "NOOOO…"

She nodded proudly. "It's true—and what about Rosie? What should I get her for her big day?"

Rosie? You mean my mother, Rosemary? It was as if they were good old friends. The thought made me shiver with discomfort, but I scolded myself for being so negative about the possibility of it. Stranger things have happened.

Margaret pulled her phone out of her bathrobe pocket with a flourish. "Did you know," she announced, glancing back up from its screen, "that according to the weather app right here on my phone, it'll be hot and steamy in Florida. I mean, of course, but—"

I held up my hand, clearing my throat. "Hang on a second, Margaret, I was just talking to Cam, and—"

"I'm going to Zelda's," Cameron cut me off abruptly. "She's still upset about how you treated her last night," he said, tucking his phone into his back pocket.

Margaret immediately straightened her shoulders and scratched the side of her head. "She's not upset with me, is she?"

I shook my head, exasperation dragging at my limbs as Cameron stalked off without so much as a goodbye. After he slammed the front door shut, Margaret turned to me.

"You know," she drew in her breath, "you should get to know Zelda, maybe just give her a chance."

I was suddenly livid. The heat was rushing up my body, reaching my eyebrows. "Are you kidding me right now? That girl is *probably* another Penny. She's probably just trying to drive a wedge between us so that she can take advantage of him without us being there to protect him. And Cam's so blinded by..." I heard my voice trail off when Margaret's gaze shifted intently past me. *I had heard the front door close, hadn't I?* I clenched my fists and shut my eyes tight when I heard the kitchen cabinet drawer open and Samantha's keys jingle. I held my breath, and by some miracle, I managed to avoid flinching as he slammed the drawer shut, causing the picture frames on the wall to rattle. I turned to face him.

"Are you serious, Mother?!"

Mother?

"YOU. DON'T. EVEN. KNOW. HER." He punctuated each word with a shake of his hand and the jingling of keys.

Without thinking, I lunged forward and grabbed his arm as he spun around to storm out. "Cam, wait. Wait. WAIT!" I pleaded, my voice growing desperate. "I didn't mean anything bad by that. You're so young and so sweet and I *won't* let you get hurt again like you did before." I wasn't sorry for wanting to protect Cameron. But was it possible that I was rushing to judgment with Zelda? Possibly, yes. I wished I could be more like my mother. She always seemed able to accept whatever life threw her way. And keep whatever thoughts that popped into her head from simply flying out of her mouth. This certainly didn't feel like my kinder, gentler self at work. "Okay, so, bring her to Florida!" I blurted out.

Cameron didn't answer. Instead, he turned his head back and with a scowl, waited for me to say more.

Okay, he's listening. Better make it good! "It'll be an opportunity for us to get to know Zelda," I said. "And with your dad and Sam not coming, it only makes sense that she and your grandma take their place. Everything's already paid for, and we're supposed to be spending quality time together, so…" I couldn't bring myself to add 'the more the merrier' bit. At the moment, I was feeling anything but merry.

Cameron maintained his scowl, but he *did* look me straight in the eyes with some deepness. "Really?"

I had, of course, smiled all the while, my body growing…hot. "Yes, really. But…you have to bring your laptop and work on schoolwork while we're there. I don't want you falling further behind."

Miraculously, Cameron was already nodding in agreement. I felt the tension in his body dissipate as I rubbed his upper arm and then gave him a reassuring hug. With my eyes bouncing back to Margaret, I shook my head as Cameron slipped past me, making his way toward the basement. "Not one word," I warned her.

Kindness. Patience. Openness. Just because I said Zelda could come, and that I was going to get to know her, didn't mean I had to accept her into the family, right? If it would make Cameron happy, I could keep an eye on Zelda and make sure she didn't hurt Cameron. Who knows, maybe she'd turn out not to be another Penny. Mercury *was* in retrograde, after all. Anything was possible. I mean, who needs logic when you've got astrology?

After a few minutes, Cameron came back upstairs, lugging one of my suitcases. He went straight to the front door and left, again, without saying goodbye. Maybe it was for the best. Or maybe I should just send everyone *else* to Florida and stay here with Hank. I was sure I could come up with a plausible excuse for why I couldn't go. Of course, as soon as everyone got back, I'd head down there solo to see my mother. Of all people, she would understand.

When Margaret went back downstairs, I grabbed my phone off the counter. Okay, Google, let's see what you've got.

[search] convincing excuses to get out of travel plans

I chewed my bottom lip and envisioned a few possibilities:

Bailey ate ALL my ID!

A very, very important business thing came up.

My doctor said I have a really bad sinus infection, and traveling is not advisable.

I've been exposed. #neverendingpandemic

I let out a deep sigh as my stomach let out a rather impatient growl, reminding me just how hungry I was. I poured myself some coffee, tossed some pancakes and bacon onto a plate, and sat down to enjoy a rare moment of peace and quiet. Forget Wheaties. These chocolate chip pancakes with crispy bacon were the true Breakfast of Champions.

5 – A Case of the Mondays

Monday mornings. They have this uncanny ability to mess with your mind, leaving behind a special kind of weekend regret. And on this particular Monday morning, what I felt was, hungover. I felt drained and depleted, but not from some wild weekend. No, this was an emotional hangover from learning about Zelda and arguing with Cameron and discovering that Samantha might be gone for good. And, of course, there was Margaret's unexpected 'excitement' about coming to Florida with us too.

I merged into traffic and all I could think about was just how much my life had changed in two days. With everything that'd happened, I hadn't accomplished anything I'd planned to do yesterday. In fact, I spent most of it sitting like a lifeless lump, mindlessly flipping channels in a desperate attempt to avoid thoughts of our impending trip to Florida and feelings of abandonment after Cameron didn't even bother coming back from Zelda's until almost midnight. I was hoping we would have 'carbed out' and binged the new Star Wars series.

As I rounded the corner and came to a stop at the traffic light, I took a long, deep cleansing breath. But even with the effort, my chest still ached, and the weight of Cameron's new love life loomed over me. It was my duty to protect him, but I didn't want to lose him in the process. *How do I expose Zelda without pushing Cameron away too?*

That question burned inside me until I reached the office. The second I got there, Bea ran up to greet me, complete with her green, one 'gallon' water jug as she jumped around like an over-anxious toddler.

"Allie!" she said, her face a mix of fear and hope. I returned Bea's greeting with a slight smile. The ache in my chest migrated to the back of my skull and settled in as a pounding headache.

"Morning, Bea," I said, my attention momentarily drawn to the brightly colored dangling earrings she had hanging down from her numerous piercings. I sometimes wondered if they ever got tangled up given the way she tended to bounce her head while talking or while taking massive gulps from her motivational time-management water jug.

At 9:00 a.m., it read **REMEMBER YOUR GOALS!**

"So, um, the Johnsons called," she started, absentmindedly picking at the baby blue nail polish on her thumb. My stomach instantly dropped.

"I gather they weren't calling to thank us for the tremendous job we did, were they?" I said, quite curtly. She lowered her head and started digging more aggressively at the already peeling nail polish. After letting out a huge sigh, she dropped her arms to her sides, and looked up, deflated.

"Not exactly…" she confessed.

The throbbing in the back of my head was joined by a twitching in my right eye. I fought hard to suppress my surging frustration. *Breathe, Allie. Breathe.* "What happened, Bea?" I asked calmly. She then began listing reasons behind the latest 'screw up' when I noticed she took a small step back, perhaps anticipating my reaction.

Bea's been Samantha's friend since kindergarten. Before Samantha left for Europe, she'd convinced us to let Bea take over for her while she was away. She'd even spent a couple of weeks training Bea to help with the transition. It soon became apparent that Samantha's training hadn't quite stuck. Bea was an absolute disaster, making one careless mistake after another. It's been like a slow business death by a thousand cuts with her.

My smile faded as Bea's explanation went on, and on, *and on*. It was mostly incoherent ramblings and nonsensical details. After she followed me to my office without pausing to take a breath, I dropped my purse on the desk and threw off my coat in an attempt to cool down. I couldn't tell if I was having a hot flash or if my blood pressure was skyrocketing. We had three homes to stage this weekend and two more for the weekend after. Each project carried its own set of challenges and expectations. I was already nervous enough about going to Florida for a week. But with Margaret now going, and leaving Bea on her own, could mean we may not have a business to come back to. Okay, maybe it wouldn't be *that* bad, but it was still going to be *bad*.

"Honestly, Allie, this wasn't my fault…but I told them we'd give them a discount," she said, "and then I—"

"I'll take care of it," I said, holding my hand up in hopes she'd shut up. It was simply too much for a Monday morning.

Bea stopped talking. At least she was smart enough to recognize when I'd had enough. She took a much-needed breath, a giant gulp of water, and then stood there silently waiting. When I met her with my best blank stare, she slowly backed out of my office, turned, and with a little squeak, scurried back to her desk.

I leaned back in my chair and massaged the base of my skull, waiting as my computer hummed to life. No matter what happened, you've got to keep moving forward, I reminded myself. So, I downed two extra-strength painkillers, rolled up my sleeves, and then picked up the phone to call the client.

At exactly 12:00 p.m., a sharp knock on my office door pulled me away from the email I was struggling to write. Before I could respond, the door swung open and there was Val. She had a gleam in her eyes and a big grin plastered on her face.

"Well, good afternoon, Mrs. Montgomery!" she purred in a sultry, Southern accent. Val had a penchant for speaking in different accents, depending on her mood. With one hand on her stylish, slender hip, she leaned into the doorway. "I know I don't have an appointment," she said in that slow Southern drawl, "but I was wondering if you'd do me the honor of accompanying me for a bit of lunch on this fine day." Her invitation, delivered with such theatrical flair, left me flattered and amused.

I leaped to my feet, slammed my computer shut and grabbed my coat and purse. "There better be wine," I said, quickly crossing the room, looping my arm in hers and practically dragging her out of the office. Lunch with Val, along with a little liquid courage, was exactly what I needed. Besides, Bea's water jug read **12:00 P.M. - DRINK UP**. Who was I to argue with an obviously wise and all-knowing beverage container?

Soon, we headed outside and climbed into our Uber, a sleek black sedan that pulled up to the curb. "Well, it looks like someone's got a case of the Mondays," Val said. "I didn't want to interrupt your day, but it's been almost a week since we got together, and you've sent me a scary lack of texts."

My mouth was hanging open. "What do you mean *'scary'*?" I finally asked as we made our way to Justina's, our favorite restaurant.

"Oh, well…I heard through the grapevine that your friend back there gave you some more trouble last week, but I haven't heard anything from *you* about it. So, yeah. *Scary*."

"Last week?" I couldn't help but roll my eyes. "It seems like there's something every other day," I lamented with only a hint of sarcasm. I get that the universe sometimes tests our resilience and ability to navigate through the chaos by throwing the odd curveball our way, but this was getting ridiculous.

"Yeah, okay, but the point is I had to hear about it through the grapevine, Al," she said pointedly.

The grapevine was my clients, who also happened to be *her* clients. Val was the one who encouraged me to get into the staging business in the first place. Without her, none of this would have happened.

"Yeah, sorry. It wasn't intentional," I said with an apologetic smile. Amid our conversation, our attention waned. Momentarily forgetting our discussion, we became swept up in the bustling energy and the vibrant tableau of human interaction along the streets in our small but charming downtown.

Ten minutes later, we grabbed our regular spot by the window. It was perfect for people-watching. "So, things have been kind of crazy, huh?" Val asked. She gracefully slipped off her coat and arranged it on the back of her chair before sitting down. Val had an effortless elegance about her and somehow managed to maintain her stunning figure despite a thriving career, an active social life, and a healthy appetite for all things sensual, especially wine. I, on the other hand, was far less graceful. I plopped myself down on my chair, throwing my coat over my lap.

"Yeah, crazy is an understatement, actually," I said.

Her eyes shot to my face as she wagged her finger in front of it. "Yeah, see, this vague, glossed over version of events isn't working for me. I need details, Allie. Vivid descriptions and maybe even a skit. C'mon, out with it. What's going on?"

"Well, where do I start?" I said after the server returned with our wine and took our lunch orders. "The business is falling apart. How about we start with that."

"Wait, what do you mean falling apart?" She looked surprised. "I know you've been having troubles with Bea, but everyone I talk to says how much they love your work. What's going on?"

I held her gaze. "Okay, yes, the staging work is great and we're getting clients, but Bea is *killing* me," I said, balling up my fists and shaking them. "Look, don't get me wrong, she's a sweet girl. But as an employee, she's horrendous. It's been over a month, and she still hasn't got a clue," I said. "What happened last week is just the tip of the iceberg. I've already scaled back her role so she can't hurt us *too* badly, but it means that I'm having to take on most of what Sam was doing. And, I have to keep checking up on Bea and smoothing things over every time she makes a mistake—not to mention all the money I'm spending on apology discounts and headache pills. I mean, I should be excited about how the business is growing—*Better Homes* just signed on for seven houses, by the way—but I'm worried about whether we can handle it the way things are going."

Val looked shocked. She pushed my wine glass toward me. "Allie, you taught a bunch of screaming children for years. You put up with Margaret, for Christ's sake, and you even managed to stay sane while Samantha was going through her 'bad boy' phase," she said supportively. "You can handle *this*. All you need to do is hang on 'til Sam gets back. What's that, another couple of weeks?"

I shook my head. "Ah, yeah, well, she might not be coming back for a while. Apparently, she got this great job opportunity and wants to pursue it," I said, taking a long sip of my wine before telling her more.

She stared hard at me, then snorted. "Well, then, you're just going to have to go ahead and find someone else to take over for Sam."

My heart was pounding. As frustrated as I was with Bea, the thought of going through the hassle of finding someone new, didn't exactly fill me with a sense of relief. Still, I knew Val was right. "Yeah, well," I said, "the business isn't even half of it."

"Oh?" Val asked, raising an eyebrow and leaning in. "Do tell..." she said, momentarily switching back to her Southern accent.

I took a breath and laid my palms flat on the table for support. "The Florida vacation has fallen apart. Obviously, Sam's not coming because of this job thing, and neither is Hank. He has to stay behind to babysit the merger so he can get that promotion he's been hoping for. That's all bad enough but now Margaret is taking Hank's spot and," I said, watching for her reaction as I dropped the bomb, "Cameron's *fiancé*, Zelda, is taking Sam's spot."

"His WHAT?!" she practically shouted as she smacked both of her palms on the table.

"Yep, you heard me..." I said.

Val leaned in closer, her eyes widening in anticipation. She finally spoke, "We're going to need more wine for this. I want the full scoop. Tell me everything."

Dan, our server, arrived with our salads and Val ordered a carafe. With our conversation temporarily on hold, she stared at him with a slightly predatory look in her eyes as he wielded his long wooden grinder and sprinkled a generous dose of fresh black pepper onto our plates. When she saw that I noticed her sizing Dan up, she smiled and gave me a quick wink.

"...So, when I got home from the *Better Homes* meeting on Saturday," I went on as soon as Dan left, "I found out from Margaret that Cam was coming back, and she'd made him his favorite dinner..." Val refilled our glasses and then settled back comfortably into her chair as I unloaded for a good half-hour. I figured the more I spoke, the better I'd feel but, instead, my anxiety over Cameron's future increasingly tightened its grip on my chest. Then she started asking questions. And the more she asked, the more I heard myself sounding sad and angry. Suddenly, my leg started to hurt, and I started fidgeting in my seat while my fingers nervously traced invisible patterns on the tablecloth, desperately seeking some semblance of calm.

After I'd finished, Val sat quietly for a moment and then she looked directly at me and said with a deadly serious tone, "I know what's happening here. Cam was selling drugs, and she's like...his supplier. But something went wrong, and he can't pay her back so now he's letting her use him as her 'front' to make her seem more 'normal' and the whole engagement thing is part of the cover story."

I stared at her in disbelief before we both burst out laughing. The absurdity of Val's surreal conspiracy theory, and the fact that neither of us had touched our salads but the wine was almost gone, turned that laughter into full-bodied belly laughs. This caused more than a few heads to turn in our direction. Tears streamed down my face as I struggled to get my breath. On some level, I felt better.

Val looked up. "All kidding aside, Al, I understand how you feel," she said gently. "Cam went through something awful and then this Zelda—who the hell names their kid *Zelda* anyway—comes out of nowhere and you've got all of these 'red flags' popping up at dinner. I get it. You want to protect him," she said. "I think you've got to start by getting as much information as you can on this girl and really get to know her."

Just then, Dan walked by, carrying drinks to a nearby table. Val gave him a little smile.

"What are you doing?" I said, puzzled.

Eventually she cleared her throat and sat up straighter. "Ah, well, I think I'm done with Peter."

'Peter the Cheater' was Val's on again, off again husband of over twenty-five years. He was her 'Big'.

"What happened?" I left out the *'this time'*. I turned my gaze to the tiny bubbles still dancing around in my glass.

She sighed. "Well, of course, we're fighting again," she confessed, her voice tinged with weariness. "I may have finally reached the point where it's time to stop going down the same path with him. Life's too short to be constantly trying to make him happy...you know? I need someone who lifts me up, someone who brings sparks of joy into my life, who makes me feel alive and—I dunno, fulfilled, maybe."

I nodded with furrowed brows. "It takes a lot of patience and a lot of energy to be with someone who isn't happy," I said before filling my mouth with more sparkly wine. I turned to glance out the window for a second and then I froze instantly.

"VAL. IT'S HER!" I shouted, my mouth agape.

"...No way!" She immediately came around to saddle up next to me. "Where is she?"

"Right over there," I responded quickly, pointing out the window. "See the girl with the pink braid? What are the chances?" I sat in disbelief, watching Zelda just strolling down the street.

"We have to follow her! Maybe she'll take us to *her* supplier. Then, we'll call the cops, she'll get arrested, and you'll never have to worry about her ever again!" Val threw her head back and laughed. "*Or,* maybe we'll just learn a little more about her. Either way, let's go." She tugged on her coat, left Dan with an extremely generous amount of cash, and ran outside. I immediately jumped up, tossed on my coat, and ran after her.

We caught up to Zelda and began trailing behind her closely—but not too closely. We weaved through the crowd and navigated our way past colorful storefronts and ornate buildings. After about three blocks, Zelda paused and quickly looked around.

"Shit, shit, *shit*," I cursed under my breath, ducking behind a tall wintery looking planter box, and yanking Val down beside me.

We cautiously peeked out, and to our surprise, Zelda was now engrossed in a deep conversation with some guy her age. It was a lively interaction. Then, they gave each other a long, affectionate hug while swaying their bodies from side to side.

"Whoa?!" Val and I exclaimed in unison, fully facing each other before turning back.

That was not the kind of hug you gave someone you knew casually or even more closely, like a coworker, a neighbor, or an old classmate. It was crystal clear this was a relationship that ran deeper.

And then she *kissed* him. It was quick, but…

Red Flag no. 9? Definitely.

Sighing, I felt myself getting hot. "Who *is* this guy?"

"Aww, she's actually pretty," Val said. "I was envisioning more 'goth girl' meets 'deadbeat musician'."

Pretty? My heart sank but then it suddenly leaped out of my chest when, out of nowhere, Cameron's voice cut through the air, "*MOM?*"

Val and I immediately straightened up and spun around to see Cameron crossing the street and heading toward us.

"Oh, jeez," I groaned.

I felt an uncomfortable surge of panic and shame rushing through me. Val and I fidgeted with our coats, making quick adjustments as we waited to face him.

When he reached us, he looked at me, then Val and then back at me. "What are you guys doing?" he said, his voice oozing with suspicion.

Val and I exchanged a glance. "...ahh, we were just having lunch, and... I thought I'd dropped my earring. Turns out it was caught in my hair," Val said smoothly. She cleared her throat, fixed her coat collar, and stood there calmly.

"What are *you* doing down here?" I said, not quite meeting his eye.

"Shopping with Zelda for Florida," he replied stiffly, his gaze shifting down the street. I followed his line of sight as he waved to Zelda.

"Florida! Yeah, that should be loads of fun, Cam!" Val chimed in. She then stepped forward and gave him a hug. Stepping back, she looked at her watch. "Al, we better get back to it. Lunch break is over."

I managed a smile while still stunned by what we'd seen between Zelda and that unknown guy. "Right," I said. "Have fun, Cam. Do you need money?" I asked, knowing full well that Cameron wasn't much into shopping for clothes. And if he were into it, our shopping escapades would be more than just about finding clothes. It was a fun and sacred bonding time for us, roaming in and out of stores and indulging in a bit of people watching.

Cameron shook his head, said a quick goodbye, and quickly joined Zelda, who had already crossed the street and disappeared into an expensive women's clothing store.

Shortly after settling down at my desk and staring blankly at the monitor, my phone chimed. Good grief. It was a text from Margaret saying she wanted to come to the office. After processing for a moment, I glanced at my calendar and realized I had a meeting scheduled with a real estate agent in fifteen minutes. Then it dawned on me. I could kill two birds with one stone. Or maybe even three if I was lucky. I took a deep energizing breath.

[Favor. Can you pick up your G and bring her to the office? I
have a meeting in 15 mins so no time]

I brushed aside my feelings of guilt at having lied to Cameron so I
could secretly investigate Zelda's activities. I needed to know who this girl
was. Knowledge is power.

[You should bring Zelda for dinner this week. Might be good
to get to know her before the trip :) xo]

My leg bounced under the desk while I stared intently at my phone.
When his message finally came through, I released the breath I hadn't
realized I'd been holding. He'd agreed to both, and, even through text, I
could sense his happiness over the invitation to Zelda. I placed my phone
facedown on my desk. For now, that was all that mattered.

6 – Guess Who's Coming to Dinner, Again...

I hit the button repeatedly, hoping for some sign of life on the screen. But nope. Nothing. *"ARE YOU KIDDING ME?!"* I screeched, almost falling from my chair. I could have sworn I'd charged my iPad last night but here I was, faced with a stupid lifeless device, just moments away from a Zoom call with my mother. I closed my eyes and vented my annoyance and frustration with a silent scream.

Dear Nintendo,

I've got a new hero that will blow your 'Legend of Zelda' out of the water! Her name is Queen Allison Technova, *or* Queen Allie, *for short. She's a home staging superhero armed with the latest and most powerful consumer technology, and she's on a mission to save the world from the horrors of poorly staged homes. The story starts with Queen Allie about to consult the Great Oracle, Rosemary, via Zoom using her trusty iPad. Queen Allie then discovers that her iPad has no power, and she must figure out if that's because some ruthless AI has taken control of her iPad and locked her out, or if she just forgot to plug it in, again? To find out and to complete her mission, Queen Allie must survive the hell of user forums, the long wait for tech support and, if necessary, the journey to the Apple store itself. She'll also need to learn how to navigate the perils of lost chargers, blocked Wi-Fi, forgotten passwords and infuriating iOS updates. If she can do all that, get her iPad recharged, speak with the Great Rosemary, and gain the knowledge and wisdom she needs to be a better person, she'll be able to keep her kingdom safe and bring hope to home sellers everywhere!*

It's an epic journey. Let me know what you think!

Apart from iPads, my ongoing challenges with technology, and of course, my natural resistance to always having to keep up with the latest program or type of phone, was part of the reason why it took me so long to get a smartphone. Everyone's always glued to them. And plus, I was convinced I could conquer any task without the help of apps or emojis. But now that I was armed with one, I've embarked on a journey of several accidental selfies and phone calls and autocorrect mishaps. On the bright side, I've discovered a whole new world of funny baby and dog and cat videos. Who knows, maybe I'll become the unexpected beacon of hope and inspiration to others. *A tech-savvy hero and warrior ready to conquer new frontiers.* I laughed at the thought.

After abruptly closing the iPad case and letting out a frustrated sigh, I took the last sip of my lemon balm tea. *Yes,* teatime with Margaret. Who knew?

"What's wrong?" she asked.

"Oh, nothing," I said, watching as she walked across the kitchen floor with one hand holding her tea and the other scrolling through her phone. I'd have said she was an old pro with the smartphone except that she was scrolling back and forth through the app screens and risking a broken hip. "Ahh, Margaret, remember how you used to yell at Hank for running with scissors in his hands?" I said, when she finally turned in my direction.

She paused and gave me a slightly curious look. "Yes?"

I gestured to her phone. "What you're doing is not that different. Okaaay…you're not going to stab yourself if you fall while running with a smartphone," I said. "But I really don't want to be installing a wheelchair lift in here because you were too busy scrolling through Facebook to watch where you were going," I said as I reached across the table, whispering a silent thank you to Cameron for having left his laptop on it. Now, if I could only remember the password.

Margaret sniffed primly at me, lifting her chin defiantly. "Isn't that Cameron's laptop?"

Fingers poised over the keyboard, like a secret agent getting ready to crack a top-secret code, I typed in '1234' to unlock his laptop. I smiled. *Sometimes he was still just a simple, innocent boy.* I went straight to his Zoom app. "Yes, it is," I answered, looking up at her.

"Well, if he catches you snooping on it, he won't even let you live in his basement when you're my age. It'll be straight to the home for you, my dear."

"Don't worry, Margaret," I replied with a wink. "I'll tread carefully." And with a determined grin, I successfully logged into Zoom. "I'm just using it to call my mother because I forgot to charge my iPad."

Margaret looked puzzled. "Well, why don't you just use your smartphone? That's what it's for, you know," she said.

"Because I want to share my screen and show her some websites—"

"Share your screen?" Her eyebrows lifted. "Oh? How does that work?"

"It's a Zoom feature and—*oh* never mind, Margaret," I said with a hint of exasperation. "I'll show you another time." I quickly shifted my focus back to the Zoom call, hoping Margaret was satisfied with my very brief, almost non-response. She shook her head but then just continued moving across the kitchen floor. I wasn't initially planning on snooping. I only really started considering it after Margaret mentioned it. But I needed information. Whatever I could get. There were open windows on Cameron's laptop, and this was for his own good. So, I looked at what he'd been browsing. It was just something to do while I was waiting for my mother to join, I told myself. And besides, he left it open, and it's my job to protect him, I also told myself.

The first tab. **Laurent College - School Assignment Portal**

See? He's a good kid. So much for Val's drug dealer theory.

The second tab. **Gmail**

My eyes widened in surprise when I saw a PayPal receipt, showing a transaction with one thousand dollars being transferred from him to... *Zelda?* A big thick knot formed in the pit of my stomach.

The next tab. **Holly's Wedding Ideas**

The knot in my stomach tightened.

And then the next tab. **Pinterest.** Great Gifts for Great Girlfriends

Oh, boy.

The last tab. **You & Baby Co.** Cute Baby Names

I froze, feeling my heart pound through my chest.

I snapped the laptop shut and closed my eyes tight. But then took a deep breath and opened it again. I had to know more. I returned to his email and looked at one from Zelda with a message that said, *hey, check these out*, followed by a bunch of links. Of course, as any mother would do, I clicked on the first link. It went to a popular online marketplace and the page that opened was full of an eclectic assortment of handmade bags and purses, The second link went to the same marketplace, but this time showed a page full of wall art. *Oh, she's a shopper.* I was about to click on one of the interesting looking pieces made entirely of metal when Bailey jumped up and ran to the front door, barking. Moments later, the door swung open.

"Hey, buddy!" I heard Cameron saying playfully to Bailey.

Frantically, I shut the laptop again and sprang quickly to my feet. A sharp twinge shot down my leg. I hobbled over to the oven and, just in time, grabbed the towel hanging from the door and began wiping down the counter, pretending to be engrossed in cleaning.

Cameron entered the kitchen and paused for a second while he scanned the room. He must have felt that something was off, aside from the fact that I was using a decorative tea towel to wipe the counter, a big *no-no* in this house. He cast a suspicious glance at his laptop sitting in front of my 'spot' at the kitchen table, next to my empty teacup, still making noisy shut-down sounds. His eyes narrowed when he looked over to me.

I flashed him a sheepish smile, hoping to distract him from potential questions. After all, a little innocent tea towel mishap was far easier to explain than the tangled hidden truths I'd just stumbled upon. My smile stretched wider. "I wasn't expecting you home so soon," I said, my voice a touch breathless. "I hope you don't mind, I forgot to charge my iPad and had to use your laptop to Zoom your grandma."

"...OK...I actually just came back to grab it," he said.

I was only halfway through asking him if he wanted me to make his favorite snack when Zelda emerged from behind him, her tone carrying what sounded like forced politeness. "Hello, Mrs. Montgomery."

Shocked and momentarily at a loss for words, I managed only a flat, 'Oh, Zelda...' as the smile vanished from my face. But before I could regroup and follow up with something a little more welcoming, for Cameron's sake, Margaret pushed open the basement door and entered the kitchen. When she saw Cameron and Zelda, her demeanor changed to one of bright smiles and warm, welcoming energy. "Oh! Cameron. Zelda," she said, excitedly, "I didn't know you were here." Then, without so much as a glance in my direction, she went ahead and ruined my evening. "Hey, you guys should stay for dinner," she added with a clap of her hands. "Your dad has to work late, so it was just going to be me and your mom," she said, sounding as though it were part of some grand plan. She walked toward me, mumbling, almost singing, "This can help with getting to know her better."

Oh, Margaret! First, she wasn't supposed to be just waltzing in and making dinner plans for us like that. Secondly, I was looking forward to making a simple meal for myself and spending a quiet evening decompressing in front of the TV. I swallowed hard, trying to keep my rising frustration from bubbling to the surface. It was things like this that made me realize how utterly out of sync Margaret and I could still be.

Cameron looked at Zelda and then over to me, his eyes filled with anticipation and excitement. Well, I did tell him to invite Zelda for dinner *sometime* this week. But, unlike last time, I wanted to be able to prepare ahead of time for the experience. So much for that idea. At least he wasn't thinking about me using his laptop anymore.

My head snapped in Cameron's direction and then at Margaret's. "Absolutely," I said, trying to appear agreeable. "That's a great idea, Margaret." I looked over at Zelda. "We'd love to have you," I said. *Forget home staging, maybe I should get into acting!*

Zelda hesitated for a moment, looked at Cameron, and then smiling, she nodded. "That would be lovely," she said, slipping her arm around Cameron's, "thank you."

Margaret gleefully slipped past me and pulled her blue ruffled apron from its spot on the back of the pantry door. I was about to object but decided not to fight her about who was going to be doing the cooking.

"Great, you two go relax," Margaret said, assuming command of the kitchen. "I'll let you know once dinner's ready," she said as she opened the refrigerator door.

Cameron grabbed his laptop and then Zelda's hand and took her upstairs to his room.

As I watched them go, I couldn't help but wonder what else I might have discovered if I'd had a few more minutes with Cameron's laptop, and whether I was going to get another chance. For now, though, I had to get myself ready for another unexpected dinner with hurricane Zelda.

"Well," I said to Margaret as I grabbed my iPad off the counter, "since you've got everything under control down here, I'll just go upstairs and rest for a bit." Margaret was already busy bustling around the kitchen to spare the time for anything more than a quick nod. With a sigh, I slipped away in hopes of a little peace and quiet to soothe the chaos swirling around in my head.

My hip was throbbing by the time I made it to the top of the stairs. I limped past Cameron's room and saw them sitting on his bed, laughing, and poking each other playfully. He certainly seemed happy. But then again, he was happy with Penny at first, too. Right up until she ripped his heart out. I paused just outside the door to my room to see if I could hear anything else. Zelda was saying something but all I could make out was Cameron's response. "Oh, she's got a pinched nerve or something like that. I think it flares up when she's tired or stressed," he said.

Suddenly, I heard the floorboards squeak, so I dashed into my room. Cameron entered the hallway. "Okay, water and something sweet. Got it. Be right back!"

Oh, so now she likes sweets?

I closed my bedroom door and leaned up against it with my eyes shut tight until I realized I still needed to have my Zoom call with my mother. Moments after settling on the bed, I plugged in my iPad and as expected, she answered on the third ring.

We talked about the weather and then about the crocodile sighting at her golf club. I nodded absently, only half listening, as she described the creature, calling it a modern-day dinosaur. The laughter from Cameron's room and images of the things I'd seen on his computer swirled around in my head. "That sounds great," I replied flatly. Aware of my lackluster response, I injected more enthusiasm in my voice. "Sorry, so, you saw a crocodile? That must have been quite an experience."

"What's wrong, Allie?" my mother said after watching me silently for a few seconds.

For the second time today, I went through the whole story about Cameron, Zelda, all the red flags at dinner, Florida—and the impending dinner tonight.

After I finished, she finally said, "You sound very upset about this, Allie."

"I am. And I should be," I said defensively. "It's my job to protect him. Cam can't handle another Penny. After everything he's been through, why would he decide to go ahead and get engaged to a girl he barely knows?" I paused, taking a deep breath. "I need to know *why* Zelda's pushing this whole marriage thing."

"There are some big assumptions in there. Do you think, maybe, you might be jumping the gun?" she said calmly but with a hint of genuine curiosity.

My voice was tiny. "I don't know what I think right now."

After saying a quick goodbye, I relaxed into the bed, closing my eyes. Seconds later, they popped open. I'd completely forgotten about seeing Zelda brazenly hugging then kissing some guy earlier today. I rolled onto my side, hugged a pillow, and let out a long sigh. My mind was consumed with questions and uncertainty, leaving little room for anything else. I hugged the pillow tighter, seeking its familiar comfort. I tried to find solace in its softness, but in my head, the events of the day played on a loop while I drifted off into a restless sleep.

7 – AND THEN THERE WAS MARGARET...

I dreamed. And in my dream, I lived in a time before wrinkles, gray hair, and worries about my children's future. Hank and I were young and energetic, and George, my kind confidant, was still alive. And then there was Margaret. In real life, her presence loomed large, but in my dream, she was an evil queen ruling over my marriage with an iron fist. To her, *I* was an insurgent, a rebel, and she was actively looking for an opportunity to lock me in some tower and chop off my head.

Waking up with a start, I quickly realized I'd only been out for a few minutes. Still, the dream was a nightmarish reflection of the many battles I'd fought with, and wounds I'd received from Margaret in real life. All because of her controlling nature and my unwillingness to play the part of the perfectly deferential and socially acceptable wife she had had in mind for Hank. Frankly, it was only because of my mother's sage advice and Val's fiery spirit that I was able to survive life with Margaret, and her antics. Whereas my mother's wisdom—she preferred 'killing with kindness' over 'blunt force trauma'—had helped me with being patient and calm, when necessary, Val's fiery spirit had helped keep my own spirit alive. She helped plan my various subtle, and not so subtle, acts of rebellion, usually during our Chardonnay-fueled 'whine' nights.

As my head cleared, I carefully stretched out my leg and gave it a gentle rub. When I rolled over, I was greeted by the aroma of dinner wafting up from the kitchen. Even as my stomach grumbled, my mind kept going back to the dream and thoughts about my life with Margaret. Even though she'd been a *'challenging'* mother-in-law for most of my married life, she was *always* a loving and hands-on grandmother. Despite her prim and proper attitude and country-club mentality, she seemed to have quite liked changing dirty diapers and cleaning up milk vomit. Margaret had always been a consistent presence, and while she was generous with the kids, maybe too generous, she was also strict—bare feet outside and shoes inside were definite *no-nos*. It started me thinking about what kind of grandmother I'd be. Active and fun loving? Sweet and sensitive? Strict and practical? Or, maybe, like how my mother *still* is with Samantha and Cameron? The glam gran, with her winged eyeliner and stylish outfits, breezing in and out from some adventure and always more focused on nurturing their spirits than on helping with homework or providing discipline.

A shiver ran down my spine. The truth is, I have no desire to be a grandmother right now. None. I find it hard listening to women my age complaining about not having any already. Despite the pregnancy scare years ago from Samantha, which sent me to the edge and back, she's too busy right now for a family of her own, and Cameron, well, he's still my baby, struggling to find his place in the world. He isn't quite ready to celebrate his accomplishments of mundane *everydayness* tasks or being super excited about home appliances and kitchen gadgets either. And he's no where near ready for adult responsibilities of being a father. Instantly, I thought of Zelda and all the red flags. Could this be why she's pushing him to get married?

I brought my hand to my chest to steady myself as my anxiety started to build. Everyone seemed to be wearing rose-colored glasses when it came to this whole Zelda thing. I guess they couldn't see what I saw because they weren't Cameron's mother. They didn't know him like I did, and they hadn't spent the time that I had, putting him back together after Penny was done with him. But they *were* right about one thing. I needed to know more about Zelda. Tonight would be a good opportunity to get some answers, but I didn't know how I was going to do that without upsetting Cameron—

Wait a minute.

I sat straight up, realizing I'd overlooked a potential source of support and guidance. While she didn't seem overly concerned about Zelda, Margaret hates the idea that anyone might be trying to trick her. She also loves authority and control, and she loves her grandson. Maybe I could leverage that same 'protective' instinct she demonstrated for decades after Hank brought me home by playing into her suspicious and controlling nature. It's exactly what worked in the business. As soon as I put her in charge of vetting suppliers and handling collections, she latched onto it, like a dog with a bone—and we've both been happier since. It was time to 'activate' my mother-in-law. Take action, Margaret. *Be yourself!*

I heard Cameron and Zelda laughing again when I passed by his room on my way downstairs. Still irritating, but it meant the coast was clear for my little chat with Margaret. I entered the kitchen and saw her busy rummaging through the vegetable drawer in the fridge. She looked back when she heard me.

"Oh, there you are," she said.

I walked over to the counter where she had two long thick carrots resembling sturdy orange batons sitting on a cutting board. I pulled a knife from the block, grabbed one of the carrots and gave it a satisfying whack.

"You have to peel it first, Allison. No one wants a dirty carrot in their salad," she said, looking as though she was weighing whether to expel me from my own kitchen.

"You know, Margaret," I started, my voice dripping with sweetness as I began to meticulously peel the first carrot. "I've been thinking about what you said earlier, and you're a hundred percent right," I said.

"Oh?" Margaret said, washing the lettuce. Out of the corner of my eye, I could see her standing just a little bit taller. *Excellent.*

I chopped the carrot into salad-ready slices. "Yes," I said. "Tonight *is* a good opportunity to get to know Zelda better. Thanks for suggesting it,"

I added, trying to sound as humble and grateful as I could. "All I want is for Cam to be happy, but I just seem to be making him more and more upset." I paused with a slightly exaggerated sigh before continuing. "Maybe you should do the talking tonight…"

Margaret stopped what she was doing and looked over at me.

I put my knife down and turned to meet her gaze. "Let's face it, Margaret," I said, laying on the flattery thick, "you're way better at getting people to 'come clean' than I am. Remember how you got that painting company guy to admit that their references were fake? Imagine what would have happened if we'd gone ahead and hired them like *I* wanted to?"

Margaret stared at me for what seemed like a very long time. But then, she snorted, shook her head, and went back to assembling the salad. "Yes, well, it's all about reading people, Allison. Nobody pulls the wool over my eyes," she said with a slight smile.

Now that she was all puffed up and proud, it was time to push the final 'activation' button. "Anyway, maybe I'm overreacting," I said, "and maybe Zelda's not another Penny, but if she *is* a threat to Cam, there's no one better than you at finding out the truth."

"Oh, don't you worry," she responded immediately, "I'll find out if 'little miss Zelda' is up to something."

I nodded, and with a flick of my wrist, I dumped the rest of the carrots into the salad bowl. "I know you will," I said. And she might even give me an opening to slip in a few questions of my own. Questions like, *Who the hell was that guy you were hugging and kissing earlier today? Why did Cameron send you a thousand-dollar transfer?* and *Are you carrying my grandchild?* Even if that didn't happen, I knew that at least Margaret wasn't going to accept any cryptic or evasive responses this time. And if Cameron got upset, well, better for him to be angry with her than at me.

I grabbed the plates from the cabinet and was passing them to Margaret when Zelda walked into the kitchen, rubbing her palms against her tight jeans.

"Do you need any help?" she asked, forcing a smile as she stopped at the opposite end of the counter from me. I heard the water running upstairs. Cameron's having a shower, now? Margaret and I exchanged looks.

"Actually, yes," Margaret said, quickly taking charge. "Grab the salad bowl over there, please, dear." She then turned, and after digging through the drawer where we kept the placemats and napkins, she pulled out the white linen set usually reserved for formal occasions at the dining room table.

"*Oh*, Margaret. Let's just eat at the kitchen table," I said.

"Nonsense! I'm making up the dining room table—we have a guest, Allison."

"Oh, please, don't go to any trouble on my account," Zelda said, picking up the salad bowl.

"Well, since it's just the four of us tonight, let's stick with the kitchen table," I said. Zelda was more likely to let something slip if things were light and casual. I looked at Margaret and quickly added, "but we can still use the linens." It was a small victory for her. She gets a kick out of ironing and folding them.

Zelda was biting the inner corner of her lip when she looked first at me and then at Margaret, for direction.

"Fine," Margaret said, accepting my terms.

"Fine," I confirmed.

"So, where should I...?" Zelda held out the salad bowl, looking slightly confused before Margaret pointed to the kitchen table, smiling.

The table was set, and we were already seated when Cameron came down looking fresh, clean, and surprisingly polished. After some small talk and obligatory compliments about Margaret's cooking, she sat back and gave me a slight nod. Margaret then pushed her plate forward, put her hands flat on the table, and leaned forward looking intently at both Cameron and Zelda. *Here we go!*

"So," she started, "we're obviously *thrilled* you're both so deeply in love, but I am curious about something. I hear most kids these days are avoiding relationships altogether. So, what made you two decide you wanted to get engaged?"

Zelda looked over at Cameron, then at me, and then back to Margaret. Covering Cameron's hand with hers, she smiled warmly and said, "Well, I think we both just felt it was the right thing for *us*, you know? I mean, we love each other very much, and we're both better together than we are apart. Getting married is just a sign of our commitment."

Cameron shifted in his chair, looking uncomfortable with the turn the conversation had taken. Meanwhile, 'work' Margaret was in full-on interrogation mode. I could see she had her follow up question ready, so instead of secretly flashing her a double thumbs-up sign, I kept my focus on my plate while she did her thing.

"Yes, but why now? What's the hurry?" she asked with a probing tone. "You're both still so young and there's still so much you don't know. You haven't even finished school yet. It's not like one of you is going off to war or getting deported or… something serious like that. Why the rush?"

Yes, that's it, Margaret, go for the jugular! Okay, so Margaret was nineteen when she married George, and I was twenty-five when I married Hank. No, wait, twenty-four. But we weren't being hypocritical, those were just different times.

Clearly better prepared than she was on Saturday, Zelda smiled and nodded. "I understand. But we *are* better together and that helps with all kinds of things like finishing school, getting established and living up to family responsibilities. Getting engaged also adds a sense of certainty and stability about the future. We're just 'locking it in' now."

'Family responsibilities' and 'locking it in'?

"That sounds very romantic," Margaret said, "but being married can also be *very* stressful, especially while you're still trying to get yourselves established. Why take on the added stress so early on, why not wait?"

"Marriage definitely isn't for everyone," Zelda said, "I understand that. But for HSPs like Cam, being married to someone who gets them and who provides the proper support makes life easier."

My head snapped up and I immediately turned to Zelda. First things first. "Cam's a *what*?!"

"An HSP," she repeated slowly. "It stands for a 'highly sensitive person'. I learned about them in one of my psychology courses at school. They're people with highly active nervous systems and high levels of sensory processing. They're very smart, highly empathetic, notice what most people miss, and tend to think more deeply than others. But they can also get easily overwhelmed and exhausted. They tend to do best with deep, stable, supportive relationships. It didn't take long for me to see these traits in Cam," she said, calm, matter-of-fact.

"Yes, well, Cam's always been a very smart and sensitive child," I said, feeling irritated by her armchair psychology. Honestly, I had no idea what the hell 'Dr. Zelda' was talking about, but I could easily take it up with 'Dr. Google' later.

"An HSP," said Margaret, trying it on. She looked at Cameron thoughtfully and then said, "Well, I guess it makes sense. You did cry a lot as a child, now that I think about it."

"Yeah, well, Sam used to pinch me while you guys weren't looking," Cameron said, smiling, "so there's that, too."

Sighing dramatically, I started grabbing plates. This wasn't working out the way I'd hoped. Margaret didn't get a 'confession' and there was no grand opening for me to jump in with my questions. At least, not without it looking to Cameron like a repeat of Saturday's dinner.

At the sink, Zelda came up to me with the half-empty salad bowl, biting the inner corner of her lip again. My eye twitched, most likely from her energy invading my personal space. Irritated and slightly angry about her 'diagnosis and prescription' for Cameron, I grabbed the bowl from her. Our eyes met once more and then she said quietly, "I wanted to tell you—"

Just then, my phone buzzed on the counter, and I quickly reached for it, grateful for the distraction. I didn't want to hear any more about this HSP business. It sounded like an excuse for Cameron's fragile personality. *Everyone's got some sort of mental health condition these days it seems.*

"Sorry, I *really* need to get this," I lied, glancing at the number, and trying not to look too relieved.

Zelda nodded and went back to the table to join Cameron and Margaret. I held the phone up to my ear, making sure to speak loudly enough for everyone to hear. "This is Allie," I said, signaling to them with a pointed finger that I needed to leave the room.

"Hey, just checking in," Val started as I hurried up the stairs. *"Did you find out who that guy was that Zelda was with today?"*

"No," I said, rubbing my temple. "Cam came home, with Zelda, and then Margaret invited her to stay for dinner. We're just finishing up now." When I finally reached my bedroom, I updated Val on everything that had happened since I got back from work. Then, suddenly remembering, I said, "Oh, wait. His name might be Oliver. I saw it come up on Zelda's phone while we were setting the table."

"Oliver?" Val's voice softened. *"Hmmm, not much to go on, but it's a start. We need to find out who he is."* I heard her sigh. *"By the way, I have some clothes for you for the trip—"*

"Thanks, Val—"

"And a birthday gift for your mom."

"*Oh*, she'll be thrilled!"

"I know," she said, with a hint of smugness. It was love at first sight when she had met my mother. We were probably kindred spirits in another lifetime, she liked to say.

After hanging up with Val, I made my way back to the kitchen. Even though I tried to focus on how happy Cameron seemed, there were things about Zelda that rubbed me the wrong way. The drop out, the street hug, the money transfer, to name a few. There were so many red flags. I basically needed to keep a running list at this point. Well, for now, I had to play nice to avoid upsetting Cameron. So, I put a smile back on my face and turned into the kitchen. It was empty. The dishes were put away, Cameron and Zelda were gone, and Margaret was back downstairs with her door closed. The only thing I found was a note on the kitchen table. I snatched it up quickly and read Cameron's message.

Had to go. Staying at Zelda's tonight. Back tomorrow.

8 – Project Zelda

Are you there, George? It's me, Allie.

They say the almighty 'Universe' sends signs or messages you need to pay attention to. Well, I've seen a couple lately and they've really got me thinking.

Right before Cameron brought Zelda home and dropped this whole 'fiancé' bombshell on us, I saw a big, orange, construction sign that read 'Caution: Rough Road Ahead'. I swear, George, the second I saw that sign, I knew deep down in my bones it was a message for me.

And then this morning, when I was passing by St. Andrew's church like I do everyday,

I felt something compelling me to look at their sign. Normally, they have something funny or about love or forgiveness. Today, it was all fire and brimstone. It said 'The Road to Hell is Paved with Good Intentions'. What the actual hell? I'm not an expert when it comes to emotional intelligence, but those big white letters on the bold blue sign made me feel uncomfortable. No disrespect for when a church shows up in your neighborhood with hopes of attracting new visitors, but it should be welcoming, don't you think?

I'm sure this sign is about Zelda too. She's pushing Cameron into getting married and claims it's because it's what's best for him, but I know there's something else going on. Either way, I'm sure this will end badly. And it'll be hell for Cameron.

Honestly, I don't really know how to navigate either of these roads.
I just know I have to protect Cameron. Funny enough, the one person
who I think could help, is Margaret.
I wish you were here.
Allie xoxo

After roaming the aisles for last-minute trip stuff, I pushed the cart over to a beautiful display of oranges. I tossed five in a bag for Hank and could feel my mouth watering, imagining a tasty burst of tangy sweetness. Even if for a second, it was nice to have a break from my dark and gloomy thoughts. I missed *my* Cameron. Thanks to Zelda, he seemed to have taken a one-way ticket to *Transformation Ville*. That sweet, mild-mannered, scruffy-looking, couch potato of a boy had turned overnight into an opinionated, hipster-like, wanna-be Zen master. It was as if we were in some stupid reality show where one family member suddenly starts meditating, playing spa music, and burning incense, and everyone else is left standing around trying to figure out what the hell's going on. I half-expected a camera crew to leap out from behind the curtains, and the host appearing with a microphone following us around.

Cameron's mannerisms had undergone a noticeable change too. He'd been challenging me and correcting *every little thing* I said. *Every* single statement needed to be approved or validated by Zelda's opinion. *Zelda says this…* or *Zelda says that… Blah, blah, blah.* It was always 'Zelda, Zelda, Zelda'.

I mean, this week was supposed to be our time to hang out together and start getting ready for Florida. Instead, Cameron was with Zelda—at her place, going shopping, taking her to and from work, it didn't matter. Even when he was here, he wasn't. Either she was here with him, or he was on the phone, or he had his head down texting her. I've become mere furniture in his world.

What troubled me the most was the money. How was he paying for his new wardrobe, for the meals out and for the gas to drive Zelda back and forth? Was he depleting his summer savings and tapping into what we sent him each month for living expenses? And what about that thousand-dollar transfer? This felt like Penny all over again.

I hefted the grocery bags onto the kitchen counter and then separated out the items for delivery downstairs. Anyone going on a grocery run had to accept that Margaret was going to need something. This time, it was Cheerios, dental floss, and licorice for the plane ride tomorrow. *And make sure to get the red licorice, Allison, you know I don't like black licorice.* Margaret had said this three times, like I'd never bought licorice for her before, or was some kind of idiot.

"Margaret? I'm coming down!" I announced, knocking loudly on the wall, descending the stairs.

Seconds later, there she was, eagerly waiting for me to hand her the bag at the bottom of them. "Did you remember the red licorice?"

I nodded, and then she rummaged through the bag. My eyes wandered past her, and I remembered the extensive, six-month-long renovation we'd endured as our once dingy basement was transferred into a cozy, luxurious suite for her. She'd spared no expense. She had a fully equipped kitchen and bathroom, complete with granite, marble, and high-end fixtures. She also had a separate living room and bedroom, which was windowless, but still. It was furnished with cherished pieces from her old condo and the walls were adorned with colorful artwork, remnants of the kids' younger years, and framed photos of George and Hank. For Christmas last year, we got her a large flat-screen TV, however I deeply regretted getting her one with a surround sound system.

Margaret grabbed her purse. "Thanks for getting these. How much?"

"Oh... let's take care of that later," I said, my attention momentarily drawn to the sight of Margaret's suitcase looking packed and ready to go next to the fridge. "Let's focus on more pressing matters for now," I said, steering the conversation in a different direction. I took a seat in George's beloved old recliner. Reaching over and grabbing the remote, I turned the TV down before turning my attention back to her and offered her a warm smile. "How about some tea?"

She smiled and hurried to the kitchen to turn on the kettle. "A big talk, huh? Is this about Bea?"

"No...no, it's not," I replied. "But we'll definitely need to have *that* talk when we get back."

Ten minutes later, Margaret brought the tea over and settled herself on the couch. I leaned in closer to her. "We need to take things up a notch with our little project."

Her eyes lit up. "Our little project? Do you mean the business?"

I picked up my cup and warmed my hands around it. "No," I said, lowering my voice. "I'm talking about 'Project Zelda'."

Margaret's eyes narrowed. "Okay..." she said, tentatively.

"Obviously, things didn't work out the way we wanted at dinner on Monday, so I switched our plane seats around. Now, instead of us sitting together, I'll sit next to Cameron, and *you'll* be next to Zelda."

"You switched seats? So, you'll be sitting next to Cameron, and I'll be sitting next to Zelda," she repeated to herself, like she sometimes does when trying to make sense of any decision made without her.

"Yes," I said, confirming her understanding. "I thought it would give you another shot at Zelda and allow me some time alone with Cam."

Margaret raised an eyebrow. "That's clever. She'll be stuck in her seat beside me for two whole hours."

"Exactly," I said, nodding as I set my teacup down. "Now, make sure to ask about her past relationships and future ambitions. You know, like, does she want a big house and is she planning on having a career or does she expect Cameron to provide everything?" I really wanted to add...*just be as horrible as you were to me*, but I managed to bite my tongue.

Margaret sat silently studying me for a moment, then smiled and said, "Alright, I think I could manage that. Project Zelda, it is. It sounds like a spy movie." She gulped down the rest of her tea and then added, "I feel like Helen Mirren or maybe Judy Dench!"

I chuckled softly and stood up. "Well, it isn't exactly international espionage but if you can get Zelda to talk, you'll definitely be my hero."

"Hi, Sue," I said, switching to the speaker phone. "I wanted to confirm a few things for tomorrow," I said a little more loudly while scowling, ill-temperedly, at the devastatingly empty suitcase sitting on my bed. I picked up another one of Val's dresses and held it up against myself, turning to look in the mirror. *Definitely not me.* "Can we add an extra room to our package?" I asked. The thought of sharing a room with Margaret was making me anxious.

"Sure, Allie, let me check," Sue said cheerfully.

While I waited, I grabbed a flowery skirt and attempted to try it on over my yoga pants. As expected, it didn't fit. Of course, it didn't fit. I let out an exasperated sigh. Damn Val and that perfectly svelte body of hers. Feeling utterly defeated by my overwhelming clothing crisis, I looked at everything strewn about. *There's got to be something that still fits!*

"*Allison?*" Sue's voice called out. I quickly grabbed my phone and took it off speaker.

"Oh, really? I understand." *Damnit.* "Well, can you confirm again that we got the sporty Jeep with the luggage rack you mentioned?"

"*Of course,*" she said, "*one second.*"

I waited patiently while Sue checked the file and tossed another shirt onto the 'can't take because I haven't exercised in months' pile. I smiled when Sue finally confirmed the Jeep. Okay, so I wasn't getting my own room, but at least I got the Jeep, Margaret was on board with 'Project Zelda' and in less than twenty-four hours, I was going to be enjoying a real, freshly picked orange in Florida.

Hanging up, I dug through the 'maybe' pile one more time. With a heavy sigh, I picked up an old pair of linen pants. I sucked in my gut and held my breath, slipping them on. Much to my surprise, they were only a tiny bit snug. At least I now had one thing in the 'yes' pile.

9 – Up, Up and Away!

"*Bailey!*" I shouted once more across the backyard. I was growing increasingly impatient, wrestling with the stubborn zipper on my rather large toiletry bag. Leaning further through the open kitchen door and welcoming the cold air on my face, Bailey, completely ignoring my existence, continued barking at a squirrel perched on the fence.

"*Stupid...*bag!" I screamed through clenched teeth. The zipper wasn't moving, so this time, I yanked it, pulling it off its track. I barely caught my deodorant before it flew through the doorway. My nail polish and toothpaste, however, were successfully launched across the patio, and onto a pile of dirty snow. *Stupid bag! Stupid squirrel!*

I shoved my deodorant back into my now broken bag and tossed it onto the kitchen table. Grabbing Bailey's bag of shrimp bites from the pantry, I called out again, hoping to lure him with his favorite treats. The squirrel flicked its bushy tail and watched me step out onto the snow, while Bailey continued barking like a lunatic. I vigorously shook the treat bag and he immediately forgot all about the squirrel, darting back to the door. Honestly, I could have sworn the stupid squirrel was smirking at me, as if he had orchestrated the whole kerfuffle for its own amusement.

"Hank?!" I called out, and then heard the sound of a heavy suitcase crashing against the basement stairs.

"Jesus, Margaret!" I exclaimed when I saw her standing in front of the basement door with not one, but *two* suitcases.

"I'm all ready," she declared confidently, setting the suitcases down alongside her matching carry-on bag that was strapped around her neck.

"You should have asked for help," I scolded her, glancing at the oversized luggage, and shaking my head in disbelief. "I'm not sure they're going to fit—*oh*, what now?" I sighed and pulled my phone from my back pocket, noticing a new text message from Cameron.

[B there soon. Zelda still getting ready]

My stress headache began to throb behind my eyes. "Of course she isn't ready yet," I muttered. The more I thought about it, the more her audacity made my blood boil. Not only had she brainwashed Cameron and turned him into a doting disciple, but she'd also managed to insert herself into our family trip but couldn't be bothered to be ready on time.

"*Uh*, Mom?" Hank's voice brought me back to the present. I turned to see him standing behind me with one hand on his hip and the other rubbing the back of his neck, looking at his mother's suitcases. "We can't fit all of this *and* everyone else's stuff in my car." He then looked expectantly at me, like I had all the answers.

"Can you fix this?" I gave him my problem bag and the zipper. I shrugged irritably. "Maybe we should just call an Uber."

He gave me a patient smile. "I'll order a minivan," he said, reaching out to gently tuck a loose strand of hair behind my ear.

I smiled. "That'd be great, thanks." My tension eased slightly but was replaced by a sudden pang of sadness at the fact that he wasn't coming with us. I turned back to Margaret. She was busy tying multiple-colored ribbons she'd knitted herself onto her luggage handles *and* zipper pulls. "Do you really need all those, Margaret?"

"*Oh*, Allison," she said, looking up at me, "haven't you been watching the news? You can't take any chances at airports these days. You need to mark your luggage so that you can tell right away which ones are yours.

Some people make mistakes, but *some* people are actually trying to *steal* your suitcases. Either way, you really can't be too careful!"

I looked at her old, worn-out, oversized Caribbean blue luggage and nodded with a mix of amusement and respect. It's *highly* unlikely anyone would ever mistake those suitcases for their own, much less willingly choose to be seen with them.

She tapped the suitcase beside her. "In this one, I've got my hair dryer, curlers, magnifying mirror, three pairs of shoes, my memory foam pillow, *oh*, a rain jacket, my umbrella, bed sheets in case the hotel maids get lazy–"

I held up my hand for her to stop. "We don't say 'maids' anymore," I said, unsure if she'd ever be able to let go of some of her more 'dated' vocabulary. "We can say 'hotel staff', 'cleaning staff' or simply 'cleaners', just not 'maids'."

She shook her head in a mighty sour way, grumbled a bit but then said, "*Fine*. I've got my own bed sheets in case the *cleaning staff* get lazy."

Hoping to avoid a potential argument, I quickly pointed to her other suitcase. "So then, what's in this one?"

"Well, my clothes, of course, Silly."

Studying her face, I couldn't help but smirk. "Right. Of course, Margaret," I said. "What else would it be." I took a deep breath and refocused. "Alright," I said slowly, "I need to go upstairs and change."

"The Uber will be here in twenty minutes, Al," Hank announced. He started carrying our suitcases to the front door. "Even with a minivan, space is going to be tight, so I'm afraid I won't be able to go with you to the airport."

"What, you're not going to see us off?" I said plaintively.

"Oh, for heaven's sake, Allison. He'll see us off from the house. If there's no room, there's no room. What's he going to do, drive there and back on his own just to say goodbye there, instead of here?"

I just nodded, let out a big sigh and went upstairs to change. Margaret started dragging 'Suitcase No. 2' to the front door.

Fifteen minutes later, I was back in the kitchen. Hank came up to me. "Don't forget to pack this," he said, handing me my toiletry bag with the zipper as good as new.

"*Aw*, thank you," I said softly.

He wrapped his arms around me and brought me in close. "You're going to have a great time," he said, like he was trying to wish that for the both of us. "Give your mother a big hug and apologize again for me." He then kissed the top of my head.

"I will," I said, returning his warm smile. Seconds later, he grabbed his phone off the counter and announced that Dev, our driver, was in the driveway.

Hank gave his mother a squeeze. "Have fun, you guys," he said, and then blew me a kiss and walked back inside the house.

"Sorry, we're still waiting on two people," I said to our Uber driver after settling in the front seat.

In the back, Margaret was deeply engrossed in her phone. I could feel the frustration bubbling up inside me. "Can you call him again?" I snapped. I squinted at the clock on the dashboard and realized that I'd left my reading glasses on the kitchen counter. "I'll be right back," I said and quickly rushed into the house. I sighed when I heard the shower running upstairs. *He'll be okay on his own for one week, won't he?* Hank was under an awful lot of stress at work again. And he was tired. Probably *too* tired and distracted to give another moment's thought to Cameron and Zelda and how she was already ruining our trip. Grabbing my glasses, I got a pen, pulled a sticky note off the stack, and started writing Hank a series of messages.

Leah, <u>not</u> Mel, will walk Bailey all next week - 12 pm ish.

No extra treats for Bailey! or YOU! ;)

Don't forget the garbage - Wednesday morning <u>before</u> 7am.

Call me every single day! xoxo

When I tugged open the fridge to make sure he'd see the oranges I got him, I was taken aback by the number of labeled meals Margaret had arranged neatly on the shelf. I shook my head. *Of course she did that.*

Cameron was busy loading their suitcases into the back of the van. He grunted loudly as he rearranged Margaret's luggage to create more space while Zelda just stood there watching, casually taking tiny sips of the *venti*-sized coffee, or tea, or whatever the hell it was she had. *You've got to be kidding me.* They were probably late because they were waiting in the drive-thru just so that 'Princess Zelda' could get her fix.

Fuming, I jerked the side door back open, glancing at the unusual looking purse hanging off Zelda's arm. Oblivious to my arrival, she was now pacing back and forth while talking on her phone. She looked stressed. Zelda wasn't brazenly talking to the boy that Val and I saw her with, when she was supposed to be shopping with Cameron, was she? Maybe it was yet another guy she was nurturing until it came time to harvest.

Cameron came over to the side of the door and whispered, "Sorry we're late."

I forced a smile, leaning in slightly. "Who's she talking to?"

"Her mother," Cameron replied, looking concerned.

Her mother? The oddness of that struck me as Zelda ended the call and slightly turned away from the van to wipe a tear from her cheek. And then moments later, after barely acknowledging my presence, she climbed into the van and huddled close to Cameron in the back row. Forget Hank, I was beginning to wonder if *I* was going to be alright with *them* for one week.

"You switched our seats?!" Cameron said, angrily shoving his backpack into the overhead bin. I expected him to be upset. He then gave me an icy look.

"I'm sorry, Cam. I just thought it'd be nice to spend some time together," I said affectionately. He forced the cabin bin closed and stood there for a moment, shaking his head. "Oh, c'mon. Surely, you can spare me a couple of hours," I pleaded. "You can always sit with Zelda on the way back. Besides, it'll give her some time to bond with your grandma," I said, trying not to sound too desperate. I glanced apologetically at the serious looking older man sitting in the window seat, who clearly had no interest in listening to our family drama for the next two-and-a-half-hours.

Cameron looked back in Zelda's direction before letting out a deep breath. "Fine," he said and then sat down beside me.

"Thank you, sweetie," I whispered, patting his forearm. Relieved, I double checked to make sure there was a vomit bag secured in its pocket in front of me. Being thirty-five thousand feet in the air, without a real understanding of how planes work, makes me an anxious flier. I whipped my head to him. "You know, for a while there, I was afraid we weren't going to make it," I said, trying to strike up an easy conversation.

"Yeah," he agreed, "sorry about that. Zelda had to take care of something last minute."

'Something'…or… 'someone'?

Sighing deeply, I sat back and tightened my seatbelt again, trying hard not to focus on the feeling of being confined in a small space, with a bunch of strangers all breathing the same air. "I'm sure the drive-thru was busy this morning."

Cameron took another deep breath. He glanced at me, then beyond me, until we were off the ground.

Once in the air, I tried again to start a conversation. "Did you manage to get enough sleep last night?" I asked with genuine concern, realizing that getting him to engage in conversation was going to be like pulling teeth.

"Not really. Actually, I think I'm going to close my eyes for a bit," he said, putting in his earbuds.

I nodded slowly. Maybe he'd be more amiable after a nap. "…Oh…OK." In fairness, he was up late last night working on a school project and then up early this morning to pack, and then to get Zelda. So, I let him be. I desperately wanted to knock down this wall that seemed to have sprung up between us. It was killing me.

Thirty minutes later, the flight attendants came by with the beverage cart. I shook Cameron's arm gently. He popped one eye open, removing his earbud and turning toward me.

"Want anything?" I asked. He squeezed his eyes together and then opened them again.

"Ahh, just water, please." he said politely to the attendant.

Moments later, I got my Bloody Mary—which was surprisingly but wonderfully strong. I took a long sip of my drink. I leaned over. "Are you excited to see Grandma Rosemary?"

"Yeah, I can't wait for her to meet Zelda." He played with the ice in his cup.

"Cam…" I hesitated, waiting for him to take a drink. "Do you really think she's the one? You haven't really known her for that long." *There, I said it.*

He sat silently, staring straight ahead and then said, "Mom, I just can't have this conversation again." He then put his ear buds in, shook his head and turned away from me.

I stared at him for a moment and then downed the rest of my drink. I could feel the heat of the vodka rising within, filling me, and strengthening my resolve. Cameron wasn't even trying to sleep now. He was just ignoring me and constantly looking over at Zelda, three rows back. *It's a plane, Cameron. Where is she going to go?* I scoffed under my breath, then reached up, tugging his left ear bud free. "Look Cam, if nothing else, you need to understand how important school is for your future. I see how distracted and exhausted you are. You can't keep burning the candle at both ends because you're too busy taking her places to be able to study during the day. This isn't helping you or making you feel *'better'*," I said.

I braced myself for his reaction but all he did was reach over, take the earbud from me, and give me a long-suffering silent stare, before popping it back in his ear and closing his eyes. *Great, the silent treatment.* He was lucky I needed to use the bathroom. I squeezed past him, hobbling my way up the narrow aisle. Maybe chugging that drink on an empty stomach wasn't the best idea.

After squeezing myself out of the tiny bathroom and making my way back down the aisle, I saw Margaret sitting in Cameron's seat, waving at me.

"Well, are you going to sit?" she said when I got to her.

I stared for a moment, then awkwardly stepped over her stretched-out legs, and sat back down. Drawing a deep shaky breath, I quickly fastened my seatbelt.

"I had a good chat with Zelda," Margaret said enthusiastically.

"You mean 'good' as in informative?" I leaned in eagerly, nearly bumping my head against hers, grabbing the armrest between us.

"Well, I'm not sure how we got onto the topic, but she's getting a kitten for her mother," she hummed thoughtfully. "I'm not sure why. Something about her mother struggling with being tired. Or was it retired?" She reclined her seat back. "Did you know there are *nine* different kinds of Tabby cats, probably more? She showed me the pictures. But I wouldn't be able to put up with all that cat hair. Can you imagine?"

"A *kitten?*" I said slowly.

"Yes, and she showed me a bunch of adorable baby girl names—she's leaning toward getting a female cat. We ended up choosing Tabatha if it's a Tabby cat. It's so cute and makes perfect sense, doesn't it?" Margaret said excitedly. "However, we also liked Abby since Tabby cats are formerly called Abyssinian cats..."

Baby names? I recalled seeing the Baby & Co. site open on Cameron's computer.

"And guess what—"

"What, Margaret?" I said, looking out the plane window and feeling uneasy.

"She's offered to help me get an iPad, so I don't always have to look at Facebook on this tiny screen." She held up her phone and waved it back and forth. "That's pretty much all we had a chance to talk about before Cameron showed up. He looked so eager to sit next to her." She chuckled, shaking her head from side to side.

Just then, the flight attendant stopped next to Margaret, clearing her throat gently. "Ma'am, would you mind moving your leg out of the aisle? We certainly wouldn't want someone tripping over it now, would we?" she said with a sweet tone.

Margaret moved her leg and then glanced my way, crossing her arms indignantly with a slight huff. Clearly flustered, she muttered in my ear, "That *stewardess* is really starting to get on my nerves—when we were taking off, she kicked my purse under the seat and then almost spilled hot tea all over Zelda and me."

"'Flight attendant'," I corrected her under my breath, sinking further into my seat. I silently counted the minutes until we landed while trying my best to tune out Margaret's continuous complaints about the plane and the service. I dug my earphones out of my purse and, pretending to have a migraine, closed my eyes. Yes, okay, it was good to know that *maybe* they were looking at baby names because Zelda was getting a kitten. *Maybe. But I still didn't trust her.*

Margaret squeezed her way between Cameron and me, pointing at her bag. "There it is!" she exclaimed. Before I could react, I heard Zelda's voice behind me, offering to get it for her. They reached for the bag together like best friends and pulled it off the conveyor belt. As they did, Zelda noticed another matching suitcase coming and swiftly darted ahead to grab it before it could circle back around.

I shook my head and then looked at Cameron standing beside me. I leaned over. "You know, you didn't have to ditch me while I was in the bathroom."

"Zelda needed me," he said, clenching his jaw. "She doesn't like flying."

"Yeah, well, *I* don't like flying either, Cam, and you know that. All I asked for was a couple of hours," I said, feeling genuinely hurt.

The look he gave me was sullen and childish. "Mom—"

"There's yours, Allie!" Margaret shouted. She looked back and smiled proudly. "Aren't you glad I marked it," she said.

"I'll get it," Cameron volunteered, stepping forward before Zelda could grab it.

We spent the next ten minutes waiting for Cameron's and Zelda's bags to appear, the luggage carousel going round and round. I stood slightly behind the love birds caressing each other's backs. They were lost in their own little world, while I felt abandoned and all alone in mine.

10 – The Eagle Has Landed

I tapped my foot against the cheap laminate floor, feeling a slight degree of chaos. Cameron, Margaret, and Zelda lingered outside of the Florida Rent-A-Car office, seemingly enjoying the hot sun, and looking rather cheerful while engaged in conversation.

Meanwhile, the man behind the counter, Greg, with his brownish red hair—completely devoid of any style—gave me a curt smile. "Yes, she's waiting here," he said, turning away slightly with the phone held against his ear with both hands.

"For twenty-five minutes, Greg," I interjected, filling in that missing detail for whoever was on the opposite end of the phone. He completely turned his back to me.

"For twenty-five minutes. Yes, she said she made a reservation for a Jeep... Of course, yes. No, I told her that..." he whispered.

I turned to look out the front window and saw Cameron in a fit of laughter with his arm draped casually around Zelda's shoulders as Margaret gestured animatedly.

My agitation grew.

"Ma'am?"

Turning back to Greg, I looked at him expectantly. "Yes?"

He scratched his head while clearing his throat. "I'm afraid we won't have a Jeep available until Wednesday," he confessed. "As I said before, your reservation isn't in the system, and we rented our last Jeep this morning. We're so very sorry about all of this," he said, and then quickly added, "but we can offer you a discount on something else."

A mix of anger, frustration and disappointment filled me. Shaking my head from side to side, I tried my best to keep calm. I took a deep breath and exhaled slowly, and deliberately, before responding. "So, what *do* you have available then?" His face paled a little more as he made eye contact.

"We have a spacious minivan," he said timidly.

Great. I tried hard not to roll my eyes. Images of kids and hotdogs and carpooling came to mind. "And my question about adding drivers?"

After a moment, Greg turned his screen slightly toward me, revealing, with his pen, the cost of adding an extra driver. My jaw dropped in disbelief. That absolutely wasn't in the budget. Taking another deep breath, I shook my head and reminded myself to stay calm. "Never mind," I said, reaching out to sign the paperwork.

Soon, a cherry red Dodge minivan rolled up out front. I gave everyone the go ahead to get in. Margaret settled herself in the back with Zelda. Cameron took the passenger's seat. After we all got situated, Margaret, being Margaret, and a little out of touch with why people hate minivans, commented from the back. "Well, this is very spacious. And stylish. It really suits you, Allison," she said.

Fifty minutes later, there I was, in the hotel lobby, my credit card rhythmically tapping on the glossy marble front desk. Between the rush-hour traffic, a couple of wrong turns, and a sudden downpour that left the air thick with suffocating humidity, the ride here did little to alleviate my growing frustration.

The perky brunette with ultra-red lipstick who had greeted us leisurely sipped her smoothie, leaving a perfect imprint on her plastic straw. "Hmmm, no," she said, slowly shaking her head as her equally red nails clicked against the keyboard, "...no open rooms."

Suppressing a sigh, I tried putting on a friendly face. "Nothing at all? I spoke to someone named Sue yesterday, and she mentioned the possibility of suites available today. I'm happy to pay more if that would help," I implored, my hope teetering on the edge of desperation.

As if thinking quite hard, she glanced at the computer and then back at me, her expression bearing apologetic condescension. "I'm sorry, Mrs. Montgomery. Unfortunately, we've got back-to-back conferences until Wednesday and there's just nothing available. We were expecting some cancellations but that hasn't happened." There was clear subtext in her voice, like I should have planned better. But how was I supposed to know everything was going to change the week before our trip?

"Can you let me know if one opens up?" As tempting as it was to switch hotels, it didn't make sense. My mother's retirement residence, Whispering Palms, was across the street, and this was the closest hotel that fit within our budget.

When I turned to give everyone their keycards, Zelda was waving down a hotel employee. "Excuse me. Do the floors have ice machines?" I heard her say.

Seriously? I tried not to react, hefting my bag higher on my shoulder and grabbing the bellhop's cart to wheel our suitcases, and Margaret's entire closet, to our rooms. Zelda had a free plane ticket *and* hotel room, and she's concerned about ice?

"Here, I got it," Cameron said, taking over the cart. He maneuvered it through the lobby and then into the elevator behind Margaret. That placed Zelda and me at the front. I made an effort to push aside my feelings and try to be more positive. I offered her a genuine smile through the reflection of the elevator door. Zelda's lips curved into a slight smile. Before I knew it, the elevator door opened, and we all stepped out onto the plush carpet of the hallway. After some confusion, we turned right and headed past the avant-garde artwork, down the dimly lit hallway, and past a series of doors with shiny brass numbers to our rooms.

Instead of connecting through a door, Cameron's and Zelda's room was across the hall from mine and Margaret's. It still bothered me that they were bunking together. I waited patiently for them to unload their bags from the cart. Zelda was enthusiastically running down her meticulously planned itinerary with Cameron. It sounded an awful lot like a carefully orchestrated symphony of sightseeing and exploration with little consideration for spending time with me, my mother or Margaret. This was supposed to be a family vacation with my mother's birthday celebration at the heart of it, and here she was treating it like some honeymoon vacation.

Interrupting, I grabbed Cameron's arm. "We'll see you down in the lobby at 6:00 p.m., right?"

He nodded slowly. "Don't worry, we'll be there," he replied, his tone reassuring.

My eyes flitted from Cameron to Zelda and then back to Cameron. "Sharp, okay," I said, smiling broadly.

After unloading our bags in our room and letting out a frustrated sigh at the sight of the king-sized bed meant for Hank and me, I turned to Margaret. "I'll be right back," I told her and made my way to the elevator with the cart. As soon as I reached the lobby, I quickly delivered it to the front desk and then made a beeline to the hotel's complimentary snack bar, where a gorgeous basket of fruit sat. I needed a little self-care and grabbed the biggest orange I could find.

Moments later, I stepped into the elevator and found myself face to face with a lanky gentleman around my age with a bright white smile and dark tan. He looked like a seasoned golfer, and with an air of confidence, he grinned. "Beautiful," he said.

I straightened my shoulders. "I'm sorry?"

He nodded toward my hand and winked. "The orange. Enjoy it," he said slyly.

With an awkward smile and a clearing of my throat, I replied, "Oh, yes, Valencia oranges are my favorite." I then stared at the illuminated elevator buttons in silence until the doors opened.

After stepping out of the elevator, I looked over my shoulder and he smiled again. "It's almost as beautiful as you," he said smoothly.

Um...okay. That was wholly unexpected. I stood there staring at the closed elevator doors for another few seconds. It was a touch of charm to an otherwise chaotic day.

Back in the room, I wasn't in the mood to unpack, so I sat with my orange at the small table in the corner, watching Margaret as she ping-ponged back and forth between the bathroom and the closet, frantically organizing her belongings.

"Allison, did you see the size of *this* television? Wow!" she said, gesturing toward it before disappearing back into the bathroom.

"Uh, you know it's smaller than yours, right?" I said in response, peeling my orange and relishing the release of its zestiness into the air.

"Oh, I know, but this is a hotel room, Allison," she said, briefly popping her head out of the bathroom and then back into it. A few seconds later, she emerged again and darted back to her suitcases. She filled another drawer and then sat on the bed with the room service menu.

"Mmhmm," I murmured with a mouthful of orange. I savored the juicy sweetness as I chewed and focused on letting the taste and texture soothe my senses. Once the last piece was gone, I stood up and turned to Margaret. "She's got him wrapped around her little finger," I said. Before she could respond, my phone rang. It was Hank. My discussion with Margaret and my growing suspicions of Zelda would have to wait. I needed to hear his voice.

"Welcome back, Allison! It's so nice to see you again," said Cindy, a longstanding staff member at Whispering Palms and one of my favorites. Her smile was infectious.

"Nice to see you again too, Cindy," I said with a warm smile while taking in the grandeur of the lobby—complete with its warm lighting and plush chairs arranged in cozy clusters.

Wearing a lavender chiffon blouse, Cindy was, as always, ready to assist. "Would you like me to ring your mother?"

"No, it's okay. She knows we're here," I reassured her. "Is it alright if I give them a little tour of the floor while we wait?" I said, gesturing to the three behind me.

"Of course. And please, help yourself to some refreshments," she added, pointing just past Cameron's shoulder to the counter.

Once Cindy was out of sight, I turned around and said in Margaret's ear, "Can you believe this place?" I breathed out in awe. "It's like a five-star resort here," I said. "And apparently they just upgraded the spa."

"Yes, well," Margaret scoffed loud enough for everyone in the vicinity to hear, "it all looks crushingly expensive, if you ask me." Her attention was suddenly drawn to a handsome, well-dressed older man strutting like a peacock toward a tall lobby chair. It was Bob, the resident gadabout. When he noticed Margaret, he turned toward her and winked mischievously.

I tried to hide the smile on my face, watching her blush. It seemed our stay was about to get a little more interesting. According to my mother, Whispering Palms had its fair share of intriguing characters and 'romantic' entanglements.

Across the lobby, I saw Zelda helping a couple of residents with coffee and then quickly rushing to help another resident who almost tripped on the rug while carrying his coffee back to his chair. Who was she trying to impress?

"She's certainly very helpful," I heard Margaret commenting to Cameron.

"Yeah, she really likes helping people," he said.

Margaret laughed, almost snorting. "Well, it seems like she's awfully good at helping *old* people."

Cameron smiled affectionately. "Yeah, she's used to working with seniors," he said and then added quickly, "but, it's not really what she wants to do long term, *you know*."

How could Margaret possibly know what Zelda did or did not want to do? *I certainly didn't.* I strategically positioned myself in front of the gold-framed social activities schedule on the wall, pretending to be deeply engrossed in next week's lineup so I could hear more of Margaret and Cameron's conversation. I mean, c'mon. *Chair Dancing, Balloon Badminton, Kooky Karaoke...* Who knew retirement living could be this exciting? It's a full-blown carnival around here.

"...she had to drop out for financial reasons, Grandma, so she picked up that job to—"

"Hello, everyone!" my mother's voice radiated joy and happiness from behind us. I turned around, and before I knew it, she had me all wrapped up in a tight hug. "You made it!" she said, her eyes sparkling and her pink coral dress flowing. She then turned to Margaret and gave her a heartfelt hug before turning to smile warmly at Cameron and Zelda. "You must be Zelda," she said. Cameron beamed, and Zelda blushed as my mother took her hand, seeming to forget she was holding onto it as she eagerly hugged Cameron before pulling Zelda in and hugging them both. She stepped back and then clapped her hands together with a look of absolute bliss. "So, where are we going?" she asked, giving Margaret a gentle rub on the back before wrapping her arm around my waist. "I'm starving!"

The world couldn't possibly be this small. I stood next to Cameron, waiting to be seated while watching Zelda throw her arms around a handsome looking waiter. She was now standing close to him, a big smile plastered on her face while she talked animatedly to this muscular, blond-haired creature.

Behind me, Margaret and my mother chatted about the weather and commiserated with each other over their various aches and pains. Suddenly, Margaret's voice grew louder. "It's downright *libidinous* the way he looked at me!"

"Well, there's a million-dollar word for you." She laughed.

I glanced at Cameron and could see the uncertainty in his eyes as he watched Zelda.

"Oh, Margaret. So what if he saw something he liked? That's exciting," my mother said.

"It's not exciting. It's improper—and who exactly *is* this 'Bob' character anyway?" Margaret said, unamused.

I turned around to see the pair appearing genuinely at ease with one another, smiling and laughing. It was a rare sight. I hoped this newfound camaraderie might last the week, but with Margaret, there were no guarantees.

Turning back, I intertwined my arm with Cameron's. I looked at Zelda. "They seem awfully friendly, don't they?" I remarked idly. He shifted uncomfortably, shooting me a quick, slightly irritated glance. Finally...*finally*, he was getting to see her true nature. Who knows, maybe what 'Project Zelda' needed to do was to create opportunities for Zelda to show who she *really* was.

"Yeah, well..." was all he said. We stood there watching Zelda saying her goodbye to this waiter guy.

"Cam?" I looked at him again. "You alright?"

He pulled his arm away from mine, nodding silently as Zelda walked toward us.

"Whew, sorry about that," she said when she got closer. Her smile softened and then she took Cameron's hand in hers. "I can't believe I just ran into someone I know, in Florida," she said.

"Who was that?" Cameron said, doing his best not to sound upset.

I leaned in slightly, pretending to be checking my phone.

"Do you remember Shelly?" she asked, continuing when he nodded. "So, back when I was in school, her best friend's cousin was visiting, and we all went out together on a 'show him the ropes' kind of night. Oh, God, I didn't even remember his name but was too embarrassed to ask—Wes, maybe? Anyway, he recognized me." She lowered her voice. "Apparently, he just got married to a girl he'd met *that night*. They moved down here a few months ago and..."

I could see a wave of relief wash over Cameron. The tension in his face was quickly replaced by a warm smile. He shot me a quick look.

"And what do you think of Allison's stylish-looking van? She was so upset when we couldn't get a Jeep, you know," Margaret said behind me.

"Well, it's a good thing she got the minivan. *How on earth* were we all supposed to be comfortable in a tiny little Jeep?" my mother said. I looked back but before I could respond, she gently pulled me toward her, linking our arms together and leaning her head on my shoulder. I could feel her reassurance and hear her thoughts. *Everything happens for a reason, Allie. Breathe.*

11 – AND ROSIE MAKES THREE

Are you there, George? It's me, Allie.

Instead of cruising along Florida's gorgeous coastline in a new, rugged, top-of-the-line Jeep looking effortlessly cool with the wind blowing through my hair, guess what I'm driving? A vibrant red boxy minivan that smells like gym socks and cotton candy and screams 'my idea of fun is a bake sale, and my idea of adventure is finding a good parking spot at the mall'. So, in case you're looking for me, look no further than the designated chauffeur of four fully grown adults (two lovebirds, and two best friends it seems), each with their own cup holder, in unparalleled comfort and space as we navigate the streets of Florida.

Apart from that, you should have seen Zelda at my mother's retirement place yesterday. She put on quite a show for everyone, helping residents with coffee and getting to their seats. She wants us to think she's this sweet, attentive, caring girl. But nobody pulls the wool over my eyes, George. I know it's all an act and before this trip is done, Margaret and I will expose her for the fraud she is before she can hurt Cameron. 'Project Zelda' is officially underway.

On a happy note, my mother seems to be living her best life here in Florida. The place is gorgeous, the staff is amazing, and she's got a social calendar that would put a twenty-year-old to shame. And get this. The resident Casanova winked at Margaret. I mean, who could possibly

resist the charms of your lovely wife, right? But don't you worry, George,
I've got my eye on her. I'll keep her safe for you!

Miss you, always.
Allie xoxo

Let me be perfectly clear. I did *not* miss the frigid, snowy winter
weather we left at home. Not one bit. But this eighty-six-degree heat and
ninety percent humidity weren't exactly the warm, breezy, relaxing escape
I had in mind. Mornings were supposed to be bright and fresh, not this
damp, clingy suffocating mess. Think cool, happy thoughts, and eating
juicy Florida oranges, I told myself when I made my way to my mother's
place.

Once at Whispering Palms, I passed through the lobby and entered
the main dining hall. I was greeted by the welcoming smell of freshly
brewed coffee along with bacon and pastries. My stomach growled. No
wonder my mother loved this place. The small breakfast buffet was a
culinary delight, which included a made-to-order omelet station. Even
though residents' guests had to pay, it was still better than the so-called
'Breakfast Extravaganza' at our hotel. Nothing but bland coffee, sugary
cereal, and stale croissants.

Spotting my mother at a table by the large window, I lifted my hand
to wave but then quickly lowered it. I froze in sudden disbelief at what I
saw before me. There, to my astonishment, was Margaret—striking a pose
in front of her phone, in a selfie-session with my mother. They sat side by
side with my mother's arm casually draped around Margaret's shoulders,
examining photos, and laughing uproariously like a couple of teenage
schoolgirls.

My emotions were difficult to pinpoint and understand. I'd already
had one surprise this morning when I saw Zelda having a secret
conversation on her stupid phone. She looked rather disheveled, and was
half-naked, wearing nothing but a skimpy nightgown while balancing a

bucket under the ice machine. A heavy sigh escaped her lips, carrying the weight of the name, Oliver.

I could have confronted her for cheating on Cameron. But I didn't. I could have confronted her for having the nerve to do it on *our* family vacation—and on one which *we* were paying for. But I didn't. And I could have snuck behind the wall and listened in on their conversation. But I didn't do that either. It took every ounce of self-restraint I had to resist the temptation to go charging in, but I needed to handle things with a little more finesse, for Cameron's sake. I needed to stick with 'Project Zelda', gather evidence, and help Cameron see for himself who Zelda *really* is.

I cleared my throat and the lump of unease lodged in it, then grabbed a cup of coffee and made my way across the dining hall. With a forced smile, I slipped into the seat opposite my mother and Margaret. "Good morning," I said. Despite my dampened mood, I would be amiable. I would be pleasant. I would be joyful, finalizing my mother's party plans and turning this into a good day.

"Allie!" my mother said, full of good cheer. She reached across the table and took my hand. "Well, don't you look lovely this morning."

I laughed slightly, downplaying the compliment. "Oh, I guess the right hat and a good pair of sunglasses can make anyone look good," I said, taking them off and placing them on the chair next to me.

My mother smiled wide and nodded before spreading some butter on her toast. "I was afraid you weren't going to make it for breakfast. Margaret said you were still sound asleep when she left this morning—"

"Oh, you had the covers pulled *way* up over your head. For a second there, I thought you were dead," Margaret said, chuckling, "but then you rolled over, sound asleep. So, I left."

I smiled. I decided not to mention that Margaret's snoring had kept me up half the night. Simply shrugging to myself, I looked at the neighboring table and saw a sweet-looking woman enjoying golden-brown French toast and a vibrant bowl of fresh fruit while chatting easily with a staff member. She exuded a warm and friendly smile, reflecting the sense of community and companionship that permeated the dining hall.

"The staff here is very attentive," my mother said, as if reading my mind. "You just let them know what you need, and they take care of everything." She brushed her thumb over the back of my hand and studied me for a moment. "Did you sleep well? You look tired."

I've said this before, and I'll say it again. It's a compliment to say you look tired in some African countries. But here, in the Western world, telling someone they look tired is considered a shit move because it usually means one of two things; you look like crap, explain yourself or you look bad—worse than usual.

"No, I'm good, just a bit tired from traveling yesterday." I leaned back in my chair and thought for a second about Margaret's snoring, her relentless throat clearing and her frequent trips to the bathroom. Either I was going to have to set up a bed in the bathtub or just accept that I wasn't going to be getting much sleep for the next six nights.

She gave my hand a comforting squeeze and shook her head sympathetically. "So, Margaret and I were talking about Cam and Zelda. Are you still worried about her?"

"Of course, I am. After what happened with Penny, after all the red flags I've seen about this girl, and given how little we know about her, I think I should be, don't you?" I said, looking at each of them expectantly.

"You're absolutely right, Allison," Margaret agreed a little more enthusiastically than I'd expected. "It's our job to protect Cameron, after all."

My mother nodded thoughtfully. "Yes, well, then we should definitely be keeping an eye on Zelda and paying close attention to not only *what* she does but *why*," she said. "But we can't be too obvious about it, or we'll end up pushing Cameron away," my mother cautioned, "and that's the last thing any of us wants. It's certainly the last thing Cameron needs."

"I agree completely," I said, taking a sip of my coffee. The light, sweet hazelnut flavor awakened my taste buds just as the satisfyingly restorative and stimulating effects of the morning's first dose of caffeine began flowing through my veins. With Margaret *and* my mother now on board, I felt even more confident that 'Project Zelda' was going to succeed.

"Okay, now that that's settled," my mother said, getting up from her chair, "let's get a golf cart today and explore the village shops!" A huge smile graced her face.

"Actually, I promised to take Cameron and Zelda to the beach this morning before the sun gets too hot," I said, my gaze meeting theirs.

"Oh, well, the beach is going to be *much* too hot for Rosie and me today," Margaret said, shaking her head, "but it does sound like a good opportunity to see how Zelda treats Cameron in public." She paused and then stood up, putting her arm around my mother's shoulder. "How about *we* take the golf cart and go check out the shops, and *you* take the kids to the beach? Zelda would probably be on her best behavior with all of us there, but if it's just you, she's more likely to be herself. Just remember, not to get too pushy. You know how you can be sometimes, Allison, and we don't want to upset Cameron."

Pushy? I was about to open my mouth and object but opted for a nod instead. "You're right, Margaret. That sounds like a good plan and, yes, I *will* be careful." I was a little hesitant about leaving my mother alone with Margaret, but I was pretty sure my mother could handle anything Margaret might throw her way. With that in mind, I sent Cameron a text telling him and Zelda to meet me in the lobby in thirty minutes.

As she and Margaret started making plans, I enjoyed the rest of my coffee while I gazed out the window. After Cameron's experience with Penny, I couldn't help but think about his future. He needed someone who was kind and supportive, like the daughter of a friend of mine. A kinesiologist. I'd envisioned Cameron with a job in IT while she improved the lives of people. They'd live nearby and—at least that was the plan before Zelda weaseled her way into our lives.

"...of course, that's a great idea!" I heard my mother say. She put a hand on Margaret's forearm and exchanged a conspiratorial grin.

"What's a great idea?" I asked.

"Oh, nothing for you to worry about, Allison," Margaret said, waving her hand dismissively. Then she turned toward me and said very intently, "You just focus on Zelda and let us know *exactly* what happens today."

"Definitely," I said with a clear sense of purpose.

Focus on Zelda? She didn't have to tell me twice!

12 – Show Me the Money

I watched Cameron effortlessly haul our bags, along with the rented beach chairs, umbrella, and cooler, out of the back of the minivan. *Okay, fine. The damn minivan was proving to be useful.*

"Oh, let me get that," Zelda said, eagerly stepping forward. Her halter top provided precious little support when she bent down to grab the umbrella and her expensive looking handbag.

Cameron smiled to himself. I rolled my eyes. Okay, I get it. Most young men would have a similar reaction to seeing a pair of barely concealed perky little breasts, but did she really need to go out of her way to impress him? I mean, they were already sharing a room. Then it occurred to me that maybe the show wasn't just for him.

"Thanks, Z," Cameron said, giving her a wink.

Z? Really? I took one of the canvas bags from Cameron while Zelda rushed on ahead.

The beach was crowded but the sand was clean, having just been freshly raked. The water looked sparkling and inviting, enough that even *I* would consider going for a swim. We reached the top of the small hill, and the refreshing ocean breeze filled my lungs. A sense of relaxation pulled me in. The balmy seventy-five-degree weather *on* the beach felt like a slice of heaven.

Zelda chose a spot, and Cameron and I worked in silence, setting up our beach retreat while she ran down to the water. Shortly after, she came racing back, full of energy and with the bottom of her tie-around skirt wet and crusted with sand.

"Oh, my goodness, it's amazing!" Zelda exclaimed, quickly tying her hair into a messy bun. "Thank you so much, Mrs. Montgomery. I've always wanted to swim in an ocean." Before I could say anything, her phone buzzed, and she immediately went to get it. Her smile faded when she picked it up. Her thumbs instantly started pounding the screen. *Oliver again?* Cameron stepped forward with a look of concern, but Zelda shook her head and, plastering a fake smile on her face, dropped her phone back into her bag. She pulled off her skirt revealing a pair of skimpy white bikini bottoms. My instant suspicion of her phone message was cut short as revulsion shot through me when she turned around. In a white thong, her hips swayed as she led Cameron down to the water. I certainly didn't think it was appropriate to be on a family beach in that attire. Who was she really trying to impress? Or attract?

I settled into one of the low chairs and dug my toes into the hot sand. My suspicions continued to grow. I glanced over at her beach bag and saw her phone sitting just inside on top of her towel. *Maybe I could just…* No. Going through Zelda's phone was not an option. It was most likely password protected anyway. Besides, this was *my* vacation too and I deserved a little rest and relaxation of my own. I closed my eyes and tried to let go of all thoughts.

No Zelda.

No Cameron.

No Margaret.

And no damn minivan. Just the feel of the sun on my face.

A few minutes passed and then I rummaged through my bag and pulled out a book that had been sitting on my shelf, unread, for far too long. I flipped to the first page of chapter one and dove in. By the time I got to the third page, Cameron came back all wet and sandy. He flopped down beside me and settled down on his towel. He dried his face, reached for his phone, and put in his earbuds without saying a single word. He looked content so I let him be and slipped back into the welcoming embrace of my cozy whodunit. By the time I got to page five, Cameron started shifting restlessly on his towel. His leg started twitching. It was clear that something was bothering him. I reminded myself that I needed to give him space. The temptation to ask him what was wrong, was there, but I resisted. Instead, I continued reading my book. Of course, it was only natural that he was unsettled. Zelda had been so controlling, so demanding and so needy that he barely got any time to himself. Thank goodness she was so taken with the ocean—or was it all the attention she was getting in that collection of loose threads she called a bikini—otherwise she'd be all over him with that pouty little 'poor me' act of hers. *Stop!* I shook my head to try and derail this runaway train of thoughts and flipped to the next page. Suddenly, Cameron sat up and pulled an earbud out.

"Mom?"

My heart delightedly skipped a beat. Was this it? Did Zelda's public display of overtly wanton behavior suddenly bring him to his senses? Was he finally going to open up to me and tell me I'd been right all along?

"Hm?" I played it cool, nonchalant even, turning the page I hadn't even read, just to really sell it.

"Can you transfer some money into my account? I added some classes this semester and need to make the final payment," he said, turning his phone screen to me. I tried not to let my disappointment show, looking at the request for payment from his school.

"*Three* classes? Don't you think that's a little much with your internship?"

"It's UX design at a software company that makes video games. I can handle it," he reassured me. "Besides, I *have* to take three so I can make up for..." he trailed off and after a moment of hesitation, he found the right words. "...because of what happened with Penny," he admitted softly.

I gave him a quick nod. "Sure sweetie, I'll send the transfer once we get back to the hotel. I don't have the app on my phone but it's on my iPad."

"Okay, thanks," he said and then rolled onto his back, holding his phone up over his face.

Looking down at my book, I turned the page mindlessly. *Didn't we just send him money?*

After the beach, we headed to the outlet mall. As soon as we found a parking spot near the front entrance, Cameron and Zelda shot out of the minivan.

"Hey, watch the cars!" I shouted, quickening my pace, and trying to catch up.

"We're good, Mom. See you in a bit," Cameron shouted back as he led Zelda through the doors while she clung tightly to his arm.

I winced when a sudden sharp pain shot through my lower leg. It was almost as bad as the pain I felt in my heart, watching them disappear into the crowd. Shopping with Cameron was always our thing. Clearly, I'd been replaced and that stung a little.

After wandering through several stores, trying on countless pairs of shoes, and ultimately failing to find anything comfortable, I pulled out my phone to text Cameron. I sighed irritably because I'd forgotten he told me his phone had died, which meant if I needed to reach him, I'd have to go through Zelda. *Shades of things to come?*

I found Zelda's 'test' text and swiftly typed a message, asking her where they were. She replied immediately:

[just finishing]

It was an irritating response that didn't answer the question. I asked what side of the mall they were on, and the second response was more irritating than the first:

[not sure. hold on]

Hold on?

I spotted a row of massage chairs, jumped out of the shopping herd, and rushed over and grabbed the only one that was empty. *Fine, I'll hold on.* With the remote control in hand, I pushed the button for setting one. The chair immediately sprang to life. I tried to maintain my composure as the rollers went to work, kneading my back with gusto. With hundreds of people walking by, and watching me it seemed, I closed my eyes and surrendered to what could only be described as an almost orgasmic experience. When the rollers finished doing their magic, I opened my eyes. I didn't see anyone waiting, so I quickly dug into my purse, paid for another session, and then texted Zelda. By the time round two was done, she'd finally replied:

[at fr ent in 15]

These kids are supposed to be our future leaders and they can't even be bothered to use proper sentences? We're doomed.

I reluctantly bid farewell to the chair and with aching feet, weaved my way through the crowd toward our meeting spot. Eventually, I found a bench near the doors and waited. And waited. Finally, they sauntered up, arm in arm, unaware of my mounting frustration. I resisted the urge to greet them with a sarcastic comment about punctuality and consideration for others. *Patience, Allison, patience.* Instead, I greeted them with a forced smile.

"We're so sorry, Mrs. Montgomery," Zelda said, waving her phone at me. "We tried to call you, but my phone died too."

"Yeah, sorry, Mom," Cameron echoed. "At least you got my texts before Zelda's phone died."

His texts? I adjusted my purse and stood up slowly, observing Cameron's apologetic expression transform into a brief look of concern when he saw the pain on my face. *Well, at least he noticed.* Then I saw all the bags he was carrying. Shaking my head in mock exasperation, I gestured for them to lead the way.

With Cameron walking in between Zelda and me, I leaned in close to Cameron and whispered, "That's a lot of bags for a student without a job. What did you get?"

"Actually, these are Zelda's," he whispered back.

Zelda's?

I bit the inside of my cheek and looked over at her. I was willing to bet that those bags were filled with expensive handbags, clothing, and other items that no dropout could possibly afford on their own.

"So, you didn't get her anything?" I asked. I tried to be subtle. I couldn't help but wonder if Cameron was spending all his money on Zelda instead of on his courses and other school expenses. If he was, it meant that we would now have to pay for them, again. Just like with Penny.

He shrugged slightly and dashed out ahead to get the door for Zelda. *Great, now he's her personal valet.*

Shortly after leaving the mall, a sudden glint from the backseat caught my attention. At a red light and with the two of them seemingly asleep, I took advantage of the momentary stop to see the sunlight reflecting off what looked like an actual engagement ring adorning Zelda's finger.

What the hell?

I swallowed the lump in my throat, my grip tightening on the steering wheel. The impatient honking from the car behind me jolted me back to reality. *Oh, fuck off!* Instead of flipping him 'the bird', I took a deep, calming breath, then slowly released it. It was better if we got back to the hotel, without any incidents. After all, I seriously doubted they had massage chairs in prison.

I opened the door to the hotel room and there was Margaret with the curtains drawn tight and all the lights on, lounging on the bed, watching TV, and casually flipping through my celebrity gossip magazine. She looked up and smiled. "Well, there you are, Allison! You've been gone for a while. How was the beach?" she asked, reaching for one of the pillows and propping it behind her head. She must have noticed my weary expression. "Oh, you look exhausted," she added.

I flopped on the bed with a heavy sigh. "The beach was busy, but the water felt so good." I kicked off my sandals and motioned for her to turn down the TV. "How was shopping?" I asked.

"Oh, we had a *lovely* time, Allison."

A '*lovely*' time? Who was this person sitting in my room and what had she done with Margaret? It really wasn't like her to use such flowery language or to show this kind of enthusiasm. But then again, I was too tired to think clearly. I don't know if I was just being polite or reflexively making conversation, but I automatically asked, "What made it so 'lovely'?" I instantly regretted the question. I didn't have the energy to actively listen to a detailed retelling of her 'lovely' adventures with my mother.

Margaret's face lit up. "Oh, well, we got one of those golf carts, just like Rosie said, and let me tell you, she drove it like an old pro!" She laughed, clapping her hands together. "Don't tell anyone, but she let me drive it! I mean, it was in the parking lot. But can you imagine me driving? Oh, if only George could have seen me." Her eyes filled with tears of joy. "Anyway, we went three blocks up to the new shopping plaza. They had a Portuguese bakery, a bookstore I wouldn't mind going back to, and oh, a nail salon." Her eyes shifted to my feet, and I could feel her staring disapprovingly at the bright aqua green color that Lucy at Tips to Pretty Toes talked me into getting last week. "I would imagine you're probably dying to get your nails redone," she said, lowering her voice as though speaking in confidence. "Anyway," she said when I didn't respond, "there was a store with these very fancy clothes that were just far too pricey, so we walked right out of there. Oh, I almost forgot, we went into a Yarn Barn that was even bigger than the one we have back home." She pointed at the large paper bag sitting on the floor beside her. "Look at the colors I got..."

Before I could look down at the bag, Margaret continued with her tale. "Anyway, after we got back to her place, Rosie and I made some decorations and party bags. Don't tell her, but I made her a special party hat and on Wednesday morning," she paused, reconsidering the timing, "or maybe better in the afternoon. Whatever, I'll sneak over there in the back and cut some of those hibiscus flowers we saw last night and glue them on..."

She continued talking, and I couldn't help but feel a little taken aback. *I* was supposed to help decorate. I mean, I used to be a kindergarten teacher for God's sake. *Making crafty things is my thing*!

"...we had a good time. That Whispering Palms is an impressive place. And Rosie's apartment is quite spacious. The kitchen could use a little sprucing up, but I suppose she doesn't need to cook all that often."

"No...I suppose not," I agreed, distractedly.

Again, I found myself wondering how everyone and everything could have changed so much in just two weeks. Cameron, Zelda, Samantha, Hank and now Margaret and my mother, or 'Rosie' as Margaret now called her. They were getting along like a couple of besties on spring break. And now Margaret is talking about Whispering Palms as 'impressive' when just last week she sarcastically referred to places like these as 'God's waiting room'. I had a sudden feeling that there was something going on with Margaret. Maybe this was just 'Vacation Margaret', but something seemed odd.

"Were you at the beach this whole time?" she asked.

"No, actually, we went to an outlet mall," I said and then paused. "Margaret, we need to step up Project Zelda."

She immediately turned to face me. "Did something happen?"

I nodded slowly, closing my eyes. "I *really* think Zelda is taking money from Cam," I said. I'd had my suspicions before but our trip to the mall confirmed it. "While we were at the beach, Cam asked me for money to finish paying for his courses. Then, right after I agreed, he goes on a shopping spree at the mall. And it was all for her. He even bought her a *real* engagement ring."

Margaret sat silently with her hands on her thighs, her expression unreadable.

"She's a thief and a con artist," I said, "just like Penny."

Margaret sat quietly for a moment longer. "Alright, but we still need Cameron to see it, right?"

I nodded and then hesitated before saying, "What if we actually caught her taking money and could prove it to him?"

"Well, if she *did* and there was *proof*, that should work. What do you have in mind?" she asked, looking intrigued.

"Okay," I started, "so, when we go out to dinner tonight, we put some money on one of our chairs or drop it on the floor beside her as we walk past her, and then see what she does. If she takes it, we confront her in front of him. We just need to mark the bills ahead of time so we can prove that it was ours. I saw it in a movie once."

"Well, I suppose that *could* work," she said, nodding thoughtfully.

I appreciated her willingness to turn our dinner into an undercover mission. Then, suddenly feeling utterly drained, I rolled over onto my stomach. "I'm sorry, but I really need to take a nap," I said, burying my face into the pillow. And the last thing I remember before drifting off to sleep was feeling Margaret's hand gently patting me on my back. It was a strangely caring and comforting gesture. *Honestly, who was this person and where the heck was the Margaret I'd known all these years?*

13 – So Much for That Idea

Alex Trebek, the legendary and beloved Jeopardy! host, held up his cue card and gave his signature patient, but expectant, look. He'd given me the answer, and I needed to come up with the question. It felt like I was teetering on the edge of a steep cliff in the middle of a hurricane. With the buzzer in my trembling hand, the timer ticking down, my mind raced to come up with the right question. If I didn't get this right, I was going to lose the game and, for some unknown reason, my whole family. *What is...?*

"What is...*oh*...a HOBBIT!" Margaret shouted excitedly, her voice filling the room.

I bolted upright, looking around frantically. Where was Alex? It took me a minute to gather myself and get my bearings amidst the steady droning of the stupid air conditioner and the sounds of the Jeopardy! rerun Margaret was watching on the television.

...New Zealand for $1,000 and to close out the category. This body of water is renowned for being the world's clearest, Alex's voice said smoothly.

"*Oh*, come on now, how are any of us supposed to know that one?" Margaret said as if I'd been actively participating in the game show with her all along. With a hint of uncertainty, one of the contestants ventured, *What is Blue Lake?* Their response was met with a smile from Alex, who confirmed their correct answer and awarded them the well-deserved points.

I rubbed my eyes and then slid out of bed and stood up, attempting a stretch. Thankfully, my hip and leg felt considerably better. "Margaret, why do you have it so cold and dark in here? You know, we came on this trip to get away from all that."

"It's not cold. It's good for—oh, *the MOON!* What is…the moon?!" she shouted at the television. I looked at her for a moment then shook my head, walked into the bathroom, and shut the door behind me. The coldness of the tile floor sent a shiver up my spine as I reluctantly sat down on the frigid toilet seat. Margaret, burrowing in our basement, watching game shows, and scrolling through Facebook all day, was affecting her. At least she seemed to be enjoying herself here in Florida.

I took my time washing my face, brushing my hair, and applying a tiny bit of makeup. By the time I walked back out, Alex had been replaced by Pat, and the ever-popular Wheel of Fortune. Margaret was now standing in front of the closet looking for an outfit.

"Oh, I forgot to tell you, Rosie and I are going on a tour," she declared over her shoulder.

"Of what?" I asked, surprised. *Now they were going on a tour together?*

"There's an alligator sanctuary right down the street. Can you believe that? They have a tour at 5:30 sharp, so I have to meet her downstairs in…" She glanced at her watch. "Twenty minutes," she said, popping her head up with a smile.

"*Oh*, well…I was just about to call her and see if she wanted to join me for a drink by the pool before dinner, but that's fine. I'll just wait for her there until you're back," I said. "Do you have any cash? I really want to get this thing with Zelda done tonight."

Margaret smacked her lips.

My brows knitted together. "I'll pay you back, of course."

She waved a hand. "No need—I don't have any."

I glanced over at her purse on the dresser beside the TV, trying not to let my disappointment show. I distinctly remembered seeing her shove some wadded up cash inside. Maybe she just forgot about it.

"I can get some at the front desk," she said, carefully selecting a neatly pressed pair of beige pants with a green blouse.

"That's okay," I said, "I can get it."

Just then, my phone buzzed. It was a text from Cameron. Still feeling a little groggy, I read his message.

[hey mom Z and I are heading to dinner now. have a great time tonight with grans M&R text you later xo]

Wait, what?! What did he mean they were 'heading to dinner'? I quickly texted him back and asked what he was talking about.

[having dinner with that waiter Z saw last night and his fiancé they made a reservation…told grandma M while you were sleeping. she said ok]

Feeling frustrated, I replied with a short response. There was nothing I could do. We hadn't made plans for tonight. I just assumed we'd all have dinner together. But why didn't Margaret tell me? Especially since I *just* mentioned getting cash for our plan tonight.

"Um, Margaret?" I said, trying to get her attention. "Why didn't you tell me that Cameron and Zelda weren't coming to dinner—we just talked about getting cash for our plan?"

"Oh, I completely forgot," she said, chuckling to herself. She turned around fully to face me. "What do you think, Allison, the green blouse or the burgundy one?"

The little girl squealed with delight, leaping into her father's waiting arms. He joined in her laughter, spinning her around before gently lowering her into the water. With another squeal of delight, she splash-kicked her way back to the edge, eager to do it all over again. *And again.* Their playful water dance brought back memories of Samantha at that age and all the fun she'd had with Hank. I tried to picture Cameron as a father. There's no 'off' switch when it comes to being a parent. You can't just do *whatever* you want, *whenever* you want. It's like an eternal subscription, with no cancellation policy. He's just not ready for that kind of responsibility. And why should he be? He's still just a kid himself.

I shifted in the lounge chair, curling my feet up and feeling the slightly cooler breeze rustling my hair as I adjusted the phone against my ear. *"...but it's going really well,"* Hank said, filling me in on the happenings back home. His passion and excitement came through loud and clear. I was proud of his hard work and dedication, and hoped *our* sacrifice would soon be rewarded. *"So, tell me,"* he said, *"how was dinner?"*

I took a moment to gather my thoughts, deciding how much I should reveal. *Dinner was...* "It was good," I said guardedly, still feeling disappointed at being ditched by Cameron and Zelda. Then, to avoid the topic for now and with a genuine sense of amusement, I changed the subject. "By the way, your mother has an admirer."

Silence.

"Hank?"

"Oh my God, can you imagine?" He laughed.

I pictured Hank's amused face on the other end of the phone. "Oh, I'm not kidding," I said, sipping my Pina Colada and savoring the refreshing blend of flavors. "Do you remember Bob?"

"Bob? Oh, c'mon, you're joking, right?!"

I laughed. "Actually, I'm not! He's been 'ogling' her since we got here. Your mother's words, not mine."

"Okay," Hank said, letting out a low chuckle. *"She's taking it well, I gather?"*

"Like a champ." A broad grin spread across my face. "She says it's all so scandalous, but I think she likes the attention."

"Okay, well, keep me posted," he said, somewhat tentatively. *"How's your mother?"*

"Loving life. After dinner, we met some of her friends. I didn't stay too long after that, but she dragged Margaret away for a card game or something. Who knows, maybe strip poker with Bob," I said, trying to sound a little scandalous myself.

"*Hmm, maybe we should move there when we retire,*" Hank said playfully.

"Only if the kids come too," I countered.

"*Speaking of kids, how're things with Cam and Zelda?*"

I fidgeted with my bracelet. I hadn't planned on going into this with him, but I couldn't help myself. "Hank...she's taking advantage of him." I waited for his reaction, but he didn't say anything. "They wanted to go to the mall, so I took them. And the amount of stuff Cam bought her was insane. She must have hit like half the stores."

"*And you're sure he bought everything for her?*" he asked.

I told him that Cameron had asked for more money for his courses, but I didn't tell him about the ring. "What if she's stealing from him, just like Penny did?"

"*I think we're jumping to conclusions here.*" His voice was full of patience and empathy. "*Remember, the more focused you are on your suspicions, the more likely you'll be looking at things in a way that only supports them. Believe me, I don't want Cameron getting hurt again any more than you do, but we don't want our fears to deny him an opportunity to be happy, right?*"

I took a deep breath and exhaled slowly. "I hear you, Hank," I said while absently taking in the romantic ambiance created by the sparkling of the fairy lights off the water in the pool.

"*I just think we need to give Zelda a chance, Al. I'm not saying we shouldn't be vigilant, just that we want to draw conclusions based on evidence, not try to find evidence to support our conclusions. Keep watching, keep asking questions, but try to keep an open mind, okay,*" he said.

"You're right. I'll do my best," I promised. I love Hank dearly and he *is* a great father, much like his father George, who had accepted me with open arms from the moment we first met. But Hank wasn't here, and he hadn't seen what I'd seen.

I could hear him smiling through the phone. *"It's one of the many things I love about you!"* he said.

Even with my afternoon nap, I was still tired. By the time I got off the phone with Hank, all I could think about was crawling back into bed. I made my way out of the pool area, meandering through the enchanting pathway and past the outdoor gas fireplace which was nestled in the corner of a seating area filled with deep, comfortable looking sofas. I nodded pleasantly at a couple enjoying a nightcap, then headed for the front desk to check, again, if any rooms had become available. Sadly, nothing. I thought about Margaret's tractor-like snoring and the frigid icebox she'd turned our room into, but as tired as I was, there was a chance I *might* not even notice.

"Well, well, well." I turned around to find that same guy I'd met yesterday, sitting by the elevator. "Now *there's* a sight for sore eyes," he said. Despite his lecherous grin, I was flattered, but at the same time, a little put off since he had that unmistaken aura of a serial seducer. He was about to speak again when, thankfully, the elevator doors opened. I got in quickly and pushed the button for my floor, avoiding eye contact. I certainly didn't want to encourage him.

When I stepped out of the elevator, Zelda and Cameron were about to board. I recoiled, my eyes blinking rapidly while I took in Zelda's revealing outfit. Maybe it was a bit extreme of me to think, but she looked like she'd just stepped off a New York street corner.

"Oh, hey, Mrs. Montgomery," Zelda exclaimed, her eyebrows rising in. "We thought you'd still be with your mother."

Be kind, Allie. "No," I said, looking at Cameron while he kept the elevator door from closing. "Margaret is, though. They're playing cards with some of the residents."

Cameron looked awfully dapper with his sun-kissed glow. "Oh, that's great," he said. "We're just going to check out this bar down the street. There's supposed to be a live band tonight."

"Ah, okay," was all I could manage. I had an overwhelming urge to unleash my inner 'helicopter-parent' and ask if he'd eaten a proper dinner, how much he'd had to drink and how late they were planning on staying out. But I didn't. I didn't have the energy and I didn't want to embarrass him in front of Zelda.

"Have a good night, Mrs. Montgomery," Zelda said, almost hesitantly.

I was suddenly seized by an irresistible impulse. "Who's Oliver?" I blurted out. My eyes jumped to Cameron then back to Zelda.

They stepped out into the hall, letting the elevator doors close behind them. Cameron's head tilted slightly. "How do *you* know about Oliver?" he drawled.

Zelda put her hand on Cameron's arm. "He's just a friend from back home. We've known each other for...for a while," she added, her voice trailing off. Just then, Zelda pulled out her phone and let out a deep sigh. "I'm sorry," she said, pressing the elevator button again. "But I better take this." And then, to my surprise, she stepped forward and gave me a hug. Before I could react, she tugged Cameron's shirt, signalling him into the elevator. Slightly bewildered, two things occurred to me. First, at least now the whole 'Oliver' matter was in the open and fair game for discussion. Second, I didn't recall hearing her phone ringing or vibrating. As I walked down the oddly quiet hallway to my room, I felt a sudden pang of loneliness emerging. I missed Hank.

14 – Zelda to the Rescue?

Are you there, George? It's me, Allie.

My oh-so-neurotic mind is in full swing. I was right. Zelda is using Cam. Yesterday, he asked me to send him money to pay for his school fees but then hours later, she made him take her on a shopping spree which included an expensive ring! She's going to break his heart, George, and I might be the only one focused on him enough to do anything about it. Meanwhile, she keeps shaking her little tail in his face and he follows along blindly. It wouldn't surprise me if she plans to take him away from us so I can't protect him. You know, turn me into a mere footnote in his life, reduced to sending cash and care packages, and obsessively stalking their social media profiles for updates. Nothing can take the place of a mother's love. I guess I could still send him messages and show up unannounced at his doorstep, right? Right?! Oh George, why couldn't she just be the sweet, caring person that Cam and everyone else seems to think she is? I miss him.

And tomorrow will be the first time Hank and I will have ever spent a Valentine's Day apart. What happened to my family?! I wish you were here.

Love, Allie. xoxo

I wonder if outdoor malls were one of those great ideas over beer scenarios, like Uber. And if it was, who ever thought a never-ending maze of scattered shops that left you exposed to the scorching sun and burning hot pavement was a good idea? Not me. Everyone knows that effective 'retail therapy' requires wide open store fronts, marble floors and air conditioning. Just ask any *good* psychologist. I promised to myself I wouldn't complain about the weather here in Florida after leaving the frigid cold of home, but I failed. The heat was pressing down on me like a heavy blanket while I followed my mother past various scattered benches and the occasional ice cream cart to the many shops she'd had on her list. It was draining every ounce of energy and enthusiasm in me.

In a stylish boutique dress shop, I stood there and let out an exasperated sigh, waiting for my mother to emerge from the dressing room with yet another possibility.

"Oh, I think this could be the one!" she said, excitedly swaying from side to side, letting the silky fabric flow gracefully. "What do you think?"

"I know you like purple, Mom, but I didn't know you liked it enough to wear an entire outfit of it," I said.

Ignoring the snarkiness in my response, she admired herself in the full-length mirror. "Well, seventy-five is a *bit* of a milestone," she said, "so it might be a good time to try something new."

I stepped behind her to get a better look at her reflection. Momentarily disregarding my tired, raccoon-like eyes, I focused on the dress and tried to see what she saw. "But purple?" I questioned, raising an eyebrow.

"Well, purple is the color of royalty, and since it *is* my birthday, why *shouldn't* I be queen for a day?" she said, smiling in the mirror. "Were you thinking, maybe, yellow?"

I watched her move over to a nearby rack and lift a flattering A-line silhouette that exuded a cheerful energy. I nodded, quickly covering my mouth to suppress a yawn. She looked at it for a moment but then put it back and grabbed an emerald, green dress that made her light auburn hair pop. That would definitely make her the sparkling jewel at the party.

"I like it," I said mildly, not wanting to influence her decision overly much, even though I *really* liked it.

"Do you?" she said absently, taking the dress back to the mirror and looking at it thoughtfully. "I'll go try it on," she said quickly.

I nodded slowly, trying unsuccessfully to stifle another yawn.

She nudged me with her hip. "Did Margaret keep you up again last night?"

I pulled a face. "She's killing me," I said, "and still no vacant rooms."

She clucked her tongue in sympathy and then gave me a quick peck on my cheek before disappearing into the dressing room.

My phone buzzed and I rummaged through my purse feeling slightly irritated by the interruption. My irritation spiked as I read the text message, twice, making sure I understood it correctly:

[Hi Mrs. M...we're busy at a day spa and then going to the shoe museum. If you need to talk to Cam, you can call or text me :)]

Oh, so now if I wanted to talk to *my* son, I had to go through *her? What the actual hell?* I threw my phone back in my purse, closed my eyes and let out a scoff, causing the lady at the front desk to shoot me a curious look. Talk about the straw that broke the camel's back. The nerve of this girl, thinking *she* had the right to tell me when I could or couldn't speak to my own son.

When my mother came out of the dressing room, she was back in her clothes. A smug of satisfaction in finding the perfect dressed played on her lips. However, when she saw my face, she stopped in her tracks. "What happened?"

"I'll tell you later," I said. "Where's the green dress?"

She pointed to the dressing room with her eyes. "I like the purple one better," she said confidently. Then she looked at her watch. "My goodness, look at the time."

Damn. We had just thirty minutes to get to my mother's hair appointment and since the salon was a twenty-minute drive away, we were cutting it close. After paying for the dress and then waiting for the agonizingly slow sales lady to fold it, wrap it in layers of tissue paper, put it in an elegant box and then, finally, in a bag that looked more expensive than my entire wardrobe, we made a mad dash for the car. All the while, the heat was causing beads of sweat to trickle down my body and into the most inconvenient of places.

Thirty-five minutes later, I was sitting in the hair salon breathing in a mix of fragrant smells with a touch of distinct chemical undertones. I sat back on the soft leather sofa, enjoying a complimentary cappuccino, and watched Miranda, my mother's friendly stylist, wash my mother's hair. I thought about Zelda and her passive aggressive text and decided it was time to 'call a friend'. I pulled out my phone and messaged Samantha.

[Hey darling. Anything on Zelda's social media or the website address I gave you? Did you see the name Oliver anywhere?]

I chewed on my thumbnail, waiting for her response. Ten minutes later, my phone buzzed. Unlocking it—after two unsuccessful attempts (*damn cappuccino*)—I opened the messaging app to see what she'd discovered.

[Hello to you too Mom. I'm doing really well and having a great time thanks!]

Okay, maybe I deserved a bit of sarcasm, but it wasn't like *she* ever messaged *me* to ask how *I* was doing.

[Like I said before she doesn't have SM profiles]

I scowled at my phone before my thumbs danced across the keyboard again.

[Okay. I need you to do something else for me. I'll send her phone number]

Three minutes later.

[For you or for Cam?]

Well, she was in a mood.

[For Cam. They went out last night to a bar. Can you text Zelda and pretend you're someone who saw her at the bar and wants to take her out?]

Seconds later.

[No!!!! Bad plan. I don't think Z would give her number out. Nobody does that now. Give her a chance mom. C is happy]

Give her a chance? What the hell was with everyone? Halfway through responding to her, my heart skipped a beat when my phone rang, and Bea's name flashed on the screen. A wave of panic slammed into me as a series of nightmare scenarios flashed before my eyes.

She's burned down the office…

Or worse, someone's house…

Someone's house with someone in it…

Oh, dear God.

After taking a deep breath, I steadied my hand over the answer button and tapped it. "Bea? *Is everything okay?*" I asked cautiously, hoping to avoid another long, meandering explanation.

"Allie! Oh, thank *God*," Bea said frantically. "I was so worried I wasn't going to be able to reach you, with you being on vacation and all. I was going to call Margaret, but I thought I should try you first—you always know what to do and Margaret sometimes gets angry when things—"

"What happened?" I said.

"We're out of furniture for the Chan showings!" she blurted out.

Out of furniture?! I mentally ran through our schedule and then it hit me. The first of the new Better Homes jobs may have had us temporarily overbooked. "Never mind, I think I know what happened. I'll get back to you," I assured her.

She let out a long breath. "Thank you. Thank you so much, Allie. I'm so sorry to disturb your vacation, and I just got so worried, and I didn't want—"

"It's okay, Bea." I stood up, feeling incredibly antsy. "Can you send me this week's client files and the most recent inventory spreadsheet? I'll let you know when everything is going to arrive at the warehouse."

"Thank you. Thank you, Allie," she said.

I ended the call and paced back and forth, problem-solving in my head. I had to get in front of a computer, fast. Once I got back to the hotel, I could borrow Cameron's laptop, call in a favor for a rush order, go over the details with Bea, and everything would be fine.

Fine.

Fine.

Fine.

At least, that's what I hoped.

Trying to rush my mother with anything was like trying to push a rope. Uphill. Fortunately, Miranda was able to finish styling my mother's hair in record time and I was able to get us back to Whispering Palms in twenty minutes.

"Oh look," my mother exclaimed, tugging on my elbow as I helped her with her bags. "There's Margaret and Bob."

Despite a potentially disastrous situation with an important client, I stopped dead in my tracks and immediately whipped my head around. Sure enough, Margaret and Bob were seated on a nearby bench in front of a colorful rock garden, deeply engrossed in conversation. While the look on Margaret's face implied she was merely being polite, her body language told a very different story.

When Bob caught sight of us and waved, Margaret immediately jumped up off the bench and hurried over.

"*Well, well, well*, Ms. Margaret. What, *pray tell*, is going on over there?" my mother said with a slightly mischievous grin on her face.

"Oh, Rosie, that Bob sure is a character. I just came by to drop off a book and borrow this one," she said, waving a well-thumbed paperback in the air, "and there he was, following me. Oh, he's relentless!" She swiped her hand dismissively but gave my mother what she thought was a secret smile. Changing the subject, Margaret interlocked her arm with my mother's and declared, "Now, come on Rosie, why don't you show me your new dress!"

A dress! I squeezed my eyes tight and groaned. I hadn't managed to get one for myself.

"Alright, I've got to head back—" I started to excuse myself, but they were already halfway to the doors, practically skipping, arm in arm. Neither one of them looked back.

I stared at Cameron's stern and unyielding face, his arms crossed defiantly over his chest.

"Why can't you just use your phone?" he said, positioning himself firmly in the doorway of his hotel room, effectively blocking my entry. I stood helplessly in the hallway, clasping my hands in frustration.

"Cam, please," I begged. "This is for *my business*." I could see Zelda behind him sitting on the edge of the bed and talking on the hotel phone.

"Yeah, I got that, Mom. But that's the problem. The last time you used my computer, you didn't exactly mind 'your business', did you?"

"Cameron, you're being completely unreasonable. I'm your mother and I *need* to use your computer *right now*." My tone shifted from pleading to demanding as Zelda stepped up from behind him, placing her hand on his shoulder and gently pushing him aside.

"Mrs. Montgomery, I just talked to the front desk," she started. *Wait, did she just call hotel security on me?* Before I could finish the thought, she added, "They have a business office downstairs. They even have printers and a photocopier." She brushed past Cameron, giving him a slightly disapproving look, and put her hand on my shoulder. She flashed me a reassuring smile and led me toward the elevator, leaving Cameron standing in the doorway and scratching his head.

Zelda apologized for Cameron. "He's just tired and upset that he can't find his phone," she said. That was hardly an excuse for the way he'd just treated me, but I wasn't about to get into it with her. Besides, I was still dumbfounded by her sudden compassion and willingness to help.

In the lobby, she veered right, led me past the busy main desk, and guided me into a small office located behind it. Inside the brightly lit room, sure enough, were two tables with office chairs, desktop computers, a large printer, and a photocopier.

"Just type in your last name and then your room number," Zelda said, sitting down in the chair next to me. "Make sure to capitalize the first letter," she pointed to the screen.

My mind reeled with confusion and gratitude, staring ahead. "Thank you," I whispered, quickly logging in and noting how much faster this computer was than the one I had at the office.

I accessed our inventory spreadsheet and furniture dashboard, successfully. This was one thing Samantha took care of, and Bea was supposed to have learned. Margaret was right. What was the point of paying Bea if I wasn't going to let her do the job? The problem is she *can't* do it.

With each click in Zoom, I felt like I was stumbling blindfolded through a maze. When I glanced at Zelda, she looked up from her phone with another reassuring smile. "Everything okay?"

For the good of the client and the business, I admitted my struggle. "I...I need to set up a Zoom meeting so I can share my screen with Bea."

"Oh, I can help with that." She slid her chair closer, ready to take the helm. I awkwardly scooted aside to give her full control.

"Does Bea know you're zooming her?" she asked me.

"Oh, no," I confessed, grabbing my phone, and quickly messaging her.

Leaning back in my chair, I waited for Bea to join while Zelda expertly enabled the share feature.

"Here you go, you can maximize your screen too," she pointed to the icon with her long, slender, finger.

With a grateful nod, I followed her guidance and expanded my workspace. Seconds later, Bea's voice came through the speakers. "Allie?" I watched her hunching over her phone, trying to find the perfect position. First, her nose took center stage, then her cleavage. After a series of adjustments, Bea seemed to have found the right angle. "Sorry about that," she said, catching her breath. "I'm using my phone, so I can watch what you're doing and order at the same time." She showed me a glimpse of her computer screen before bringing her phone back to her face and struggling to find the right angle again.

"Great idea!" I said with forced enthusiasm. Being encouraging was essential to prevent Bea from getting overwhelmed. "Do you see it?" I asked, pulling up the purchasing page. She nodded eagerly. I scrolled through the furniture options, keeping budget considerations and storage capacity in mind. Bea wasn't much help.

"Allie?" she said, sounding confused.

Lost in my thoughts, I didn't realize how much time had passed. I cleared my throat and refocused. "Hang on a sec, Bea. I'm trying to figure this out." Given the short notice, there weren't a lot of options that fit within our budget. Well, we'd have to take the hit on this one. Of course, even without the short notice, décor costs were going up. We were going to need to find options or start raising prices. I felt a wave of nausea rising inside me. I'd made a mistake coming here.

As if Zelda read my mind, she sat up straighter. "Oh wow, that stuff's really expensive," she said. It took everything I had to keep myself from telling her to mind her own business. But then she added, "You know, Mrs. Montgomery, I have a friend who upsells furniture a lot like this— and it's much cheaper. I bet she'd be willing to do trade-ins if you're looking to change the older looking pieces."

I whipped my head around so quickly I almost snapped my neck. "Really?!" I asked, feeling a sudden mix of curiosity and hope.

Zelda nodded. "Oh yeah! She's been doing it for a few years now. Her dad's a retired carpenter. He helped her get started and I think he still helps from time to time."

"That sounds like something worth exploring," I said, looking at her thoughtfully. "Thank you."

But before she had a chance to respond, I turned back to the computer screen. "Okay, Bea, let's go ahead and order the pieces I've highlighted, and I'll call Dave to make sure he puts a rush on it," I said, relaxing my shoulders. "I'll talk to Margaret and sort the rest out with her."

"Okay, I'm on it, Allie. You can count on me!" she said enthusiastically.

With a decisive click, I ended the Zoom call and collapsed back in the chair, feeling drained. I glanced over at Zelda, who was busy tapping on her phone. My gaze inadvertently landed on her engagement ring. I let out a sigh, sinking deeper into the chair, unsure of what to make of this unexpected kindness and connection with her.

And then. "Oh, thank *God*," she said, wearing a big bright smile.

"What happened?" I asked wearily.

"Oh, when we went to dinner last night, Cam left his cell phone in the Uber," she said incredulously. "But the driver just dropped it off to him. He was so stressed out and upset with himself, especially being so far from home," she said. "That's why I sent you that text earlier and why he was so hostile upstairs."

"Ahh, well I guess that makes sense," I said, stumbling slightly when I stood up.

"I'm so happy he got it back. We've got to keep in touch—you never know what could happen here," she said.

"Maybe he'll be up for grabbing some lunch with me," I replied with a smile, quickly typing him a message. "I could use his help this afternoon with a few things too." However, just after I hit send, Zelda swiftly made her way to the door.

"We're actually heading to the museum now." And with a burst of energy, she said goodbye, and disappeared.

Alone again, I sat back and thought about what had just happened. Minutes later, my phone buzzed. It was Cameron.

[What about dinner? Just us. xoxo]

Dinner with Cameron? And just the two of us? I messaged him back with a smile spread across my face.

15 – Hey Cupid, You're Fired!

'Love is in the air
Everywhere I look around
Love is in the air
Every sight and every sound...'

Happy Valentine's Day, George!
I know today is supposed to be a day for love, but I can't help being in a bit of a mood. Cameron and I had a great dinner last night. We were reminiscing and laughing like we used to and there was not a single mention of Zelda! It made me feel like maybe, just maybe, things could go back to normal. But as soon as we returned to the hotel, there she was, eagerly waiting for him, all perky and excited. As soon as he saw her, he left me standing there like some dull, boring, and completely unnecessary old woman. All I could do was watch them leave, hand in hand, laughing like they didn't have a care in the world because they were finally free of me. When Cameron said he didn't want dessert, I thought it was because we'd had such a great dinner, and he was just too stuffed. But no. It was all just an act because he'd made plans to have dessert with Zelda. I can't believe I almost fell for her 'I'm so caring and helpful' routine. She was probably just trying to throw me off so I wouldn't see the way she's been manipulating Cameron.

And to make things worse, everywhere I look today, everyone is walking around with that 'lovey-dovey' Valentine's Day glow. Even the hotel lobby is full of hearts, balloons, and the sounds of romantic love songs being played by an actual piano player. And it looks like Samantha has a new love interest too. I saw a photo of her with some guy on social media. And Hank? Well, he hasn't bothered to call or text me yet. I tried reaching him, but he's gone MIA. I get that his work is important, but it's Valentine's Day and he knows how important that is to me. And, of all people, Margaret got flowers today. Bob sent them (but don't worry, we'll be out of here soon). On top of this, it's been over a week now and my sciatica has not gone away. If my fairy godmother ever comes back, she's fired!

I miss you, George. I know if you were here, you'd know just what to say to lift my spirits and make me feel better. But, sadly, here I am, on my own, on one of my favorite days of the year. Sorry, but that son of yours is going to get an ear full when he finally calls!

Send me positive vibes if you can.

Allie xoxo

Her treat. Margaret insisted we all go to Captain Tom's, a highly rated seafood restaurant with an impressive wine list. As we sat there perusing the menu, my eyes widened listening to the conversation unfolding between Margaret and Cameron at the end of the table.

"I thought you were waiting until today to give Zelda her new ring?" Margaret said, her voice barely audible amidst the buzz of the restaurant.

I snapped my menu shut, staring at Margaret with a look of utter disappointment and disbelief. "So, you knew about all this? And what, just decided I didn't need to know?!" I said accusingly.

Margaret swiftly lifted her menu but then looked up from it. "I'm sorry, Allie, but Cameron wanted it to be a surprise and I promised not to say anything," she said with a surprising degree of compassion. Unless she was feigning innocence.

Caught off guard, I looked at Margaret and then at Cameron. My mother put her hand on my arm when Zelda returned after a quick trip to the washroom. Margaret pretended to be studying the menu while Zelda, all smiles and oblivious to the undercurrent of tension, settled back into her seat before commenting on the restaurant's décor. I quickly re-opened the menu and hid behind it, struggling to regain my composure. The last thing I wanted was to lose it in the middle of the restaurant on Valentine's Day. Regaining my inner calm, I locked eyes with Cameron. With a forced smile and a heavy heart, I silently hid my feelings of hurt and betrayal.

"This place is so charming," Zelda said to no one in particular.

"Well, it had a lot of great reviews," Margaret declared proudly. "I found it on my phone. Here, let me show you—"

"Oh, look, there's Bob!" my mother suddenly exclaimed. She then waved to him enthusiastically.

Margaret's semi-horrified expression remained in place while she quickly fluffed her hair and adjusted her glasses. Failing miserably in her attempts to look displeased, she whispered to my mother, "What's he doing *here*?!"

With that same mischievous grin she'd had earlier, my mother said, loud enough for us all to hear, "Oh, it must be some lovely coincidence. And we just happen to have an extra seat!" She gestured Bob to the empty chair, inviting him to join us. "It's the least we could do, Margaret, after he got you those roses."

"Well, I won't be paying for his dinner, that's for sure," Margaret huffed, trying, and failing, to sound offended.

Dressed impeccably and with a broad smile on his face, Bob flowed gracefully through the dining area, exuding an aura of sophistication and self-assuredness. His gaze was focused directly on Margaret as he approached our table. "Ladies," he said, smoothing his hand down the front of his sleek black vest. "And gentleman," he added, acknowledging Cameron's presence.

After shaking Bob's hand firmly, Cameron sat back down, a little straighter, a little taller. Meanwhile, Margaret, seemingly trying to navigate Bob's unexpected presence and her feeling of unwavering loyalty to George, had her head down and was secretly shooting me an embarrassed, apologetic, and slightly guilty look. I leaned back in my chair, entertained by Margaret's secret Morse code winks to me and her attempts to maintain her composure.

Bob sat in the vacant seat right beside Margaret, his arrival creating an interesting twist to the table dynamics. Before anyone could say anything, Margaret declared loudly and formally, "Thank you for the roses, Bob. They're lovely."

His grin stretched from ear to ear and his perfectly white teeth made for a sharp contrast with his tanned, weathered skin. He had all the charm and charisma of a dashing young Robert Redford but with the same depth and maturity in his eyes that the older version had. He leaned in closer to Margaret with his head tilted toward her. "Well, they're not nearly as lovely as you, my dear. But I just wanted to make sure you knew that you were being thought of today. That's all."

Margaret blushed, despite herself.

Zelda giggled, but quickly stifled it with a cough.

And my mother declared emphatically, "Well said, Bob!"

Oh boy.

Around us, the clicking of glasses and the murmur of patrons continued. Margaret's ears turned a shade of red. She took a sip of water, attempting to distract herself with the menu again.

That's when I saw the subtle wink exchanged between Bob and my mother.

"Thank you, Rosemary, and thank you all for allowing me to join you this evening," Bob said, making eye contact with each of us. "By the way, dinner is on me."

As dinner progressed, Margaret remained unusually quiet and reserved. Bob, on the other hand, was the life of the party. A skilled conversationalist with a genuine interest in others, he effortlessly steered the conversation using his wit and charm, managing to get everyone talking, including Zelda.

"I couldn't help but notice you helping a few of the residents at Whispering Palms the other day," he remarked to Zelda after our waiter refilled our water glasses. "It was quite impressive."

Zelda's cheeks flushed, her hand instinctively covering her mouth to finish chewing. "Oh, thank you," she responded, after a while. "I work at a senior's residence back home, so it's just second nature to me."

"Oh, is that a part-time job?" Bob asked. I glanced at Margaret and saw her looking at Bob with what seemed like admiration.

"No, it's full-time. Eight-to-four, Monday to Friday," she said, placing her napkin back in her lap, "but I do have a part-time job. I work four nights a week from six-to-one at a popular bar."

Oh, he was good. That's more than I got after two whole dinners.

"I also have a store on Etsy where I upcycle clothes, purses, and accessories. I make wall art too." She paused for a moment before exchanging a smile with Cameron. "I started doing it for fun a few years ago but it's actually turned into a pretty good side hustle."

She has two jobs and an Etsy store?

Bob's eyebrow shot up. He was clearly intrigued. "You certainly are one industrious young lady," he said. "But, forgive me, what exactly is 'Etsy' and what do you mean by 'upcycle'?"

"Well, thank you," she said, blushing slightly. "Etsy's an online marketplace for handmade or vintage items—nothing mass produced, and upcycling is just taking something older and making changes to it that increases its value. Everything's so expensive these days and a lot of people are getting turned off by the big brand names. They're looking for less expensive alternatives that still look stylish and cool. So, I buy a lot of older, discounted items, update them, and then resell them," she explained. Bob nodded with exaggerated enthusiasm.

"Turning trash into treasure, huh? You're a modern-day alchemist," he said grinning.

I started connecting the dots in my mind. Some things made sense. The Etsy website address on the PayPal invoice and why she'd looked so sleep-deprived.

"So, if you're making such good money, why do you need Cameron to drive you around all the time?" I blurted out.

Everyone stopped doing what they were doing and looked at me in stunned silence.

"Mom, seriously?" Cameron said, looking mortified.

Zelda looked at him, putting her hand on his arm. "Our car died recently. My mom and I decided it's not worth getting it fixed but we haven't decided what we're going to get next. I actually prefer taking the bus, to be honest. It gives me time to work on my business and it *is* better for the environment," she said, glancing at Cameron before her eyes found mine again. "But Cam insists on driving me."

Cameron nudged her playfully with his shoulder. "Yeah, well, it's the least I could do," he said, sounding awfully grown up. "She works hard."

"I need to use the ladies' room," Margaret announced, quickly rising from her seat. "Are you coming, Rosemary?" she said, looking expectantly at my mother while Bob gallantly helped her with her chair.

Bob, watching the two of them leave, smiled broadly. "Oh, that Margaret is a very 'spirited' woman." He chuckled to himself and sat back down.

"So, Zelda, are you looking to make a career out of looking after seniors or do your interests lie elsewhere?" he asked.

"I do enjoy working with seniors," she replied, "but I'd like to finish my degree at some point. I had to take some time off for personal reasons. I'm also really enjoying running my business. I'm just trying to save money now to get some new equipment and maybe hire some help."

"Well, that sounds very exciting," Bob said, smiling. "I get the sense that you're the kind of girl who's not afraid to go after what she wants."

Zelda smiled and Cameron nodded in agreement. Well, she certainly went after Cameron and managed to get him to fall head over heels in love with her. *Okay, so she could be helpful when she wanted to be, and she sounds smart, works hard, and has some ambition. Fine.* But there were things that just didn't seem right. And who *is* Oliver?

Washing my face, I replayed Bob's conversation with Zelda in my mind. There were still unanswered questions about her. One thing was clear though, Margaret knew more than she was letting on. Closing my eyes, I let go of the lingering anger I felt over her keeping Cameron's buying an engagement ring a secret. I patted my face dry with a towel and stepped out of the bathroom. It was time I had a chat with Margaret.

She was tucked under the covers with her phone. I cleared my throat, softly, to get her attention. When she looked up, I jumped right in. "We need to talk. I know we learned a lot more about Zelda tonight, thanks to Bob, but there are still things that don't make sense. I mean, you knew about the ring but what about their shopping spree? Where did she get all that money? And what about that guy, Oliver?"

Margaret sat up. "I don't know anything about the shopping or about this 'Oliver'," she responded. "Cameron *did* tell me about the ring, but he also made me promise not to say anything."

"Okay, well, there *is* something else," I started. "Last Monday, I happened to see that Cam sent Zelda a thousand-dollar transfer. Do you know anything about *that*?"

"Oh, where did you *happen* to see this?" she asked, putting down her phone.

"I saw the receipt in Cameron's emails," I confessed.

Margaret tilted her head slightly, her eyes narrowing. "That was the day you were using Cam's computer to Zoom with your mother, wasn't it?" she said, shaking her head disapprovingly. "You actually snooped around on his computer?"

"*Really*, Margaret," I retorted, putting my hands on my hips. And then I sighed, feeling a twinge of guilt. "Okay, yes, I *was* using his computer for the Zoom call, but I happened to notice the email."

"Oh, so, you just happened to go into his email—" she started to argue.

"Margaret!" I stomped my foot in frustration.

"Alright, alright," she said defensively. "Well, a thousand dollars *is* a lot of money. Did you ask him about it?"

"No, of course not," I said, shaking my head. "How could I possibly do that without him knowing that I was looking at his emails?"

"Exactly—" Margaret chuckled slightly.

Taking a deep breath, I continued. "I just need to know if *you* know anything about it," I said. "After all her talk tonight about buying and hiring staff, it just seems...suspicious, doesn't it?"

Margaret processed my words, her expression serious. "Hmm...let me think about how we can ask Cameron about it."

I felt the tension in my shoulders ease a little. "Maybe you can tell him *you* found it in his emails," I suggested, hopefully. "Play dumb, like you were trying to look up a recipe or something, or you were about to email someone and accidentally opened up his inbox. He'd probably believe you."

"*Oh, no, no, no,* Allison. He wouldn't be too thrilled with me if he thought I'd been looking at his emails," she said right away.

"Okay," I said, grabbing my phone from the dresser, "I've got an idea."

Margaret furrowed her brows.

"Maybe we should recruit Bob," I said.

"What?!" Margaret said, sounding suddenly panic-stricken. She watched me slip into my sandals.

"I'm kidding," I said. "But he does seem pretty good at getting people to talk."

"Yes, well, I'll admit he does have a certain *charm*," she said with a slight smile, but then quickly added, "So what's your idea?"

"Let's put a pin in that. I need to think about it more," I answered. "Anyway, it's still early, so I'm going to sit by the pool for a while and try Hank again."

Margaret looked at her watch. "You know it's dangerous to be out at night alone, especially if you're drinking by that pool. You could fall in and drown or end up getting carried off by some crazy person."

"I'll be fine," I said, catching a glimpse of myself in the long mirror on the wall. I reached up and undid my hair tie, allowing my hair to fall past my shoulders. That simple act felt liberating. Not as much as taking off a bra, but it was still good. I turned back to say good night. "Margaret, I—" I paused, observing her. Her chest rose and fell in a steady rhythm. Not wanting to wake her, I quietly tiptoed out of the room and headed to the lobby.

I decided to treat myself to a well-deserved drink in the hotel bar. While waiting for it, I left a message for Hank, expressing my frustration at his lack of responsiveness today, of all days. I also lamented that I would likely have to endure yet another sleepless night, plagued by his mother's incessant snoring, along with her numerous bathroom trips.

Thirty minutes later, my head was spinning. I stumbled out of the noisy bar, realizing the drinks here had been much stronger than what I was used to. That's when my sandal's strap suddenly snapped. There I was, with it dangling awkwardly. When I looked back up, the lecherous elevator guy was looking my way while also flirting with the front desk girl. In a desperate attempt to avoid him seeing me, I made my way to a lounge chair by the pool—as quickly as my compromised balance and uncooperative sandal would allow.

I felt an odd sense of relief hearing her voice. *"Tell me everything,"* said Val, instead of the more traditional 'hello'. *"Okay, maybe not everything. Let's start with Zelda."* Before I could respond, she blurted out, *"So, is she pregnant?"*

"I don't think so. She had a drink at dinner tonight. Bob ordered champagne—"

"Wait—who's Bob?" she interrupted.

"Oh, well that's another story *entirely*," I said, unable to believe Margaret had an admirer. "He lives at Whispering Palms—"

"I thought Zelda said she didn't drink?"

I considered this. "Yeah, uh, I think she said she wasn't *much* of a drinker," I corrected, thinking back to the list of cute baby names I'd seen on Cameron's computer, only to discover later that it was for the kitten she was getting. Besides, Zelda seemed more focused on building her empire than starting a family. With a dismissive wave of my hand, I changed the topic. "Anyway, it's Valentine's Day. What did you do?"

"Ahh, well, funny you should ask," she said. *"Now, don't get mad, but…"*

I already knew what was coming.

"…I spent it with Peter."

Bingo!

"I know, I know!" she groaned after I sighed loudly. *"But you have no idea just how frickin' dismal it is out there in the dating world these days, Allie!"*

"It can't be any more dismal than being married to a man that doesn't bother to call you, or text you or even return your messages… on Valentine's Day!" I said, my voice rising.

"Oh no, trouble in paradise?" she asked. Curious as ever.

"Yeah, it's almost nine o'clock, and so far, nothing. Not even a measly text. Hell, at this point, I'd settle for a damn heart emoji."

"Well, it's Hank, after all, so I'm sure he's not out getting drunk with some twenty-year-old."

"Great, thanks. I wasn't considering that until now," I said, doubling up on the sarcasm.

"Seriously, he's probably been going full speed all day and just passed out on the couch or something," she said firmly.

I knew she was right. I did.

By the time our call ended, I felt slightly better about Zelda but also slightly worse about Hank. I pulled myself out of the chair and shuffled back to the lobby. When I got to the elevator, I heard a sharp whistle from behind me. I know I'd felt flattered before, but I was in no mood for him tonight. And not because I'd seen him flirting with that front desk girl. Fueled by my disappointment with Hank and my irritation with Margaret's snoring, I was going to tell him exactly what he could do with those puckered lips of his. But when I turned around, my words failed me.

"What's a beautiful woman like you doing here all by herself on Valentine's Day?"

I stood there, blinking rapidly. Without saying another word, he pulled me in close and kissed me, deeply. Momentarily stunned, I felt a surge of exhilaration as my body tingled. Letting go of my inhibitions, I threw my arms around him and returned his kiss. His scent filled my nostrils and my heart raced. We separated, breathlessly. I barely managed to stifle a giggle.

"Happy Valentines," he whispered in a low playful voice while slipping a room card into my hand.

It was my Hank!

16 – Forget Waldo, Where's Margaret?

Are you there, George? It's me, Allie.

I woke up this morning feeling refreshed and energized. I should have had more faith in Hank and known he would have surprised me on Valentine's Day. He always does, every single time. You've raised a good son, George. Have I ever told you that?

His being here will mean a lot to my mother too. She adores him and the fact that he made it for her big celebration, even though he's in the middle of a huge change at work, won't be lost on her.

Hank got us our own room. And when I went to tell Margaret last night so she wouldn't think I fell in the pool or got abducted by aliens, she had a rather peculiar reaction. I assumed she would have jumped out of bed the moment I mentioned Hank's name, but instead, she grumbled something unintelligible, rolled over and went back to sleep. Perhaps she's been keeping herself up with that snoring of hers too. At any rate, she's going to be happy when she sees him today!

I love you, George.

Allie xoxo

"Margaret?" I called out, stepping into the dark and chilly room. I closed the door behind me and reached for the switch to flick on the bathroom light. With a quick glance to ensure she was still sleeping, I tiptoed into the bathroom to pack my toiletries.

Today was a special day, a double meaning for my mother and me. Not only was it her birthday, but it was the fifteenth anniversary of my father's death. I know most people respond to the death of a loved one with a deep and enduring sadness. Especially if, like in my mother's case, their spouse died on their birthday. For her, she celebrates life and joy, wherever she can find it. She affectionately called him a 'jack-ass' for 'choosing' to die on such a day. *Leave it to that man to pick my birthday so I'd have to remember him at least one day a year for the rest of my life*, she'd said, laughing through her tears. Every year, we'd raise a glass in celebration of him, the eternal joker, whose passing on my mother's birthday became part of our family lore—a story we'd retell with fondness for the way that its unique character reflected his own.

I mentally ticked off the things I hadn't grabbed last night and needed for today. *Face wash, hairbrush, makeup bag, and of course, my trusty tweezers.* With a final check to ensure I hadn't missed anything, I moved onto the closet while Margaret remained sound asleep. Thankfully, the light came on when I opened the double French doors, saving me from fumbling around in the dark. I picked out my outfit for the day, deciding to move the rest of my things to my new room with Hank later. Maneuvering around proved to be more challenging than I expected. Eventually I got what I needed, including my book, and reading glasses.

I made my way back to the door and just as I was about to turn the doorknob, a sudden realization hit me. It was 9:30 a.m. and Margaret never, *ever*, sleeps in. "Margaret, are you okay?" I said, reaching out to shake her shoulder. But when I got to where her shoulder should have been, my hand sank down to the bed. "*What the hell?!*" I muttered, half-expecting her to pop up from behind me and yell, 'Gotcha'! I quickly turned on the bedside lamp. Margaret wasn't there.

I pulled out my phone and sent her a text. I was hoping for an immediate response. But nothing. Giving her time to return from wherever it was she went, or at least to respond to my text, I decided to take a shower. But even after I was done, she still hadn't returned and there was still no reply from her. Slightly concerned, I called her. But nothing. Just her long and unnecessary detailed voicemail greeting.

"*...okay, now leave me your message after the beep—Hank, isn't there supposed to be a beep...*" her voice trailed off as her greeting finally ended.

"Margaret, where are you? Call me back. Hank and I are going for breakfast soon and of course he wants to see you," I said into the phone.

Where was she? I texted Cameron, but he hadn't seen her either. I sent a text to my mother for the second time today, even though she hadn't responded to the first one. The knot in my stomach tightened. Maybe she was having breakfast or lounging by the pool.

I chewed on my lip thoughtfully on the elevator down to the lobby. For the first time since I'd been in Florida, I resisted the urge to grab an orange from the big glass bowl on the front desk counter. My mind was on Margaret.

A nice-looking staff member with stylish glasses and smooth hair looked up when she saw me. "Can I help you?" she asked, her tone turning cautious when she read my expression.

"I was wondering if you've seen my mother-in-law, Margaret," I said, flashing her a smile and showing her Margaret's picture on my phone.

"I'm sorry. I don't believe I have," she replied, shaking her head apologetically.

I nodded appreciatively, stepping back to read my mother's incoming text. The first part was a thank-you for the birthday wishes, but the second part raised my level of concern. She hadn't seen Margaret either.

Taking a deep breath, I scanned the lobby, checked the restaurant and then the pool area. Still no Margaret. Maybe she'd gone for a walk. If she did, maybe she got chased by an alligator and ended up as its breakfast. I gave my head a good shake. That sounded like something Margaret would say. Although amusing, it also terrified me. Then it occurred to me. She could be off sulking because Hank didn't come up to see her himself last night. That didn't make sense. I mean, I thought we were past that 'craving his undivided attention' bit.

Suddenly, my phone buzzed. I looked eagerly at the screen, hoping it was Margaret. I frowned. "Hey, Sam," I said, trying my best to smile as her face lit up the screen, "how are you?"

She smiled with tired eyes, giving me a detailed account of her day, and then abruptly changed the subject and asked about Bea.

Resisting the urge to roll my eyes, I forced a smile and lied, "Oh, she's doing great. She's really holding down the fort while we're here."

"Okay, *phew*. I know she's had a bit of a rough start, but she'll get better at it. Anyway, that's what I told her when she called me. You know, she's so worried you're going to fire her."

When I asked Samantha about her plans next week, I couldn't help but feel envious of how light her schedule was compared to the hectic week I'd be going home to. We continued talking as I made my way up to what was now Margaret's room. I'd missed my chats with Samantha. However, when she asked how everything was going here, I kept it light. I told her about her father's surprise arrival but didn't mention Margaret's mysterious disappearance. I didn't want to talk about Zelda either. Based on our recent text conversation, she was clearly on the 'Z' team.

She abruptly changed the subject again. "Zelda's birthday's next month, and Cameron wanted some advice on what to get her."

"Oh?" I responded, hiding my disappointment. Cameron hadn't bothered to ask me, his shopping buddy, for advice.

"Yeah..." Samantha nodded slowly, clearly distracted. She spoke again. "He wants to get her something special and asked me for suggestions."

What, the engagement ring wasn't enough?

I managed a smile. "Well, I'm sure you'll come up with some great ideas."

"I dunno. She's not on social media so it's hard to tell what she likes or doesn't like. And, obviously, I don't want to come right out and ask her." *So now she's having conversations with Zelda?*

"I'm sure you'll figure something out, Sam," I said.

Margaret's disappearance, and now my feelings over Samantha's easy acceptance of Zelda, was souring my mood. It seemed like Zelda was making her way into every corner of the family. First Cameron, now Samantha and maybe even Margaret. Who was next, Hank? My mother? Val?

"I mean, yeah," she said, sounding disappointed with my unenthusiastic responses. Again, she glanced away, seemingly distracted. "Anyway—"

"Am I keeping you from something?" I asked, letting a little more irritation show than I'd meant to.

Her expression was uncertain. "No, sorry," she said, shrugging. I heard her take a deep breath. "So, um, I'm going to Australia in two weeks…"

I blinked. For a dizzying moment, I felt surprised at just how unsurprised I was. "Australia?" I repeated. "What happened to Europe and that whole plan to work or volunteer or whatever it was? And how are you affording all this globetrotting?"

"Oh Mom, don't worry about it. My friend told me about this working holiday visa. His friend already works there bartending and said they're *always* hiring…" she explained. "And I'd really love to see Australia. It seems so nice," she added. It sounded like a complex plan.

As Samantha continued talking, I realized I missed Cameron more. My connection with him had always been stronger. Samantha marched to the beat of her own drummer. She was bold and spontaneous. She could be out enjoying coffee with a friend one minute, and the next…who knows? *She* doesn't even know. Samantha would always live fearlessly, making decisions without anyone's approval.

Alone in Margaret's room, I stretched out on her bed and listened to Samantha's latest plans. I knew I'd told myself that nothing was going to bring me down today, but I was already physically and emotionally exhausted, and my leg ached. Where *was* Margaret and how could I *possibly* regain my party mood now?

17 – Confessions

I paced back and forth in Margaret's room, waiting for the tiny coffee machine to work its magic and deliver me my first cup of the day. I called her again, and for the third time, it went straight to voicemail. Unable to sit still, I spun on my heels and drew back the thick, heavy curtains. As the midmorning light flooded the room, my eyes fell upon the dresser and there, right next to the TV, sat Margaret's cell phone, devoid of any life. *She left without her phone?* I mean, sure, she could have been taking a momentary break from Facebook, I supposed. But unlikely. Something didn't feel right.

I typed out a message to Cameron.

[Have you heard from your grandmother yet?]

No, of course he hadn't, I thought, even before I hit send. I looked around the room for anything else that might provide a clue of her whereabouts. When nothing jumped out at me, I flopped down onto the bed. *Think, think, think.* Thankfully, Hank was busy with work. I wasn't ready to tell him, just yet.

I called my mother. "Happy birthday, again!" I said, keeping my tone cheerful. "You haven't seen or heard from Margaret yet, have you?"

"No…" she answered slowly. "Why? Is everything okay?"

There should be some kind of amber alert for missing seniors. #WhereIsMargaret? I was getting more and more worried with each passing minute. We had a toothbrush that was dry and her preferred shoes at the door. *If anyone knows where she is, please speak up.*

Back in the bathroom, I splashed cold water on my face. *Maybe she went shopping*, I mumbled to my reflection in the mirror. *Oh no, shopping!* I braced myself against the counter as another wave of panic flooded through me. I was dressless and presentless for my mother's big day.

First things first. #WhereIsMargaret? I couldn't help but think about how Bailey had slipped out of our back gate, pulling his own disappearing act years ago. He hadn't 'run away', per se. Why would he? He's got the perfect setup, complete with personal chefs, unlimited treats, and countless cuddles. It was more like an adventure gone awry when he got lost. Obviously, Margaret hadn't 'run away' either. And why on earth would she? She knows the grass isn't always greener on the other side. It's just more grass. I grabbed the room key and marched out of the room.

I smacked the elevator button repeatedly while #WhereIsMargaret? screamed in my head. Alligators kill people down here. What about sharks? How close do *they* come to the beach? Can Margaret even swim? When the doors finally opened, I rushed inside, and let out a long sigh as they slid closed again. I couldn't shake the whirlwind of emotions and irrational fears that her disappearance had triggered.

I power walked toward the main entrance, quickly scanning the lobby. I was a woman on a mission but with no clear destination. When I passed the front desk, I caught sight of Zelda, her back pressed up against the lobby's majestic marble pillars. I hesitated for a moment but then headed over to her.

"Oh, Mrs. Montgomery," she said, gently rubbing her finger under her eye.

"Hi," I said hurriedly, smiling of course. "Have you seen Margaret?"

"Ahh, no, I'm sorry. I haven't seen her," she said. "Is everything okay?"

I suddenly noticed that she looked…plain awful. Stress tugged at the corners of her teary eyes, her mouth drooping. Something was amiss. I couldn't help but wonder if she and Cameron were fighting. "Are you okay?" I quickly asked, putting my concern for Margaret aside.

"I'm okay, thanks. But Cam's not feeling well," she said.

I gripped the tall chair next to her. "Is he sick? I'll go—"

"No. No," she quickly interjected, her eyes wide. "I mean, he's just a little under the weather. It's nothing serious, really. He'll be okay. There's no need to check on him unless you really want to," she said, her words laced with an odd sense of reassurance.

Yes, I wanted to check in on him. That was exactly what I wanted to do. "I'll just drop in for a second," I said.

Zelda smiled weakly as she pulled her room key out of her back pocket and held it out to me. "Just in case he's sleeping and doesn't hear you," she offered, her voice softening.

"Thank you," I said gratefully. There was something about her sad eyes that made me want to reach out—maybe even hug her, but knowing Cameron was sick consumed any other thoughts. I spun around and nearly sprinted to the elevator.

When I got to the door, I made sure to knock. Once inside, I found Cameron lying on the bed with his hand resting on his stomach.

"Hey you," I whispered. "I just—"

"Hey, Mom," he murmured, sounding relieved to see me.

I took a good look at his face before instinctively putting my hand gently on his forehead. "Zelda said you weren't feeling well," I said, checking for signs of a fever.

"Yeah, it's probably something I ate," he moaned, before rolling onto his side and making room for me.

He reached out and put his hand on my forearm. "Did you find Grandma?"

Who?

I shook my head, and we sat in silence for a few moments. My heart swelled with joy when I realized that all Cameron wanted was the comfort of his mother. I think.

"I can't remember the last time my stomach felt like this," he said, managing a small smile.

I rummaged through my purse and triumphantly found a tiny pink nausea tablet. I handed it to him along with a glass of warm water and then sat back down on the bed. I gave his hand a gentle squeeze before leaning over and picking up the hotel phone on the side table. After three rings, a courteous voice answered.

"Hi, yes. I'd like to order some room service," I said. "Yes…ah, Ginger Ale and plain toast, please."

Cameron settled back into the pillows, yawning. "Thanks, Mom. I'm glad you're here," he said, giving me a sweet smile before closing his eyes.

Feeling a sense of calmness, I nestled beside him. If he wanted quiet company, I could be that. "You're welcome," I whispered.

To my surprise, the room itself was clean and organized. I half-expected to see suitcases left open, clothes strewn across the floor, and snack wrappers and food containers scattered about. Everything was neatly in its place. Given their empty suitcases, I was almost certain their clothes were folded and stowed away in the glossy dresser or pressed and hung up in the tiny closet.

"Wow," I said, breaking the silence.

Cameron's eyes popped open. "What?"

"This room is…clean," I said.

His laugh sounded rusty.

"I mean, it's *so* tidy, I could probably eat off of every surface with no worries," I said.

He wrinkled his nose. "You'd eat off a hotel carpet?"

"Yeah, well, you got me there," I said, "but your grandma would certainly approve of how clean this room is." Suddenly #WhereIsMargaret? played in my mind again. I needed to find her, but for right now, I needed to be here with Cameron. Margaret was a grown woman who was perfectly capable of taking care of herself, wasn't she?

Cameron and I locked eyes again and laughed. His laughter quickly faded, and a look of pain crossed his face. I felt it in my heart so sharply that I sat straight up.

"Oh, Cam, what is it?"

"Mom," he said, his voice trembling, "I think getting married now might be a mistake." There it was. The truth.

I sat there, stunned by his confession. Disbelief, hope and an odd streak of heartache shot through me. *Was this why Zelda looked so upset downstairs?* I squeezed his hand tightly to ground myself.

For the next ten minutes, Cameron opened up to me. He stumbled, searching for the right words to convey his emotions. I needed to tread carefully, so I made a conscious effort to remain silent and let him speak. He told me how much he loved Zelda but that maybe they *were* too young. School should come first, he said. He paused, seemingly waiting for a response. I simply nodded supportively and encouraged him to go on. When he finished, I chose my words carefully, being mindful not to challenge anything he'd said as his eyes filled with tears. Keeping my face calm, my tone soothing, I ran my hand through his hair. I swallowed all other questions swirling in my head, except for one. "So, what now?"

18 – Celebrate Good Times, Come On!

Are you there, George? It's me, Allie.

So, I have some good news and some bad news—which do you want first?

…Well, let's start off with the bad news and say that Margaret is missing. We're not talking 'missing persons' missing, like, with police, helicopters, and breaking news headlines. More like 'MIA' kinda missing. At least I hope so. I mean, Margaret's a grown woman with a mind of her own, and if she wants to go off somewhere without telling anyone, that's really no one's business but hers, right? Still, I'm a bit worried. Maybe I should have kept a closer eye on her. I dunno. Anyway, I haven't said anything to Hank yet but I'm sure she's fine, especially with you watching over her.

Let's move on to the good news. Cameron came to his senses and changed his mind about getting married. Can you believe it? I mean, love is a fickle thing, but it's still hard to wrap my head around the fact that he fought so hard for this, and he only just bought her a ring. So why is he backing out now? It's not like they had a major fight or anything, at least not that I know of. It makes me wonder why they were in such a hurry to get married in the first place. Was Zelda pressuring him into it or was he originally just trying to keep her from leaving him like Penny did? Well, I guess all that really matters now is that I got my son back. He confided in me again, George. All it took

*was a little patience, love, and understanding, which we both know I'm
absolutely full of. Right?*

Love you, talk soon!

Allie xoxo

"Oh." My mother paused, pinching the neck of a purple balloon before continuing, "I forgot to tell you that Cathy, you know her, she's the nosey one down the hall from me, saw Margaret late last night. Does that help?" she asked, smiling as she expertly tied a knot in the base of the balloon.

"And you're just telling me this *now?*" I said, getting mad. "*What time?!*"

She stopped what she was doing, raised her eyebrows and gave me 'the look'.

I took a slow, deep breath and tried again. "Sorry. Did Cathy say when and where she saw Margaret?"

"Much better," she said smiling as the balloon bobbed in her hand. "Well, according to Cathy, Margaret was here for our 'Night Owls' movie night."

"But how? She was sleeping when I went down to the lobby last night, *and* when I came back up to get my pajamas and tell her Hank was here. That was around ten-thirty," I said, feeling confused. I watched absentmindedly as the balloon floated up toward the end of its tether after my mother released it. "I can't believe she'd just go running off without telling anyone," I said, still staring at the balloon and silently wishing it would pop.

My mother laughed, shaking her head slightly. "Allie, it's been a while since she's really been free to enjoy the company of people her own age and do things on her own. You need to relax and cut her a little slack. Who knows, maybe she just woke up and felt like a little company. 'Night Owls' movies don't start until eleven."

So, Margaret *could* have gone to the movie after I came by. And my mother *wasn't* wrong about my cutting her some slack. It was Margaret's vacation too, after all. So, if she felt like prancing around at all hours of the night, well, who was I to stand in her way?

I relaxed and sat down. "So, did Cathy say anything else?" I asked while creating an eye-catching streamer out of pink and purple crepe paper.

"Well, yes," my mother said hesitantly, "she said it looked like Margaret was having *lots of fun* with her new friend." She barely tried to suppress the big grin plastered on her face.

"*Bob?!*"

My mother just shrugged as she continued twisting and twirling a silver ribbon around another purple balloon she was holding. She glanced at me out of the corner of her eye and then burst out laughing. "Oh Allie, *of course* she means Bob."

With the 'party room' now fully decorated and ready for tonight's festivities, my mother and I enjoyed a light lunch in the dining room. Soon after, I headed back to the hotel, hoping to find Margaret or at least find some sign she'd returned. I made a mental note not to mention her little late-night escapade to Hank. As long as she was safe and sound, there was no harm in "Florida Margaret' spreading her wings.

As I made my way down the quiet hallway, I was startled by a sudden clinking of ice cubes. I turned to my right and there was Zelda, hunched over and diligently filling a bucket with ice in the dimly lit alcove. She jumped in surprise when she noticed me, a slight, fragile smile appearing on her face.

"I have to ask…what's all the ice for?" I said.

She clutched the metal bucket against her chest, clearing her throat. "Um, I'm trying a new technique. It's something I saw online," she said, sounding guarded.

I hoisted my heavy purse further up onto my shoulder, keeping my eyes fixed on her. "Oh, I see," I replied awkwardly, although I had no idea what this 'technique' could possibly be. It occurred to me she could be using the ice for some kind of weird sex thing. Maybe this was the 'real' reason Cameron changed his mind about getting married. Poor guy, no wonder he was feeling sick. "Ah, well, good luck," I said, suddenly feeling uncomfortable. She responded with another weak smile as I made my way back down the hallway.

Once back in Margaret's room, it was clear she hadn't returned. I sat on the edge of the bed, pulled out my phone and typed in *ice technique* to which Google added ...*for anxiety*. Anxiety. Okay, not great, but better than some bizarre and disturbing possibility that'd been running through my head. This 'technique' for dealing with anxiety amounted to little more than plunging your face or body into ice water. *Who needs Valium when you can find solace in the depths of your freezer?* I laughed at the absurdity of it all.

I was about to dive deeper down this rabbit hole when there was a sharp knock on the door. Startled, I heard Hank calling out from the other side. "Mom? Allie?"

I jumped up and quickly opened the door to find Hank standing there with a concerned look on his face. He placed his hand on my shoulder, poking his head into the room. "Is my mother here?"

A sudden rush of guilt surged through me. "Actually, no," I said slowly. "I just came to grab the rest of my stuff—"

"Well, do you know where she is?" he asked impatiently. "I've been calling and texting her for a while now to see if she wants to have lunch, but she hasn't been answering her phone or responding to any of my texts. I tried Cam, too, but he hasn't been answering his phone either. Have you heard from either of them?"

I took a deep breath and exhaled slowly. *Okay, here we go.* "Well, Cam isn't feeling well," I said. "It's nothing serious. He's probably just sleeping right now." I hesitated a moment. "As for your mother, I've been looking for her too," I confessed. "She's been gone all morning. I tried contacting her too but then found her phone here. Looks like she forgot to charge it." I paused and then added, "I think she's out with Bob."

For a second, he stood there looking at me with a puzzled expression. "You mean, 'Bob' from across the street?" he finally said.

I nodded slowly. "I'm not sure but I think so."

"Okay, but why would she go off without telling anyone?" he said, his lips forming a thin line.

"Well, if she wants to go see a movie or whatever with Bob, or anyone else for that matter, that's her business, right?"

"A movie?"

Oops.

He glanced at his watch. "Well, I don't think any movies start this early and it's not like her to just go off without at least saying something to someone, is it?"

"Well, actually, the movie was last..." I paused for a half-second. "Hank, I'm sure she's fine. She's been pretty independent this week. And she really seems to be enjoying herself. Honestly, I don't think she's looked this happy for a long time. There's probably nothing to worry about," I said, although I wasn't sure who I was trying to convince more, him or me.

Hank thought for a moment and then nodded slowly. "You're probably right," he said with a sigh. "I just want to make sure she's okay. It's strange to think of her out somewhere without us. And with *Bob*—"

"I know, but we'll see her soon. She's not going to miss the party," I said, leaning in and squeezing him tight. I thought about that amber alert for seniors. Time to add Bob. #MargaretAndBobAreMIA

When Hank and I stepped into the party room at Whispering Palms, the smell of Italian cuisine filled my nostrils. James Brown's 'I Got You' resonated throughout the room, courtesy of an impressive little sound system set up earlier by a pair of enthusiastic staff members. Even though the party was just getting started, the room was filled with a vibrant energy. It seemed the early birds had wasted no time in kicking things off. Many of the balloons we'd taped to the walls were floating freely around the room like little pink and purple orbs, adding an unexpected touch of playfulness to the space. On the makeshift dance floor, a couple of the more spirited residents had taken center stage, swaying, twirling, and showing off their surprisingly spry dance moves, despite their slightly hunched postures. In the far corner, a tall male resident with a blindfold was being cheered on as he wobbled unsteadily, attempting to 'pin the tail on the donkey'.

I scanned the room for my mother and found her surrounded by a number of other ladies. She looked radiant. I waved and she waved back, flashing me a big smile. Cameron was there too. He looked noticeably better and seemed to be in better spirits. Spotting Hank and me, he made his way over to us and we settled down at our assigned table after filling our plates with savory appetizers. Cameron gave my shoulders a reassuring squeeze before taking a seat beside Hank. They wasted no time reconnecting through some light conversation and a few hearty laughs.

Meanwhile, I noticed Zelda helping some of the less able-bodied residents with getting food and settling at their tables. I spotted Cathy, the resident busy body who saw Margaret with Bob last night, reach into the pocket of her bright red blazer and pull out a handful of bills. With an outstretched hand, she flapped them at Zelda. Before I could see what happened next, my mother stepped into view.

"Not dancing?" she half shouted, slightly breathless.

I glanced up at her with a quick smile and shook my head. "It's still early," I replied, reaching over for another cheese cube, and watching Zelda. *Was Zelda taking tips from the residents?* I'd noticed how full the bartender's tip jar was already. Considering how well off many of the residents were, it would have been a clever hustle on her part.

"Yes, it is," she smiled back, "but I expect to see all four of you out there soon. Dancing's good for the soul, you know!"

And then, just like that, she fluttered off. Ever the social butterfly.

There was still no sight of Margaret, or Bob. I couldn't shake that haunting image of Margaret's pink chiffon dress still hanging in the closet when we left the hotel. Hank's outward calm was betrayed by the fact that he was already on his second drink, a clear sign he'd needed some help to steady his nerves.

A few minutes later, my mother returned and settled down beside me, waving to her friends on the dance floor. She let out a big breath, exaggeratedly fanning her face with her hands.

"Taking a breather?" I leaned in and asked.

She laughed, gently slapping my knee. "I'm saving my energy for musical chairs," she said, reaching for my glass of ice water. "I fully intend on winning that one. After all, I *am* one of the few residents here with two good knees."

I smiled warmly and drained the last bit of my wine.

Leaning in again, I said into her ear, "I forgot to tell you, Hank is taking me to Italy in the summer."

She clapped her hands together, her eyes lighting up. "Oh, my goodness, what a trip that will be!" she exclaimed. "We'll have to sit down and plan your itinerary. I just love Italy."

"Well, we certainly know you love their cuisine," I said fondly. "By the way, food tonight is excellent."

"Isn't it though?" she said excitedly, "it's so fattening, but honestly, who cares?"

"Well, as you've always said, it's all about balance, right? Some days it's vegetables and exercise…other days, it's carbs and Netflix," I said, nudging her lightly and raising my empty glass. "And good Italian wine, of course."

She nudged me back with her elbow. "Maybe you and Hank can meet up with Samantha and her new friend. His English isn't that great, but he certainly seems friendly, doesn't he?" She paused as if in deep thought.

"Although, I think they're going to Australia for work or something. At least that's what she said during our Facetime yesterday."

Sputtering and coughing, I nearly choked on my water.

She stared at me with wide eyes. "Oh my goodness, are you okay?" she asked, patting me supportively on the back.

How was it that everyone else always seemed to know what was going on before I did? "I'm fine, Mom," I said, pulling away slightly. "It just went down the wrong way—"

"Oh, there she is!" my mother gasped, jumping up from the table.

I followed her gaze and there was Margaret, grinning from ear to ear and bouncing her way across the room, arm-in-arm with Bob.

19 – MARGARITA MARGARET

Margaret was absolutely giddy. When she arrived at our table, her cheeks were flushed, and she seemed to be somewhat short of breath. "Well, hello, everyone!" she declared, still hanging off Bob's arm.

Hank jumped up out of his chair. "Mom, there you are!" he shouted, the relief obvious on his face. Margaret immediately let go of Bob's arm and wrapped herself around Hank, rocking him from side to side.

Mortified, I noticed she was wearing the same thing she had on last night. And might I just add, her deep blue paisley blouse wasn't buttoned properly. *Oh, Lord!* The thought of Margaret and Bob engaging in some sort of intimate encounter was like hopping on a mental rollercoaster.

"Where have you been?" Hank said, his tone serious when Margaret finally let him go.

She looked at me, then back at Hank, her face beaming. "Everywhere," she answered. "I've had the most wonderful day." *Was it just me, or did I detect the scent of citrus with undertones of tequila when she spoke?* "...we went shopping, played mini golf, and then we had lunch and drinks on the beach and...oh, Rosie," she breathed, her words slightly slurred, "I'm so sorry about being late. We really lost track of time."

My mother laughed as she welcomed Margaret's hug. "Better late than never," she said.

"Hi Hank, it's good to see you again," Bob said, stepping forward with his arm outstretched. After shaking Hank's hand, Bob, wide-eyed, wished my mother a happy birthday and gave her a polite hug. He then greeted each of us with a broad smile. All I could do was nod and take a big gulp of my water.

Just then, Zelda approached Hank with a smile and a polite little wave. Her cheeks were also tinged with a faint pink hue. *Had she been drinking too?* She stood beside Bob and then put her face close to his and said half-teasingly, "Oh my gosh, where were you guys?" Then, "Her family was so worried. You know, she never told anyone where she was going, and she didn't have her phone with her. *And* you guys came back *drunk?*"

"Oh my goodness, I had no idea," Bob whispered back, looking genuinely apologetic. And whatever he said next had Zelda taking a deep breath and smiling warmly.

"Cam?" Zelda called, reaching out to him. He was still pale with tired eyes, but he smiled broadly when Zelda pulled both him and Bob onto the dance floor. *She was definitely a hard one to figure out, that Zelda.* My mother quickly followed them.

I nearly stumbled when Margaret suddenly wrapped her arms around mine. She turned halfway back, taking me with her, as she gestured to the room around us. "Well, isn't this a *wonderful* party, Allison?"

I cleared my throat, struggling to keep my leftover anger from overcoming my sense of relief that she was back safe and sound. I took another sip of water, trying to keep it together. How could she just disappear all day and then waltz back in, drunk, no less? Instead of causing a scene, I breathed deep and put on a smile. "Let's get you some water," I suggested, pulling out a chair for her and handing over Hank's glass of half-melted ice water.

Hank signaled to me his need for some air. I responded with a subtle nod, and when he left, I redirected my focus to Margaret. She was now relaxing back in her chair, gulping down the water with slightly glassy eyes. In all the years I'd known Margaret, this was certainly an unexpected experience. She swayed with the music as she watched everyone out on the dance floor. Suddenly, she slapped my leg to get my attention.

"You know, Allie, I really have to thank you," she said with a big smile. I raised an eyebrow. "Oh? What exactly do you have to thank me for?" I asked, leaning in, curious to hear what the tequila had to say.

She looked at me with fondness. "Oh, for your support after George passed, for letting me be part of the business," she said, moving her head from side to side with each point, "for letting me come on this trip, for...lots of things." I took a sip of water, trying to dislodge the lump in my throat. "Did you know," she said, "that George's mother lived with us for a while before Hank was born?" She reached for my hand and gave it a gentle squeeze. "Well, she was...a difficult woman. I was never good enough for her son and nothing I did was ever right." She planted her fists firmly on her hips. "I didn't have the proper breeding, my cooking was 'too American', and no matter what I did, our house was always filthy. By the time Hank was born, she'd become too overbearing. George was such a gentle soul, but he agreed with me she just couldn't stay." Her words were flowing freely, more than usual, and punctuated by bursts of laughter. "Well, when we asked her to leave, she was *furious*. She blamed me, of course. I suppose it *was* my fault, in a way, but she was such an *awful* woman," she said, squeezing my hand again. "She just went back to Europe. George rarely saw her after that, and Hank, he never got to know his grandmother. And you would think George would have resented me for it, but he never did. He was always supportive," she said with teary eyes.

Nodding gently, I handed her a napkin from the table and then reached across it to get one for myself.

"Anyway," she said, smiling broadly, "I just wanted to say I'm grateful to you for putting up with me all these years. I never really realized how much I'd become like George's mother. But at least we turned it around in the end."

My head was buzzing, resonating with a mix of shock, compassion and even a little amusement. I mean, if I'd known that all it took was a few margaritas to turn Margaret into an open, honest, and sensitive soul, I would have started feeding them to her years ago. "Yeah, well, you're..." I started, the words getting stuck in my throat, "...you're welcome, Margaret."

Age is just a number and as the night stretched on, the party grew more vibrant and adventurous. When the early birds went to bed, the night owls took over. Once the 'golden oldies' karaoke started, a powerful 'herbal' scent wafted through the air. Moments later, a few of the more adventurous partiers came back in from the patio, giggling together as they made a beeline for the desserts. This was a lively group that showed no signs of slowing down. Even Margaret was still going strong.

"Me first!" Margaret exclaimed, passing two beautifully wrapped presents to my mother.

"*Two?* Oh, Margaret, you shouldn't have. Just having you here has been enough of a gift."

We all seemed to be holding our breath as my mother traced her fingers along the edges of the silver wrapping paper before peeling away the layers. Her eyes lit up when she saw what had been hidden inside. "An old age emergency kit?" she said, looking over at Margaret with excited curiosity. She pulled open the box and began setting the items on the table, one by one. "Let's see. *Oh*, hearing aid batteries. A magnifying glass—how useful! Large print playing cards for when I need some extra cash," she said, winking at Cameron who smiled tiredly. "A blow-up cane? Just what I need." She squinted at the small tin and then burst out laughing. "...and a compact tin of back-up underwear, in case of accidents. I love it!" she declared as she clapped her hands together, her eyes sparkling with joy and amusement.

"We all could use a pair of emergency underwear every now and then," Margaret snorted, obviously pleased with herself.

My mother straightened in her chair as she held Margaret's second gift in her hand. As if savoring the moment, she traced over the smooth and shiny surface before carefully untying the ribbon and unraveling the tape. As the wrapping fell away, her eyes were fixed on the tiny velvet box. She opened the lid slowly, lifting out a slender charm bracelet. The bracelet glimmered, its delicate chain adorned with a single charm—a letter 'M', of course. *"Oh, Margaret…"* she gasped, tearing up as she held it in her hand.

"It's clever, isn't it? Now we can all give you charms. I'll get you an 'R' next time," she said proudly.

"It's so clever! An absolutely wonderful gift. Thank you so much!" my mother gushed before she stood up to give Margaret a heartfelt hug.

Moments later, Cameron stood up and gently guided Margaret back into her seat. He then handed a colorful gift bag to my mother. "This is from Sam and me," he said, smiling.

Grinning from ear to ear, my mother pulled out the pink tissue paper from the bag and then reached into it. She gasped sharply, her eyes shooting over to him. "Oh, Cameron! No!"

He gave her a slight shrug in response.

"It's too expensive!" my mother gasped again as I leaned in to see what was inside.

I turned wide-eyed to Cameron. "You guys got her an iPad? That must have cost a small fortune—"

Well, no…actually it wasn't too expensive," he said, beaming with pride and knowing full well he'd picked the perfect gift. "Zelda got us an employee discount," he said through several coughs.

Oh, so now she works at a computer store?

As if reading my mind, Zelda quickly corrected Cameron. "Well, I have a *friend* who got the discount."

My mother smiled at her and then turned back to Cameron. "Thank you so much. I need to thank Sam too," she said, standing up to hug him.

At the same time, Margaret leaned over and whispered into my ear, "I'm sorry I didn't tell you what that thousand-dollar transfer to Zelda was for. I just didn't want you telling your mother."

I nodded mutely, sinking back in my chair as my mother pulled out her phone to message Samantha. Hopefully no one would notice I hadn't gotten anything for her from Hank and me, not even a card, for God's sake.

Hank rested his hand on Cameron's shoulder. "You okay?"

"Too much partying," he teased. "Actually, I'm not feeling all that great. Do you mind if Zelda and I head out now?"

He turned to me with warm eyes, and as he did, I put my hand on his forearm and gave it a squeeze. "Yeah, of course. You need a good night's sleep."

From what I could gather, he was feeling the effects of changing his mind about getting married. I was proud of him for finally coming around and making the right decision. Although he mentioned being too young and wanting to focus on school, maybe he'd found out something more about Oliver. Whatever it was, it really didn't matter anymore. With Zelda about to be out of the picture, Cameron would be returning to the family fold. Of course, now that I didn't have much reason to expose Zelda anymore, I supposed I should be nicer to her. At least for the remaining days in Florida.

20 – MARGARITA'S REVENGE

Margaret groans in the morning light.
Her bloodshot eyes make for quite a sight.
Too many margaritas have taken their toll.
And now she's hungover, mind, body, and soul.

Margaret winced at the morning light flooding the hotel dining room. Gingerly rubbing her temples, she struggled with a glossy brochure showcasing nearby landmarks. Her bloodshot eyes made focusing difficult. In fact, every movement seemed to be causing her some kind of discomfort. Clearly, she was feeling the effects of last night's festivities. Although I wasn't happy to see her feeling so unwell, I couldn't help but smile as I bit into my orange slice, savoring the juicy sweetness.

"Milk?" Hank asked Margaret as he poured some in my coffee.

She nodded. I assumed her dry mouth was making it difficult to speak. Although, it could have just as easily been the pounding in her head. She wrapped her hands around the warm cup and asked, slowly, "Is Rosie not joining us?"

"The party went on pretty late last night, so I figured I'd let her sleep in," I said.

"Water will help, Mom." Hank chuckled as he moved her water glass closer to her. Margaret mumbled something under her breath and then slumped in her chair, wrinkling her nose, and holding her stomach when our food arrived. The aftermath of yesterday's tequila-fueled afternoon, followed by a night of birthday cake and dancing, was taking its toll.

Hank reached out and gave Cameron's thigh a light pat. "There's a pretty nice golf course not too far from here. You up for a round?" He smiled, winking at me.

"Um, yeah, sounds good. But kinda depends on what time," Cameron said.

"Great, I'll check," Hank replied excitedly.

Cameron's smile looked a little off, so I leaned in close and quietly asked, "You okay? You're not eating."

"Yeah, I'm good. It's just—" He immediately stood up, looking toward the open doorway, as Zelda made her way to the table.

"Good morning, everyone," she said, looking subdued. "I just wanted to let you know that I have to head home this afternoon." She looked over at Cameron. "I finally managed to get a flight."

"Wait, you're leaving?" Hank said, sounding surprised and disappointed.

"Yes, I'm really sorry, but my mom isn't well, and I need to get home to her today," she said, sounding stressed, but then quickly added, "but I really wanted to thank you all for letting me join you on this trip. It really has been so nice."

"Oh no," I said, skeptical but at the same time, concerned. "Is everything okay?" Was she really leaving because of her mother or was this really all about Oliver?

"Ah, yes, thank you," she replied, sounding awfully guarded, "my mom's just…well, she just needs me home."

I kept my tone light. "Well, if she's not really *that* sick, do you really have to go back today? I mean, we're leaving in two days."

"I'm afraid I do," she said, nodding politely.

"But isn't there anyone who could—"

"Mom," Cameron said calmly, putting his hand gently on my shoulder. He then walked over to Zelda. "What time's the flight?"

"It's at four," she said.

"Dad," Cameron said, looking over at him, "can we take a rain check on golf? I want to go with Zelda to the airport."

Before Hank could answer, Zelda jumped in. "No, Cam, please don't," she said, taking his hands in hers, "your dad just got here, and you've only got a couple of days left. Please, stay and go golfing." She then smiled.

Cameron hesitated but then nodded. "Okay, well, c'mon. I'll help you pack."

After Zelda said her final goodbyes, she turned swiftly and made her way out, with Cameron following close behind. *Well, good luck, Zelda!*

As I turned back to face Hank and Margaret, their eyes were fixed on me, disapprovingly. "*What?*" I said, feeling a bit defensive. "She's rushing home, and I'm not supposed to ask why?!"

"Allison, she just told us why," Margaret said, coming back to life. "Her mother is—"

"Well, it was a vague answer," I answered sharply, dropping my last orange slice, no longer interested in it.

We finished the rest of our breakfast, mostly in silence. Hank booked a tee time for him and Cameron and then, ten minutes later, he stood up. "I'll meet you in the gift shop," he said, gently squeezing my shoulders. "Try to behave, you two." He leaned over and kissed his mother on the top of her head.

"I'm always on my best behavior," she said after him, then held her head, groaning.

I gave Margaret a long, sympathetic look before I pulled myself up from the table. "Can I assume you'll keep your phone with you from now on if you decide to have any more 'adventures'?" I said, half-serious, half-amused.

Her expression softened as she closed her eyes and nodded slowly.

In the lobby, I texted Cameron, telling him I was sorry for 'grilling' Zelda and that I could take her to the airport. Not only was it the right thing for a helpful and supportive mother to do, but it'd also be a good opportunity to dig deeper without upsetting Cameron...or Hank, Margaret, and my mother, maybe even Bob, for that matter.

As I spotted Hank browsing inside the gift shop, I also spotted elevator guy checking out at the front desk. He must've sensed me standing nearby because he turned around and flashed me a bright smile. I smiled back out of politeness. However, when he tossed me a wink, I felt my cheeks turn red.

"Made a new friend?" Hank said, sounding slightly amused.

I leaned against him, secretly flattered by the attention. "Just keeping you on your toes," I said. "By the way, I'm going to take Zelda to the airport after I have lunch with my mother."

"Good," he said. The 'and so you should' was clearly implied.

"You just go easy on Cam today," I said, "he's still not feeling a hundred percent and he hasn't golfed in a while."

"Never," Hank said with a fierce grin at the elevator doors.

"I'll be up soon," I said, waving my key card at him. "I'm going to use the computer in the office suite to check in with Bea.

"Yeah well, *you* go easy on *her*," he said with a wink.

"Always," I said, giving him the same fierce grin, he'd just given me.

Standing outside my mother's slightly opened apartment door, my curiosity got the better of me. I thought I could hear Zelda inside, talking to my mother, so I leaned in as close as I could, straining to catch every word. It was Zelda for sure, although she sounded different, almost upset. Really upset.

"It's just, sometimes she's okay, but sometimes..." Zelda's voice faded in and out. It sounded like she was pacing. I leaned a little closer to the door but then stepped back quickly when it creaked in protest. I couldn't hear what either of them were saying anymore, but I did hear what sounded like sniffling coming from one of them. Was Zelda trying to gain sympathy from my mother, maybe in a last-ditch effort to get money from her?

Suddenly, Bob's happy voice boomed down the hall. He was busy spreading joy while pushing a coffee cart and connecting with residents. I quickly stepped away from my mother's door and pretended to be checking for phone messages. When it was clear that he hadn't seen me, I hurried down the hall in the opposite direction. I was certain the 'breaking news of the day' at Whispering Palms would have been something like:

Daughter Caught Strangely Eavesdropping Outside of Mother's Door

or maybe even,

Strange Daughter Caught Eavesdropping Outside of Mother's Door

Neither would be good. Back in the lobby and seated in one of the deep chairs, I texted my mother to let her know I'd arrived for lunch. Shortly after, Zelda walked by on her way out the front door. She seemed lost in her thoughts, so I made sure not to draw attention to myself. Not long after, my mother came down, waving at me and flashing a big smile.

In the dining hall, my mother talked animatedly about the party, waving her breadstick around like a wand. "And did you know that Margaret and Bob were the last to leave?" she said, laughing.

"*Ah, no,*" I replied, slightly intrigued. "I didn't. What time was that?"

"Late late."

"You don't think she stayed with him, do you?"

She gave me a sideways glance and raised an eyebrow. "Well, you never know. They do seem quite taken with each other, and he does live alone," she said, sounding both nonchalant and scandalously mischievous at the same time. "I believe that's what they call motive *and* opportunity." She threw her head back and laughed. Desperate to block any potential visual impression from forming, I took a bite of my breadstick and quickly changed the subject.

"I thought I just saw Zelda leaving. Did she come over to say goodbye?" I asked, feeling anxious about taking her to the airport. I planned to ask her straight up what her feelings were for Cameron and what her intentions were, now that he'd decided he didn't want to get married. Was she going to hang on to the relationship until she no longer needed him? And what about this Oliver character and her mother's sudden illness? *A mother needs to know these things!*

"Oh, yes, she did," my mother said. "She's a nice girl, Allie. So sorry to hear about her mother—oh dear, is your sciatica bothering you again?" she said, noticing me shifting in my chair to pressure.

"Yeah, it feels like an angry eel has taken residence in my back and down my leg, zapping me the second I get too comfortable. I guess it serves me right for getting all Beyoncé last night," I said. "I think it might be getting worse."

She nodded thoughtfully. "You might need to see a specialist at some point. What do you think triggered it this time?"

"Could be a combination of things. I was moving heavy boxes with Bea a couple of weeks ago. But then again, I've done that many times before without any issues."

She rifled through her purse, then handed me a few tiny, flat, yellow pills. "Here, just don't drink any alcohol with them," she said, closing my hand around them. "They'll make you pretty loopy."

"Oh, well, loopy is good," I said. And then it struck me. My leg *really* started acting up the day I met Zelda. I took a sip of my water, tucking the pills into my purse. I thought back to the two signs I'd seen on my way home that Saturday afternoon. I'd certainly had my share of 'rough roads' during these past two weeks. But what about the second sign? **IN A WORLD WHERE YOU CAN BE ANYTHING, BE KIND.**

21 – Every Dark Cloud Has a Silver Lining

At the hotel, I saw Bob standing by the elevator, holding a bouquet of flowers bound together by a pink satin ribbon. When I got closer, the golden doors slid open and there was Margaret. She pressed her hand to her chest as her initial look of surprise transitioned to one of pure delight. Bob handed her the gorgeous yellow peonies. Let me tell you, it was quite a sight witnessing their sweet exchange.

Whatever was going on between them, Margaret seemed to be moving forward. She *should* be moving forward. It didn't mean she was moving on. George would always occupy a special place in her heart. Seeing her standing there, with that radiant glow as she and Bob communicated volumes without saying a word, I couldn't help but wonder if she could open her heart to love again, at this age and after a lifetime with George.

I was about to comment on the flowers when the other elevator door opened. Out stepped Zelda and Cameron, weighed down by Zelda's shopping bags and her suitcase. She looked just as stressed as she did when I saw her walking through the lobby at Whispering Palms earlier. With a teary smile, she hugged Bob, kissing his cheek, and then turned and hugged Margaret.

"I'm so happy for you, Margaret," Zelda said. "I've already told Cam I expect a full update!"

Wait, when did Zelda and Margaret become so chummy?

"Well, *you* just be safe on the way back, and let us know when you get home. I hope everything goes well with your mom," Margaret said, giving her another squeeze.

When Zelda saw me, she stood a little straighter. I gave her a little nod, pulling the van keys out of my pocket. "Ready to go?"

"Yes, thank you," she said.

The walk to the car was a quiet one, except for the scuffling of our shoes and the rhythmic thumping of the wheels of Zelda's suitcase against the pebbles and cracks in the parking lot's surface. Cameron and Zelda were a few paces behind me, holding hands but walking in silence. I guess whatever they needed to say to each other had been said upstairs.

I opened the hatch and then walked around to the driver's side as Cameron helped load her bags in the back. I watched in the rear-view mirror as they said their goodbyes. After a long hug, they both wiped away tears and walked up to the passenger side front door. Zelda got in and buckled up.

"Thanks, Mom," Cameron said, giving Zelda's hand a last squeeze before closing the door and stepping back. I smiled and then started the engine. It was stiflingly hot, so I cranked up the air conditioner and then pulled out of the lot.

Out of the corner of my eye, I watched Zelda. She looked uncomfortable, nervously rubbing her hands along her thighs. I tried to think of something to say to break the awkward silence but couldn't come up with anything.

"Looks like it's going to rain," Zelda said, staring out the window. Turning toward me, she added, "I hope Cam and Mr. Montgomery can still go golfing."

"Yeah, it does," I replied, grateful for the conversation starter. "I think they can still golf as long as there's no lightning." I kept my eyes on the road, trying to keep my voice neutral. "Did you get a good price on your ticket?"

She nodded. "I did," she said, "thankfully, another airline had a last-minute opening."

My eyes narrowed as I tightened my grip on the wheel. It made me wonder if it occurred to her that she had a two-way ticket, which in today's economy, wasn't a cheap one. All she had to do was wait to travel home as planned.

Moments later. "Thanks again for the ride, Mrs. Montgomery," she said.

I stopped and waited for a family of four to reach the middle of the crosswalk before turning the corner. "Oh, it's no problem," I said brightly, trying to lighten the mood. "I'm always happy to help Cameron, however he needs me." *Okay, that makes me sound like his goddamn personal assistant.*

After that, there was another long, uncomfortable silence. I turned on the radio for some background noise. *Okay, my turn.* "So, are you going to miss the heat?"

"Actually, I kind of like colder weather," she said, fidgeting with her seatbelt.

I shook my head. "Really? Well, I guess I don't mind the cold. I just hate *feeling* cold."

"Mmmm, yeah, me too," she agreed. "My mother always reminds me, 'there's no such thing as bad weather, just'—"

"...bad clothing," we said in unison, sharing a genuine laugh.

"You know, at my age, sometimes the cold is actually preferable," I confessed.

"At your age?"

My lips curled up a bit. "You'll understand one day," I said, feeling another wave of infernal heat deep inside reaching its way to my eyebrows.

We settled into another stretch of awkward silence. As a Zalen Jewelry commercial came on, I sent a silent prayer to George for providing the perfect segue. Enough with the pleasantries. It was time to ask some tough questions.

"Speaking of engagement rings," I said, motioning toward the radio before turning it down, "Cameron told me you guys aren't getting married. I hope you're not too upset with him."

She looked at me, seeming slightly confused. "No, I'm not upset with him at all. I understand how he feels, and I guess that's why I said 'yes' in the first place," she said. "I know he's disappointed, but I *do* think he also gets why holding off for now *is* the best thing to do."

It took me a second to process what I'd just heard and when I did, it took every ounce of control I had to keep from slamming on the brakes right then and there. I saw red. "Wait, are you saying that *you* called it off?!" My tone was sharper than I intended. "Why would you do that?"

She shifted in her seat to face me more fully. "Well, yeah, I did," she said, sounding surprised, "but I *love* Cameron and I want us to spend the rest of our lives together. But we're still young. I mean, he hasn't even finished school yet and I'm... still... trying to get myself settled," she said, wiping her cheek with her oversized turquoise t-shirt. "He may not be willing to admit it to himself, but I think the *real* reason he wants to get married *now* is because of what happened with Penny. I know he knows I'm not her, but I think, deep down, he feels that if we get married, it means that I'm in it for *him* and not for what he might have. Even though he's analytical, he feels things more deeply than others—"

"Yes, yes, I know. I read about how people with his kind of sensitivity respond to traumatic experiences," I added.

She nodded. "Yes, but on top of that, he's also strongly affected by other people's emotions. I don't want all the craziness in my life to distract him. Don't get me wrong, I really appreciate his support, but I'm not looking for him to 'save' me. But he wants to 'secure' this relationship so badly that he may get too focused on me and on getting married when he needs to be focused on his internship and on finishing school."

Hallelujah! "Well, I can't say I disagree," I said, nodding slowly.

We drove in silence for a long time. I thought about what Zelda had just said. I suddenly found myself curious about what *was* going on in her life that would make her want to hold off on marrying Cameron. "What do you mean by 'all the craziness' in your life?" I asked, tapping my fingers on the steering wheel. I was curious.

"It's my mother," she started, releasing a long breath. "I know when we first met, I said she opted for retirement, but that's not true." She paused, regaining her composure. "She's a recovering alcoholic. But she's struggling. That's why I had to drop out of school. It's just been hard lately."

Zelda opened up about her mother's struggles with alcoholism, which started after her husband died. "…because of my mother's health, I wanted to focus on her instead of school," she said. Her sincerity and vulnerability tugged at my heartstrings.

I reached out to put a comforting hand on her arm. "I'm so sorry to hear that," I said gently. "I know dealing with addiction is tough. And not just for the person struggling with it, but for their families too." It suddenly occurred to me that maybe Margaret knew more about Zelda than I did. Margaret's own mother's history with alcohol may have been the reason why she never seemed that interested in 'Project Zelda'. I couldn't say for sure when their moment of connection might've happened, maybe after we got here or, thinking back, maybe before we left. Cameron had probably tried to get them together shortly after our first dinner. "It all must be such a challenge for you," I said.

"Yeah, it has been. But I'm lucky. One of my best friends from childhood has been going through a similar experience. She…I mean *he*…" Zelda corrected herself quickly, looking over at me, "*he* is going through the same thing with her…I mean *his* father, so she…*ugh*…I mean *he*—Oliver—understands. Sorry, I'm still getting used to the pronouns—"

"Wait, *Oliver*?" I said, completely confused by what she'd just said.

"Yes, well, *now*. *He* used to be *Olivia*," she explained.

Oliver *was* Olivia and has been Zelda's friend since childhood. Okay, so I guess I misjudged that one.

I considered asking more about Oliver but decided against it. "So, why didn't you say anything about your mother before?" I asked, looking at her quickly.

"Well," she said wearily, clearing her throat, "I don't like to talk about it. People always feel sorry for *me* and think badly of *her*. And I don't want that. I can take care of myself and my mom. Just because I struggle with it or get emotional sometimes doesn't mean I can't handle it. And just because she has a disease doesn't make her a bad person." We both sat quietly for a moment looking straight ahead. Then, "I guess I also wanted you all to see me for who I am, and to see Cam and me for how we are together, without anything else getting in the way," she said, quietly.

We talked more about her mother's journey and how it affected their relationship over the years. It was obvious she carried a heavy burden. It certainly explained the stress and the buckets of ice.

"Zelda..." I said, my mind scrambling to put any sort of coherent response together. But before I could continue, my phone rang out over the minivan's speakers. It was Bea. "*Shit*. I have to take this...one sec."

"Hi Bea, what's wrong?" I said, hoping to get straight to the point.

"Oh my gosh, Allison!" her voice crackled and echoed throughout the minivan. "We've got a real problem!"

My heart pounded out of my chest. "Alright, calm down, Bea," I told her, drawing in a deep, deep breath. "What's happening?" I exhaled.

"Okay, um, that other vendor we talked about fell through, so we don't have any furniture."

"Oh no, that's not good," I replied.

"I know," Bea said, her voice trembling. "I'm so sorry!"

Zelda whipped her head toward me. "I have another friend who might be able to help," she interjected.

"Bea, hang on a second," I said quickly. "Go ahead, Zelda."

"Ah, yeah, so this guy doesn't redo furniture like the other guy so he might be a little more expensive. But he does buy interesting pieces at a pretty good discount from auctions and estate sales," she said. "I know he's looking to grow his business and is looking for new customers, so he might be able to help, especially if there's a future in it."

"Really?" I said, looking at her thoughtfully as we turned off the main road toward the airport. "Can you give me his contact information or maybe even do an email intro?" I asked, feeling excited by the possible solution Zelda was presenting, but also confused by the multitude of parking, terminal, and pick up and drop off signs as we got closer to the airport.

It took until we'd found a space in the chaotic parking garage to get Bea off the phone. "It's okay," I told her. "I'll reach out to Zelda's contact and get back to you. We have to go...my bladder's about to explode, and Zelda has a plane to catch." I didn't actually have to pee, but I wasn't ready to end this business conversation with Zelda yet. She seemed to know a lot of people.

Feeling bold and in the moment, I decided to ask Zelda what exactly she had bought when we got her bags out of the trunk. "So, what's with all the shopping?"

"Oh," she started, "that discount mall we went to, had so many clearance items and everything was so cheap. So, I grabbed whatever I could from the bins. I can make some good money upcycling all this stuff," she said, holding up the bags. "I practically cleaned out my business account, but it'll definitely be worth it." Clearly, I misjudged the shopping too.

"Ahh, well we business owners certainly need to take advantage of opportunities whenever we can," I said, impressed by her entrepreneurial nature. "So, how is it that you know so many people?" I asked as we entered the terminal and pushed our way through a swarm of excited and anxious travelers.

"Well, you meet a lot of people when you work at a bar," she said as we pushed forward. Zelda walked with a determined stride. Thanks to my mother's magic pills, I found myself trotting alongside her as if my sciatica were cured. "I've also been doing a lot of bartering for my business and other recycling projects. People in the furniture business are actually some of my best contacts."

I did my best not to let the chaos of the passengers and the incomprehensible airport intercom announcements divert my attention while she continued telling me about her business relationships. When we neared the check-out counter, she stopped and glanced down at my leg. She dug into her purse and pulled out a small envelope, her hands trembling slightly.

"When you get back home, do you want to maybe get together? We can even talk about some of the vendors I know. Maybe one or two others might be good for your business," she said.

"I'd really like that," I said as she extended her arm and offered me the envelope. "What's this?" I asked.

"It's nothing, really, just a little something to say thank you for allowing me to join you guys on your family trip," she said with a warm smile. "I really enjoyed getting to know you all. Cameron always speaks so highly about his family, especially you."

I took the envelope from her, feeling a lump building in my throat. *Cameron talked about us, especially me?* "You really didn't have to…"

Zelda shook her head. "Honestly, it's nothing much. I know your sciatica has been acting up, so I talked to the front desk and booked you a one-hour, deep tissue massage for tomorrow afternoon with Lisa. Hopefully you have time." Her eyes teared up, and she cleared her throat. "Anyway, thank you for everything, Mrs. Montgomery."

"You're welcome. And thank you, too," I said. I watched her turn and greet the attendant with the same kind smile she gave the residents at Whispering Palms. I felt another tug on my heart strings as I watched her disappear behind the wall of waiting passengers.

Soon, I was back outside walking to the parking garage. Those dark, gloomy clouds that had blanketed the sky when we left the hotel seemed to have disappeared, revealing the bright sun. The heat was already almost unbearable, but this sudden transformation lifted my spirits. I thought about this, then realized how important it was to keep an open mind and just let things unfold. Let the fairies do their magic, I told myself. I carried this odd sense of peace with me for the rest of the day.

22 – Forget Oliver, Who the Hell is Eloise?

Are you there, George? It's me, Allie.

Sooo, it seems like Margaret and Bob have become something of an item. To be honest, I wasn't sure how you might feel about it all. But then something occurred to me. You're probably the one who put him in her path. Well, it worked. I don't think I've seen her this happy and playful in a long time.

By the way, Oliver was actually a…oh, never mind. It's all a bit confusing. Speaking of confusing, as it turns out, Zelda isn't 'Penny'. Furthermore, she appears to have a big heart and an entrepreneurial spirit. Who would have guessed! Believe it or not, Zelda was the one who called off the whole 'getting married' thing. No wonder Cameron looks so miserable with Zelda's absence. And she's been looking after her mother for years. At first, I thought she was just trying to weasel her way into my good graces, but now I think she was genuinely just trying to help. I feel sorry for her, dealing with her sick mother, coming all the way here, and still attempting to tend to her from Florida. It must be hard, right? She's young, too young to get married, but also too young to have to deal with something like that on her own.

Life certainly does send us on all kinds of twists and turns, doesn't it? Well, today's our last full day here. I'm going to make the most of it.

Thanks for always watching out for us, George!

Allie xoxo

The heat was intense, so intense that the pavement could double as a sizzling grill for steaks. It's no wonder people flock to indoor malls, even if it means going in circles past the same old shops multiple times, where storefront mannequins start looking a bit judgmental. But in the cool air-conditioned bliss of the mall, none of that matters.

I trudged behind the trio in front of me, weaving through the maze of parked cars with a sweaty back. I marveled how Cameron managed to bear the weight of his grandmothers, who were flanking him on either side, arm in arm, as they marched confidently across the scorching parking lot. Determined not to fall behind, I quickened my pace. Finally, we reached the grand archway that marked one of the bigger malls in the area, famous for its post-apocalypse theme park, cutting edge restaurants, and two gigantic department stores. To my relief, a kind stranger stood there, patiently holding the tall glass door open for us. With a forced smile, I expressed my gratitude, attempting to hide the discomfort caused by a sudden jolt of pain down my leg. Sadly, no 'magic pills' today.

Like eager children about to uncover hidden treasures, Margaret and my mother stood in front of the mall directory, attempting to lift Cameron's sunken spirits or, at the very least, distract him from his thoughts. They cracked jokes about their shopping strategy, their laughter filling the air, while Cameron, the stoic audience, valiantly tried to keep a straight face. Even *he* couldn't keep from cracking a smile at their antics.

Cameron scanned the directory for a moment and then looked at the stores around us. With a spark of excitement, he pointed towards the large sale banner in front of a retro looking music store. "I'm gonna go see what they have in there," he said, waving his phone at us. "I'll meet up with you guys later." His eagerness to be on his own was obvious, but Margaret was far less enthusiastic about the idea. As he tried to leave, she protested immediately, clinging to his arm, adamant about keeping the family shopping brigade intact. It was like witnessing a comedic tug-of-war, with

Cameron pulling towards a solo shopping adventure and Margaret anchoring them to a family one.

"Oh, let him wander, Margaret. He doesn't need to be stuck with us old folks," my mother chided, playfully unwrapping Margaret's arm from Cameron's. "Besides, he'd probably just cramp our style," she said, giving us all a quick wink. "Now, Cameron, you let me know if you see something you like, and I'll get it for you," said my mother, giving him an affectionate pat on his back.

Margaret countered. "No, I'll get it for you!" she said, her determination matching my mother's affection as she planted a kiss on Cameron's cheek.

Cameron smiled warmly at both of them before he gracefully freed himself from Margaret's arm and seamlessly merged into the stream of bustling shoppers.

My mother gave Margaret a light nudge with her elbow. "We'll get it for him *together*," she said, teasingly. Margaret smiled broadly and threw her arms around my mother's shoulders.

"Just remember, we have a limited amount of room in our suitcases," I gently reminded them, in an effort to keep things from getting out of hand.

"Good point, Allie," my mother said, giving me a thoughtful look before her eyes lit up with a sudden enthusiasm. She clapped her hands together and turned to face Margaret. "Let's go pamper ourselves. What do you say, a manicure and a makeover? I can't think of a better way to end the week than with a bit of glamor!"

"Oh?" Margaret said, clearly intrigued, but also a little unsure. "A makeover? You know, I've never had one before."

"Oh my goodness, Margaret, that just *won't* do. But don't you worry, we'll take care of that, won't we, Allie?!" my mother said, turning to me and flashing another mischievous wink.

"Absolutely," I said with a big grin, watching Margaret's own smile grow even wider.

As we made our way through the mall, Margaret and my mother walked together, arm in arm, adding to its chaotic atmosphere with their own overly loud conversation and occasional raucous laughter. I followed along like a supportive, if slightly amused, chaperon and couldn't help but marvel at how this once prickly relationship had somehow blossomed into a genuine, full-blown friendship almost overnight. I felt a slight twinge of jealousy, watching them bantering and bonding together. I mean, how dare they have so much fun without me? If anything, it was nice to see that friendships could develop, heck, even grow and flourish between the most unlikely people.

I continued following along, embracing the madness of their camaraderie. They weaved their way through the crowds and into Hats and More. I was about to immortalize the scene with a photo when my mother suddenly stopped, turned around, and in one swift motion, grabbed a gorgeous, whimsical looking hat off a shelf and plopped it on my head.

"Voila!" she laughed, like a magician celebrating her grand finale. "Oh, let me get this for you!"

"I'll get one next time. Margaret would probably just 'borrow' this one anyway," I whispered to her. "Just ask Cam." We exchanged knowing glances, and then she threw her head back and laughed.

"Fair enough," she said, still laughing.

It suddenly occurred to me that it had been a while since we'd parted ways with Cameron. I checked my phone for a message from him, but there was nothing. He was most likely deep in the video game jungle, off the grid and blissfully unaware of the outside world. I stepped out of the hat shop, my worry lurking in the back of my mind. He's a big boy, I know, and perfectly capable of navigating a four-million-square-foot mall, and that was over two thousand miles from home. But it'd been nearly an hour since he ventured off on his own.

"Hey, I'll be back in a few minutes—I'm going to go get Cam," I told them. "He's probably still in that same store," I added, trying to sound completely unconcerned.

"Okay, I'm going to take Margaret to The Beauty Bar on the third floor. Meet us there?"

I nodded, and with my imaginary supermom cape fluttering behind me, I set off to find him in the wilds of Grand Circle Mall. Unfortunately, in the bazaar of chaos, it didn't take long before I felt like a fish swimming upstream. Crowds were never my thing and a dense, steady stream of noisy strangers coming in and out of my personal space gave me a kind of anxiety I'd never felt before. All those unfamiliar faces with their unfamiliar smells and incessant noise making were causing my senses to overload. So, with a quick and determined move, I took a sharp left, exiting the herd, and found myself in the serene music store. Destiny, it seemed. There stood Cameron, looking at an old vinyl album cover.

"Hey, sweetie," I said, giving him a small wave when he looked up. "Just wanted to see how you were?"

He smiled when he saw me and with his shoulders back, he held up an album like it was a precious artifact. "There's something cool about old records," he said.

I nodded in agreement. It's like each album had a soul of its own, and shops like these were sanctuaries for those whose time had passed but who still had so much left to give. As the soft rock sounds played, I was instantly transported to a simpler time in my life.

As we browsed through a collection of records from the seventies, my anxiety began to dissipate. Soothed by the relatively dim lighting, the calming music, and the vintage charm of the place, I savored the moment with Cameron. A part of me thought he felt the same. Leaning in, I said enthusiastically, "Why don't you pick a few, and when we get back home, we can pull out your grandmother's record player and have ourselves a music night?"

He shrugged and then shuffled through the rest of the stack. "I can't really squish one in my suitcase."

"True, but we could always get a few when we get back home," I said. When he just shrugged again, I put my hand gently on his arm. "Hey, I know you're sad, but—"

"Mom, don't. Please. I really don't want to talk about it." His tone sounded like a mix of defiance and desperation.

"But I spoke with Zelda. It's not like she doesn't love you or doesn't want to be with you. She just—"

"Mom, seriously," he said, giving me a double dreaded stare.

"Okay, got it," I said. I could see the turbulence of emotion swirling behind his eyes. He was right. I decided not to push the issue and let his emotions simmer until they were ready to be served.

"So, your grandmothers are going to get a makeover," I said, changing the subject with a playful grin. "I'm assuming you'll pass on getting one yourself, since you're obviously perfect as you are." I paused for dramatic effect, letting the joke land. "So, why don't I text you after we're all done?"

The corners of his lips twitched into a smile. "Sure, Mom, text me when they're ready to hit the runway," he joked.

"Oh, Cam, I swear, makeover or not, those two are going to have the paparazzi following them around in no time. Just you wait," I said laughing.

Cameron rolled his eyes, but I could tell he appreciated my attempt at humor. With that, I left him to sift through another stack of albums. I'd tried, but he wasn't in the mood to talk. So, I did what I promised myself I would do—I gave him space.

Ten minutes later, I was at The Beauty Bar watching Margaret settle into her chair. Several of their beauty experts surrounded her, eager it seemed, to turn her into their latest masterpiece. Margaret seemed thrilled and mildly terrified at the same time. As the makeup brushes and powders came out, Margaret's eyes widened in anticipation. They filled in her eyebrows so that they now resembled a couple of overfed caterpillars. Then the lipstick came out. Between the outlining, the filler, and the outer gloss layer, well, let's just say Margaret looked like some kid who'd raided their mother's makeup drawer and tried on every lipstick they could find. But the real showstopper was the eyeshadow. By the time they were done with her, Margaret's eyes looked like some long-lost *Picasso*. At one point, one of the makeup artists asked her if she wanted a smoky, sultry look instead. Margaret tilted her head slightly, looking quite perplexed. "Well, why would I want to look like I survived a bonfire?"

Meanwhile, my mother, who was seated three chairs down from Margaret, had undergone her own transformation. Her hair, usually a well-behaved bob, had been teased and curled to the point where it looked like she'd stuck her finger in a light socket. I mean, honestly, she looked like she'd just stepped out of some 1980's heavy metal band's music video. Still, as with most things in life, she took it all in stride. As Margaret saw my mother's 'new look' and then caught sight of herself in the mirror, we simultaneously burst out in laughter. My mother's wink was met with a sassy hair flip from Margaret. It was nice to see them having so much fun together, even if I did feel like a fifth wheel.

"Maybe it's too bright," Margaret said for the third time, her voice slightly exasperated, as she sat beside my mother in the back seat. She was inspecting her freshly painted nails again, trying to decide whether the pink flamingo polish was a daring fashion statement for a woman her age or a ridiculous eyesore.

My ever-supportive mother tried to reassure her, but even she couldn't hide a faint flicker of amusement. "You're in sunny Florida, Margaret. There's nothing wrong with such a bright color. It's tropical!"

"Maybe you're right," Margaret said, finally relenting as we pulled into the parking lot of Whispering Palms. Done with fussing over her nails, something else had caught her attention. "Look, there's Bob," she called out, but then fell suddenly silent.

I leaned forward, squinting through the windshield, and sure enough, there was Bob—standing outside with another woman having what seemed like a very friendly and rather intimate conversation. My heart sank, and the tension in the car was palpable.

Oh, no!

"Well, so it is," my mother said as she and Cameron climbed out of the minivan. "And that's Eloise, his old girlfriend. She was invited to my party, but she declined. She was never very fond of me. Don't worry, Margaret, she's nothing you need to worry about."

"Oh," was all Margaret said, waving goodbye to Cameron and my mother as they headed into Whispering Palms together. "Have a nice afternoon..." she said absentmindedly.

Margaret and I sat there in the minivan watching the Bob and Eloise Reunion Show. They were laughing and chatting like kindred spirits. Meanwhile, I caught a quick glance at Margaret's face in the rearview mirror and could see the doubt and uncertainty swirling in her eyes. This was like watching an unexpected plot twist in a soap opera. I half-expected a melodramatic soundtrack to start playing in the background. We sat a while longer without saying a word. I glanced back at Margaret a second time, trying to gauge her emotions without intruding on her thoughts. Her mind was clearly racing, and her expression had taken on a dark undertone.

Uh oh!

23 – See You Later, Alligator!

I followed Margaret with all her bags into the hotel, trying to keep pace. She seemed like a woman on a mission— or one with a lot on her mind. Still, I managed to slow down enough to scoop up an orange from the basket we passed. Margaret headed straight for the elevators and when she turned around, her question and her sharp tone, caught me off guard.

"What time are we going for dinner?" she said.

"Ahh, well…" I stammered, trying to gather my thoughts. "Hank and I were going to go to—*wait*, so you're not going to have dinner with Bob?" I said, feeling a pang of sympathy for her, and for myself too. Hank and I hadn't had a chance to enjoy a quiet vacation dinner together.

Margaret furrowed her brow, clearly agitated. "Why would I want to have dinner with that man?" she scolded, mashing the elevator button irritably.

"Because you genuinely enjoy his company and because, in this country, we're all presumed innocent until proven guilty," I suggested, trying to make the point without setting her off.

"I absolutely do *not* enjoy his company, Allison," she declared, stepping into the elevator, and waving impatiently for me to join her. "I was just bored. You've all been so busy with your own plans, so I had to find something, anything, to pass the time in this godforsaken place," she added quickly.

"Well, you certainly did pass an awful lot of time with him," I said, instantly regretting my words.

She shot me a warning glare. It was a look I hadn't seen for quite a while. Seeing Bob with another woman had certainly had an impact on her and, clearly, my comment had hit a nerve.

"Look, Margaret, all I'm saying is, you looked like you were having fun. And that's a good thing. You deserve to have fun. Don't let what you think you saw ruin the little time we have left here. He's a social man, after all, but that doesn't mean that you aren't special to him," I said, trying my best to turn the conversation around.

"I'd rather spend my time with Henry and you, tonight," she huffed, turning her head away.

I closed my eyes briefly and silently took a slow, deep breath. If Margaret was going to crash our date night, I may as well invite Cameron and my mother to join us as well. I was going to need a buffer. Hank was good, but, lately, my mother seemed to be much better.

"Where *are* we going for dinner?" she asked matter-of-factly, now looking straight ahead, and blinking rapidly.

I stood there silently contemplating the shift in Margaret's demeanor. The irritation and sense of entitled expectation underscored her question was clear. It was almost as if the last five years hadn't happened, and I was now standing in the elevator with the same angry and resentful woman I'd known for most of my married life.

When we stepped out of the elevator, I turned to face her. "I'm not sure yet," I said, trying to keep my tone light, "but we can decide together once we're ready to eat."

With a satisfied nod, she turned and walked down the hallway. I dutifully followed along. When we arrived at her door, I pulled out my phone to check the reservation for my massage. While Margaret fiddled with the door and its keycard, I noticed there was an extra space available in my time slot. Did that mean they had space for one more person? A grin spread across my face as a thought occurred to me.

Hank and I stood together in the change room. I couldn't tell if my excitement over my impending deep tissue massage outweighed my embarrassment at having to get mostly naked together and expose my ever expanding and distressingly doughy, fifty-year old body. I looked at Hank feeling more than a little self-conscious. Our once scorching hot romance was now more of a long simmering love. One where we got changed in private and an adventurous weekend meant ordering in and streaming a movie. And while we may not set the bedroom ablaze anymore, there's still a cozy, dependable little bonfire that keeps us plenty warm.

I slipped into the ultra-soft robe and carefully folded my clothes, placing them neatly on the chair in the corner. As I did, my phone buzzed.

Hank playfully clicked his tongue at me. "Hey, no work now," he teased. "This is supposed to be all about relaxation, remember?"

I snorted softly. "Well, isn't that the pot calling the kettle black?" I teased back.

Hank raised his eyebrows and stood there looking at me. I knew I should have just ignored it, but my curiosity got the better of me. So, I grabbed my phone and read the email. It was from Zelda. She'd sent the email introduction for me to the contact she'd mentioned at the airport. Not only had she followed through on her promise, but she did it quickly.

"Allie," he said, his voice dripping with mock patience, "put the phone down and step away from those emails." He laughed softly, stepping forward. "Again, this was your idea. So, c'mon, time to relax," he said as he gently pried my phone out of my hand.

"Right, yes. Be in the moment. Got it," I replied with a dramatic sigh.

Hank took my hand and led me into the adjoining room. It was a warm, softly lit space, with gentle music playing and the soothing aroma of lavender wafting through the air. In the center of the room stood two massage tables, side by side, with crisp, fresh linens.

Hank was right. This was our time to unwind and enjoy some quality time together. We stepped forward, removed our robes, and got on our respective tables and then waited, as instructed, for our massage therapists to arrive. After adjusting my head position in the face cradle contraption, I took a deep breath, filling my nostrils with the room's calming sweet, woody smell.

"Oh, this is great," Hank moaned. "I don't even think I need the massage."

"Mmmm, I know what you mean," I agreed. My mind kept wandering back to Zelda's email but once I heard the therapists' footsteps approaching, I closed my eyes and made a firm decision to focus on clearing my mental clutter.

Shortly after the friendly therapists made us both feel at ease, they began their magic. Lisa, my therapist, worked away the knots in my neck with the precision of a surgeon. Between her expert touch, Hank's comforting presence and the calm, soothing atmosphere, it was easy to forget about the outside world. And yet, in that moment when nothing else should have mattered, my mind fought back. Random thoughts about some of life's greatest mysteries flooded my consciousness. *Why do socks mysteriously disappear in the laundry? Where do they go?* And just as I was about to begin contemplating restaurant options for dinner, Lisa skillfully increased her pressure and pulled me back to the present moment. When she asked if the pressure was too much, the best I could come up with was something that sounded like a cross between a squeal and a sigh. Despite my best efforts, even amid ultimate relaxation, my head was playing a game of hopscotch with each stroke on my body.

Zelda.

Zelda.

Zelda.

It was strange to think that just as Cameron was doing his best to avoid thinking about her, I was starting to like the girl. But was I genuinely seeing her in a new light because of what I'd learned over the past few days? Did I just like her now because she had some business contacts? No, I wasn't *that* self-absorbed. Maybe I was just feeling better about *her* because I felt like I had *my* Cameron back. I shifted my body and tried to regain my calm by refocusing on the soothing music. *Namaste and all of that.*

After I carefully turned over under the sheet, Lisa slipped a pillow under my head and proceeded to work on my legs. I glanced over at Hank, and we shared a quick smile and a moment of bliss. I closed my eyes, desperately trying to immerse myself in the experience as Lisa found the perfect balance of firmness and gentleness on the soles of my feet. Even with this extra layer of relaxation, my mind continued to wander. There was no denying that Zelda had her merits.

Dinner was surprisingly uneventful. Cameron and Margaret were like a couple of dark clouds casting their shadows over the entire evening. When one of them sighed, the other almost immediately followed suit, creating an almost choreographed display of gloominess. Honestly, they were sapping all the light and joy out of the evening. Their food became a canvas for pushing and prodding while their drinks transformed into vehicles for miniature sips of disappointment. And as for Cameron's subdued mood, well, I could cut him some slack given the circumstances. But Margaret? I wanted to shake her out of this melodrama and remind her of the strong, confident woman she was. She wasn't a lovelorn teenager, mourning over a lost crush. She was a mother, a grandmother, a widow-with a lifetime of experiences under her belt. It had only been a week since Bob entered her life, for goodness' sake! With one glass of wine in, I had half a mind to grab her by the shoulders and give her a friendly, yet firm, reality check.

With dinner behind us, Hank led Margaret through the hotel lobby. It was hard watching her dejectedly shuffling along behind him. I considered following her up to her room, but I caught sight of Cameron strolling toward the pool and, for some reason, felt compelled to follow him instead.

He was sitting on the edge of the pool staring at the shimmering water by the time I got there. Feeling delightfully limber after my massage earlier, I managed to slip in beside him by the water's edge. When he looked at me, all I could see was the deep sadness in his face.

"The water is so warm," I said casually while I playfully bumped my arm against his.

He nodded and a slight smile formed on his lips. "We didn't really take advantage of the pool, did we?"

I leaned in. "No," I said, trying to sound chipper. "At least we made it to the beach a few times."

"Yeah, that's true," he said, still sounding somewhat distant.

I slowly moved my feet back and forth in the water and mustered up the courage to address the elephant in the room. "Cam, I know you're having a hard time right now." I immediately felt him tensing up beside me. "But I just want you to know that I'm here for you, no matter what." I started slowly rubbing his back, just like I used to when he was little and needed comforting. He didn't pull away.

"Dinner was weird," he said after a while.

"So weird." I laughed again, noticing that my chest felt lighter than it had all week. These moments of genuine laughter with him were precious to me. They were few and far in between now, but I hoped we'd get back to more of them.

"Is Grandma, like, in love with Bob?"

"I don't know if it's—"

Cameron's phone rang. He quickly pulled it out of his back pocket and stood up abruptly. I watched all the tension immediately return to his face as he answered the call. As he mentioned Zelda's name, I could hear the emotion in his voice.

"Sorry, Mom, I need to take this," he said hurriedly, covering the mouthpiece as he looked back down at me quickly. I gave him a reassuring smile and a nod, letting him know that I understood. He nodded back and then headed to the lobby.

Clearly, his insecurities had been sent into overdrive ever since Zelda changed her mind about getting married. I looked back at the water and sighed. I guess I'd have to accept we'd reached the point in his life where I simply wasn't going to be his most important relationship anymore. And it didn't matter whether it was Zelda or someone else. Cameron had to walk his own path and all I could do was be there for him when he needed me.

Slowly and carefully, I stood up, pleased to find my hip didn't give a punishing pinch, and made my way back inside the hotel too. I was ready to snuggle up next to Hank while he finished wrapping up his day, when I spotted Margaret at the front desk, looking intently at a brochure. She looked...happy, ecstatic even. This was not the same Margaret I'd seen looking miserable just thirty minutes ago. *Forget sciatica, Lisa, how are you with whiplash?*

I caught up to her as she walked back to the elevators. "I thought you were going to bed?" I said, trying to hide my curiosity.

"I was," she said with a bright smile.

"And...is everything okay?" I asked, leaning in slightly and unsuccessfully attempting to catch a glimpse of the brochure.

"Everything is wonderful!" she practically squealed.

I squinted at her, my suspicions aroused. She couldn't possibly have gotten over Bob so quickly. What could have happened?

"Oh, Allie," she said, seeing the look on my face, "I'm fine. Honestly. You don't need to worry about me." She stood there swinging her arms back and forth with childlike enthusiasm.

Did this sudden change in mood have something to do with the brochure, had she somehow patched things up with Bob or had I just stepped into the middle of an episode of The Twilight Zone?

"Did you hear what happened?" she asked, not waiting for my response. "They caught an alligator today just casually strolling near *this* hotel!" She burst into laughter "Oh this place is such a wonder, isn't it? Everyday there's something exciting going on. Well, I'm off to watch a movie in my room now," she suddenly declared as the elevator doors opened. "See you later, alligator," she said with a wink as she threw her head back and laughed.

"...in a while, crocodile," I responded as the elevator doors closed. I felt a sudden sense of relief deep inside. It appeared that *Florida Margaret* was back!

24 – BOMBS AWAY!

The week felt like a blur, with each day seamlessly melding into the next. At times, it felt like our trip was never going to end. But then, wham! Time to go home. It was as if I had blinked, and our entire Florida escapade had evaporated into thin air.

Hank and I sat in a pair of matching wingback chairs in the lobby, with our luggage forming a neat fortress between us. I felt a tinge of regret. Aside from the oranges, maybe I hadn't made the most of everything that was available here. The thought of making the shift back to daily routines and responsibilities was bittersweet.

"Guess what we've got waiting for us at home?" I said teasingly. "A lovely tray of lasagna your mother stashed in the freezer specifically for tonight's dinner."

He nodded absently, watching me wince when I shifted in my chair trying to find a comfortable position. "So," he said, reaching out to give my arm a reassuring rub, "when's your next chiro appointment? That leg of yours needs some serious attention, Allie."

"Wednesday afternoon," I said, quickly reviewing next week's schedule in my head, "right before Bailey's vet appointment—oh my God, Hank, *Bailey*!" It suddenly occurred to me that I'd been so preoccupied with everything going on with Cameron and Zelda, Margaret and Bob and my mother, that I hadn't asked how Bailey was doing. Not once.

Hank seemed amused by my sudden outburst and raised his hand in a calming gesture. "Relax. I'm sure he's having the time of his life at Paws Pet Retreat. He's probably made some new friends and caused more than his share of chaos," he chuckled. "You know, I would venture to say he would be totally fine if we got him on Monday, don't you think?"

I gave a slow and gradual nod. Bailey, bless his furry little soul, wasn't exactly the easiest dog. Despite his undeniable cuteness, he was a mischievous troublemaker with a willfully stubborn streak. Still, a wave of guilt washed over me, and I vowed to shower him with extra treats and belly rubs as soon as we got him home.

"Hello, *Earth to Allie*," Hank said, waving his hand and bringing me back to the present. "It's all good. You've been juggling while riding a unicycle and singing opera like some grand circus performer. Seriously. Bailey's just fine." And because Hank always had a knack for reading my mind, he leaned over and gave me a comforting kiss. "Okay," he said, sitting back, "now, on to more pressing matters. Any ideas about dinner next week—"

"It's too soon!" my mother called out. Her sky-blue dress flowed out behind her, and her light strappy sandals slapped the floor as she sashayed toward us with Cameron by her side. She looked exactly like what she was, a retiree on perpetual vacation who was free to lounge by the beach whenever she chose. She opened her arms wide and greeted Hank with a hug that simultaneously showed how glad she was to see him and how much she was going to miss him.

Hank hugged her right back, swaying as she vigorously rocked them from side to side. "I'm so sorry we didn't get to spend more time together, Rosemary. Next time, though, I promise I will be here, and present, for the duration," he said apologetically.

"Good. And so you should. Work is important but never lose sight of what it's all about." She smacked her lips against his cheek. "And you, my darling daughter, be sure you take care of my favorite son-in-law," she said, giving me a quick wink.

I glanced at Cameron standing to the side, quiet and subdued. I couldn't help but wonder how his conversation with Zelda went last night. From the looks of it, not that well.

"Where's Margaret?" my mother asked suddenly. As she spun around, her dress caught the air in a mesmerizing wave of fabric. "Off with Bob, maybe?" Her eyes twinkled.

I shook my head as Hank stifled a cough. Reaching over, I rubbed his back gently. I could only imagine what was going through his mind after learning about what his mother had been up to this week.

"Oh, I don't know. I got the impression she was pretty much done with Bob after the whole 'Eloise' incident," I said, though perhaps more for Hank's benefit. "Although, she was in a bit of a giddy mood when I saw her down here last night. She wouldn't say why. So, who knows?"

"Hmm," my mother said, her lips forming a playful pout.

Hank looked at my mother speculatively for a moment and then announced, "I'm going to give her a quick call."

"Allie," my mother said, wrapping me up in a hug, "thank you so much for everything. I can't tell you how wonderful this week has been."

I returned the hug and surrendered for a moment, basking in the warmth of her energy. "I feel like we didn't get to spend enough time together either…" I said after a moment but trailed off as Hank rejoined us.

"Okay, she's just finishing up with a few things. Whatever that means," he said with a slight shrug. "Do you think we should go help her out?"

I held my hands up in the air. "Hey, I offered, but she told me she had everything under control."

"Oh, I *do* enjoy her stubbornness," my mother giggled.

"Alright, well, I'm going to grab my suitcase," Cameron said. "Maybe she'll let me help her."

"Good idea. But just don't take too long," Hank said, glancing at his phone's screen again. "We're already running a bit behind."

When I turned to my mother, she was waving a sturdy looking wooden cane back and forth. "Cam was carrying it for me," she said, clearly noticing my puzzled expression. "It's for you. Should come in handy at the airport. These too," she said, suddenly producing a few more of those magic pills from her dress pocket, "they should help make the plane ride a little more bearable."

Even though her little yellow pills had turned me into a tired, and somewhat loopy version of myself, I was dreading the two hours on the plane and would gladly take any help I could get. I plucked them from her outstretched hand. "I'm not sure I'm ready for the whole cane thing just yet, though," I admitted. Smiling of course.

"Fair enough," my mother said good naturedly.

We sat and waited for Cameron to return, hopefully with Margaret and her suitcases in tow. Ten minutes later, I saw Cameron coming out of the elevator with his suitcase. He'd changed into sweatpants and an oversized, wrinkled t-shirt and his hair was disheveled. He was looking more like his pre-Zelda self.

"I knocked on her door, but she didn't answer," he said once he reached us. "I don't think she's up there," he added.

"That's strange, I just spoke to her a few minutes ago," Hank said, looking at his watch again. "We're running out of time."

I still had the other keycard to Margaret's room and gave it to Hank. Maybe she'd dozed off on the bed while watching one of her game shows. Meanwhile, I tried calling her again, growing increasingly frustrated with each unanswered ring. When Hank reappeared from the elevator looking worried, I called *again*. This time, she answered right away.

"Oh my God, Margaret, where are you?" I snapped, trying my best not to sound like a mother scolding her disobedient child. "You know we're on the verge of missing our flight?!"

"I'm coming, I'm coming!" And then, just like that, she hung up.

Standing near the hotel's front entrance, I watched as Hank loaded our bags into the minivan. I was ready to tell him we might just have to leave his mother in the middle of Florida, when the hotel doors swished open and out came Margaret shuffling our way, wearing a light, bright, flowery dress. Her face was flushed. She had a bundle of papers in one hand and a tropical drink in the other.

"Margaret, what the f—"

"Mom, where have you been?" Hank interjected, shaking his hands in the air. "Where are your suitcases—Cameron, go get your grandmother's suitcases—"

"That won't be necessary," she beamed at us. "I'm not coming."

We all froze in place. Except for my mother, that is. She looked every bit like the cat that swallowed the canary. Clearly, they were up to something.

"What do you mean you're not coming?" Hank growled, looking at Margaret, then at my mother and then back at Margaret.

"I'm going to stay for a while longer," she said simply, and a little defiantly.

"What?!" Hank gasped, "Why? For how long?"

"I don't know," she said, taking a long sip of her drink. "A few weeks, maybe longer."

"And you couldn't have mentioned this earlier?" I huffed, checking the time again.

"Well, I only made up my mind last night," she said, her voice almost whimsical. She took a deep breath, looked over at my mother and then dropped the bomb. "I'm considering moving down here and I've put my name on the waitlist at Whispering Palms," she declared.

Hank, Cameron, and I stood there, stunned. Meanwhile, my mother clapped her hands together. Laughing, she went over and gave Margaret a big hug.

"Henry, could you possibly switch my ticket for me?" Margaret asked casually with my mother still hanging off her shoulder.

"What? Ah, no. No. It doesn't work like that, Mom," Hank said, recovering somewhat from the initial shock.

"Oh? Well, don't you worry then. I'll just buy a new ticket and pay you back for the one today," she said with a nod.

"Yeah, well, you might end up paying for all our tickets if we don't hit the road in the next five minutes," I said sarcastically.

I looked over at Hank and could see the wheels turning. Ignoring my comment, he shook his head. "Mom, why move? And why haven't you said anything about this before?"

"Well, the weather here is better for my old aches and pains. And besides, I'm not dead yet, you know." She smiled, patting my mother's arm. "We've been talking about it for some time and this vacation was the perfect chance for me to see what it's really like down here."

Hank's face grew pale. It would have been a terribly inconvenient place and time for him to have another heart attack. Still, I understood how he felt. Years ago, when my father passed and my mother packed her bags for Florida, I felt like I was on an emotional rollercoaster myself. It was like a cocktail of guilt for not having spent more time together, being utterly baffled about the suddenness of the decision, and feeling a big, fat splash of sadness welling up within. How could anyone not feel like a deflated balloon when someone who had been a constant presence was now opting to be so far away with little warning?

I must admit, aside from being worried about missing our flight, I felt a certain sadness at the thought of Margaret moving here permanently. She'd been a fixture in our lives for decades and would be leaving a huge hole for all of us. But there was another emotion swirling around within me—an odd sort of happiness and sense of hope, for her. The sense of breaking free, embracing life on her own terms, was like a sparkler in the dark. It sure wouldn't be easy for Hank, I bet, or even for Margaret, but what struck me was how much she seemed to have detached from him during this trip. Funny how he appeared to be fussing over her now that she was spreading her wings a bit. *Who really needed who at this point?*

Reading our faces, Margaret let out a deep breath. "Oh, stop your fussing. All of you. I'm not moving just yet. And not to be morbid, but those spots often open up only when someone... well, you know, right Rosie?" she chuckled lightly.

"Oh, Margaret," my mother replied. "I'm not sure I'd put it quite that way, there are other reasons, but, yes, that *is* one of the more common ways that spaces open up."

"Fine," Hank sighed, "but we're going to talk more about this, okay?"

Margaret stepped forward and wrapped her arms around Hank. "Of course we will, Henry. But don't worry, I've got Rosie here to help me."

"That she does," my mother nodded emphatically.

"Okay, but if you need me..." he said with a sense of resignation.

"I won't," she promised, her hands gently cradling his cheeks. "I'll be just fine."

"Dad," Cam's voice came from behind. "We have to go."

"Right," he said. "Right. Okay. Just be safe... and keep—"

"—my phone on and with me at all times. I will. Promise." She stepped forward and hugged him again. She turned to me and gave me a hug. "Be kind to Zelda, Allie. She called me this morning to check in. She's a very sweet girl and Cam's lucky to have her," she whispered in my ear, giving me two gentle pats on the back before moving on to Cameron.

I thought quickly about what she'd just said about Zelda. What reason did I have left not to like her? Her pink braid? Occasional weak smile? Being constantly tethered to her phone? Digging into the Project Zelda case file, I couldn't come up with anything.

After saying our final goodbyes to Margaret and my mother, and persuading Hank to risk driving without insurance, I settled into the passenger seat and waved as we drove off. It was a surreal scene. There they stood, their faces sparkling with excitement, like a couple of college students being dropped off for the first time and eager to embrace a whole new chapter in their lives.

I pulled down the car's mirror to fix my hair and apply a touch of lip gloss. When I did, I caught a glimpse of Cameron's reflection in the mirror. His eyes looked heavy. Zelda was right about Cameron's sensitivity. It was a gift, but it also made dealing with him challenging at times. I didn't think he could look more miserable than he already did, but somehow, he was managing to achieve just that.

We stood by the expansive window, watching the ground crew moving luggage across the busy tarmac. Cameron's face had been buried in his phone since we got here until he suddenly shared the news. "Zelda's mom is back from the hospital," he said. "She wants me to come over when I get home." A small smile formed on his lips, a stark contrast to his demeanor over the past two days.

I looked over and noticed the background image on his phone. It was a photo of him and Zelda. He looked grown up, confident and content with her by his side. I smiled back at him encouragingly, grateful that he was communicating openly with me again. "That's great news, Cam, sounds good," I said, wrapping my arm around him with a reassuring squeeze.

Just then, my phone rang, and Bea's name flashed on the screen. I rolled my eyes. As soon as I said hello, her sharp inhale told me she was on the verge of another breakdown. "Bea, we're just about to board the plane. What's wrong?" I asked.

Bea was silent for a moment but then, as if she had been holding her breath, blurted out, "Another client didn't like the setup and they're really upset with the job I did, even though I followed exactly what you said to do. I mean, I think I did. *Oh, God*, Allie, I don't know…"

"What?" I exclaimed, taking in a deep breath. "Which client is it?"

"Um, Tom… no, Ted… no, oh sorry, just a minute," she said, sounding flustered. "It was Tom, yes, Tom Gillard. The three-bedroom condo guy. He wasn't very nice. He wants to speak directly to you or even Margaret," she added.

Me or... oh God, Margaret. I hadn't really thought about what Margaret's plans meant for the business. Aside from the possibility of her dying from heat stroke or becoming a meal for an ornery alligator, maybe Margaret would be so consumed by the Florida lifestyle that she would step out of the business. First Samantha, now Margaret? The thought of being left alone in the business with no one but Bea to rely on started my heart racing.

"Tell him I'll call him first thing tomorrow—no, wait, Monday. Okay, Monday," I said. "And don't bother Margaret," I added quickly. "I'll handle it."

"Right, okay. Sorry. Thanks, Allison. Sorry," she stammered, her voice quivering slightly.

We boarded the plane like a trio of warriors, each of us dealing with our own inner battles. Even though our seats weren't together, none of us had tried to see if changing them was possible. We were just too lost in our own thoughts to be bothered. I sat down beside a friendly yet reserved stranger and put on my seatbelt as my anxiety over flying started to rise. I slipped my hand into my pocket and retrieved one of the pills my mother gave me.

Thirty minutes later, we were airborne. The pill hadn't kicked in yet and my anxiety was piquing, so I made a conscious choice to ease my tension with a drink. It didn't take long before my head started spinning, so I reached down under my seat and grabbed an orange from my bag. Just then, the pilot's voice crackled over the intercom, announcing that our journey back to the dismally cold winter weather was going to be marked by a high degree of turbulence. I focused on the orange and its weight and smooth texture. It was a small comfort, I know, but the very act of peeling its skin had an innate ability to calm me down, lift my spirits and boldly anchor me to the present.

25 – BACK TO THE GRIND

Are you there, George? It's me, Allie.

Between the roaring headache that hit me and the icy cold air that enveloped us as we made our way out of the airport, I started to think that coming home was a mistake. Oh, and did I mention I left my bag of precious treasures under my seat too?

On another note, and I'm quite sure you're already aware of, Margaret has stumbled upon her own wellspring of joy. She downplayed her stay as merely an extended vacation, but my gut tells me that she'll end up relocating to Florida, permanently. I guess she's realized there's a whole lot more to life than hanging around here, smothering Hank and occasionally getting in my way. I can't believe I'm saying this, but I am going to miss her. But there's more to life than being here and taking care of us.

Don't you worry about her for one second, George. She's more than capable of looking out for herself.

I miss my oranges, but not as much as I miss you!

Love, Allie xoxo

Seated back at my desk on another dark, dreary, wintery morning, I couldn't help feeling a little disheartened. I slumped further in my chair. Maybe it was the mundane nature of routines, the need to wear layered clothing again, or how strangely quiet the house was when I left this morning now that the sounds from Margaret's television were no longer blaring from the basement. Of course, the fact that the cream in the office fridge had gone sour, forcing me to abandon my cup of coffee, didn't help either.

The doorbell chimed and I instinctively gripped the arms of my chair and managed to lift myself up just enough to peer over my monitor. A big part of me hoped it'd be an interaction as simple as someone looking for directions or dropping off a package. Hell, I'd even accept a couple of Jehovah's Witnesses—just no clients. Not yet. Not without coffee.

"Oh boy, you look rough," Val declared, strolling in, and placing a large, piping hot gourmet coffee right in front of me. "I was half expecting to find you with a sun-kissed glow and an army of oranges lining your desk," she said. I jumped up to give her a big hug.

"Don't get me started. I brought a bunch back with me but left them on the plane. Although I *did* manage to get the world's best sandal tan. Want to see?" I said, eager to take off my boots to show her.

"Oh, I think we're good, thanks," she said, raising her hand. She flopped down into the corner chair, casually dropping her purse, which carried a sense of adventure, down beside her. "What I'm really interested in is all the juicy details from your trip. C'mon, let's hear it!"

"Well, my friend, you asked for it," I said grinning, holding my hands up in a mock apology. But first, I greedily took a large gulp of coffee and silently savored that first jolt of caffeine hitting my system. Sufficiently fueled, I proceeded to regale Val with all the amusing tales and zany little details from the melodrama that was our vacation.

"Okay wait," she said, her expression shifted from intrigued curiosity to outright skepticism. "Hold up. Zelda called off the wedding, and you're not on the 'I told you so' train?"

I shrugged, taking another gulp of coffee. "Well, what can I tell you? Turns out she's not another Panny. In fact, I think she's a genuinely *good* person."

"Just like that?!" she said incredulously.

"Well, no. Not 'just like that'. Obviously, it took some time. But she hasn't taken a cent from him, her reasons for pulling back on the whole 'getting married' thing were all about what's best for Cam, and she still seems to be as committed to him as she was before she called it off. So, yeah, I guess that's enough for me. For now, anyway."

Val narrowed her gaze and sipped her coffee as she considered what I'd just said. After a moment, she nodded slowly. "Alright, I get it. It certainly is very *big* of you," she said with a hint of sarcasm and a slight chuckle. "Okay, so tell me more about this Bob character. And what's the deal with Margaret deciding to stay back? I didn't see that one coming."

After an hour of exchanging updates, Val rose from the chair with a completely unintentional but nonetheless sultry, cat-like stretch. Halfway out of my office doorway, she turned back. "No sign of Bea, I see. Didn't think you'd be this accommodating on your first day back."

"Unscheduled day off," I said, trying not to let my annoyance show. "She says she's got Covid—"

"*Covid?*" she balked. "Is that *still* a thing?"

I shrugged. "I think she might be avoiding me until Margaret comes back. There were a few challenges last week, and that large tomato soup looking stain on the carpet by the front door wasn't there when I left. At least, I hope it's tomato soup. I dunno," I said wearily.

Val responded with an evil grin. "Oh, I definitely noticed that when I came in. Who knows, maybe she's gone and killed an angry client, and is half-way to Mexico as we speak!"

"I highly doubt she could orchestrate a murder," I quipped.

Val gave a sympathetic nod as I mentally reminded myself to pick up rug cleaner, along with coffee creamer. If Margaret were here, she'd have already had this mess sorted out.

"I'm going to let her go," I blurted out, instantly feeling both relief and regret. "She's a good kid. And she's Sam's friend. The last thing I want to do is stir up drama. But she's killing me, Val. I don't think I have a choice."

She gestured dismissively and sauntered back toward me. "I'll take care of it," she volunteered, her eyes gleaming with a perverse kind of delight at the prospect of firing someone. No one would ever accuse Val of being soft. But she wasn't aggressive or mean. Her high EQ combined with a low guilt threshold was her superpower. Navigating delicate situations, like this one, with both tact and empathy was something I had yet to master.

"Oh, Val, thanks," I said with a relieved smile.

"I got your back," she said, raising her coffee in the air.

I survived the early morning deluge, dragged myself over the midday hump and was now well into the homestretch of the early evening. At least the office was quiet. Well, it was until my phone started ringing. Startled, I jumped slightly and raised my hand to my heart. I took a quick calming breath.

"Hello?" I said, answering the phone despite not recognizing the number that illuminated the screen.

"*Hi, Mrs. Montgomery, it's Zelda,*" she said, clearing her throat.

"Oh, hi, Zelda," I responded, hitting the speaker button and trying my best not to sound too surprised by this unexpected call. "How are you and how's your mother?"

"I'm doing well," she said warmly, hesitating again before continuing, "and, actually, I wanted to thank you for the gift basket you sent this morning. My mom was so touched by it too."

"Oh! You're very welcome. I heard the bean stew kit is good."

"Well, I can't wait to try it," she said.

"Hey," I said, my fingers deftly clicking through fields on a purchase order, closing it off and then opening another one, "I'm working late today. If you've got some time, did you want to swing by and join me for a quick dinner? Maybe we can talk about your contacts again and how best to approach them." *And maybe you can let me know how things are going with Cameron 'cause he's still not talking about it.*

"I'd love to," she said almost immediately. "And maybe we could chat about Cameron, too," she added, suddenly sounding unsure. "I haven't heard from him today."

"Oh, I talked to him a while ago. Apparently, he's only just managed to haul himself out of bed," I told her. "He's holding up, all things considered." I stretched out my legs in front of me and got a little more comfortable. "You know, Zelda, I have to admit, I'm realizing more and more just how good you are for him," I said. "You seem to understand him in ways that I'm still learning." I paused for a moment. "Look, I'm going to finish up with the day, but I'll text you the address. Okay?"

When she responded, her voice was thick with emotion. "Yes, Mrs. Montgomery, that would be great. And thank you so much for the kind words. You know Cameron means the world to me and—anyway, I'll just meet you at your office. Thank you!"

"Yes, absolutely, I completely understand," I said, trying desperately to keep my emotions in check and sound as professional as possible. Pamela, from Home Stars Realty, had always been a challenge to deal with. I swallowed hard. "But we delivered *exactly* what was agreed to in the staging plan. If there was a problem with the design, why are we only hearing—"

"You're not listening," she said, cutting me off, again.

Just then, the front door chimed, and Zelda stepped inside, unwrapping her fuzzy gray scarf from around her neck. I glanced at the clock on the wall. My nerves were frayed, almost to a breaking point. When I waved Zelda in, a sharp pain radiated down my hip. I grimaced as Pamela continued with her tirade.

"What I'm saying, *Allison*, is that your staging plan, your style, is the problem," she said, her angry voice echoing through the speaker and bouncing off the walls. "There hasn't been any interest," she said, "and given what we've spent on this staging, we expected more."

Zelda sat quietly, as if sensing my discomfort, while Pamela's accusations left me feeling exposed and full of self-doubt.

"Okay, so what do you want to do? It looks like you've only paid the deposit so far. Should we just cancel the agreement?" I said, my frustration starting to get the better of me. Handling difficult clients was Margaret's forte, not mine. I couldn't even begin to imagine how she would have handled this one, but she'd always managed to talk Pamela off the ledge *and* get the next order.

Pamela didn't respond right away. After a moment, she cleared her throat. "Well, there's no need to go *that* far. We just need the staging to make buyers fall in love with the house." Zelda remained quiet, but I could see she was listening intently.

Hearing the desperation in Pamela's voice, I suggested, "Okay, well, we're willing to make some accommodations. If you like, we can choose another theme or maybe just swap out a few pieces."

We went back and forth for several more minutes and eventually reached an agreement. "*Fuck me!*" I muttered through clenched teeth, hanging up the phone and sinking back into my chair.

"Wow, she sounds like a challenging client," Zelda said with a gentle smile, her fingers wrapped around the colorful knit bag sitting on her lap.

"Yeah, realtors are getting increasingly impatient these days and I guess it's easy to blame the staging when a place doesn't sell. But Pamela's always been a bit of a special case," I said, completely drained.

"Do you happen to have any pictures of the house she was talking about?" she asked.

"Ah—yeah, sure…" I slid my chair over, turning my computer around. I opened Pamela's site, clicked on the listing, and waited for the images to load. Meanwhile, Zelda lifted the bag she held in her hands.

"By the way, this is for you," she said.

"Really?" I said, caught completely off guard. I lifted the bag and was surprised by its weight. But that was nothing compared to the surprise I felt when I looked inside. It was filled with Valencia oranges. And atop of them, sat a small, round tin.

"Oh my God, where did you get these?" I exclaimed.

"I ordered a small crate from Hallen Grove Farms right before I left. I know you love them, and I wanted my mother to try them as well." She nodded as I held up the small tin from the bag. "That's a medicated topical pain cream my mother absolutely swears by. It might help with your leg."

"Oh, this is very thoughtful of you. Thank you. And please thank your mother for me too," I said, holding the tin closer to my chest. As much as I loved my oranges, with the way my leg had been feeling lately, I was a little more excited about the cream. "By the way, how is she doing?"

"She's doing much better, thank you," she said smiling. "Oh, and this," she said, holding up her phone, "is Obi!"

I had to step back to look at the photo. At first glance, it was just a big ball of fuzz. When my eyes finally focused, I saw a cute charcoal colored kitten with big pointy ears and piercing yellow eyes. I suddenly remembered Margaret saying that Cameron and Zelda were looking at baby names for the kitten Zelda was getting.

"Oh, how adorable! Obi? That's an interesting name. Is it a he or she?"

"He's a boy. And Cameron named him."

"Oh, he did, huh?" I chuckled. "So, then it's Obi, as in 'Obi Wan Kenobi' from *Star Wars*, right?"

"Exactly!" she said, grinning broadly. "He wanted to go with 'Vader', but I told him there was no way I was going to have a little 'sith' running around my house, so we settled on Obi. Besides, names ending in an 'i' or a 'y' sound cuter," she explained.

"Or an 'ie'," I said with a wink. "Well, no matter what you call him, I doubt they get much cuter than this little guy."

She nodded and then turned her attention back to the computer screen. "Oh wow, the staging looks *so* good," she said, sounding genuinely impressed. "You know, we watch a lot of real estate shows and, honestly, what you've done looks as good as anything I've seen on any of them."

She reached over and navigated through the rest of the photos, then looked at the details of the listing. Suddenly, she turned and looked at me wide eyed. "I don't think your staging's the issue."

"What do you mean?" I said, intrigued.

"Well," she continued, "I know this neighborhood. It's close to mine and these houses aren't going for that much. I know staging is important, but isn't price even more important? Anyway, obviously I'm no expert, but I think that could be the real issue here."

I sat there looking at her. Her speech was swift. And the way she easily transitioned between personal and professional matters was impressive, especially considering her age.

"Let's go get some dinner, shall we?"

26 – WHAT ABOUT BOB?

I practically dragged myself through the front door, wondering how it was still only Tuesday. As always, there was Bailey, his body wiggling with excitement. I reached down and gave him a few quick rubs while slipping off my coat. Satisfied, he lunged for his stuffed lama, giving it a good thrashing before it flew out of his mouth, bounced off the wall and sailed down the hallway.

Aside from Bailey's ferocious pursuit of his lama, the only other sound I could hear was from the television in the living room. I craned my neck for a quick peek as I took off my boots. Hank and Cameron were sitting on the couch, watching a Texas BBQ cookoff show.

"Oh, that looks so good," Cameron mumbled. "Did Mom say what's for dinner?"

It was late, I was tired and there was no way in hell I was going to be able to muster up the energy to cook. Before Hank could answer, I quickly stepped into the living room.

"Who's up for pizza tonight?" I didn't think either of them had heard me come in and I figured they'd be surprised by my entrance. Nope. They'd heard me alright. But instead of both jumping up to greet me with warm hugs and questions about my day, they looked back at me and raised their hands. Okay, to be fair, Cameron did give me a smile and Hank did blow me a kiss, but it was a far cry from jumping up and offering to cook dinner instead.

"Great," I said with a simple nod. "I'm going to change into something more comfortable. You guys go ahead and place the order." I leaned down and planted a kiss on the top of Cameron's mop of hair.

By the time I'd conquered the stairs, got into my pajamas, and indulged in a quick, twenty-minute lie down, giving Zelda's pain cream a chance to kick in, I heard the doorbell.

Back downstairs, Hank was meticulously dropping ice into three glasses. Easing onto my chair, I nodded as he held up a can of diet soda. Cameron joined us at the table, carrying a bottle of chili oil. I shook my head in mock disgust.

"It's amazing you still have a stomach lining," I said. The full force of the spicy-sweet steam hit me in the face when he opened the pizza box.

"Yeah, no kidding," Hank said, "I'm already breaking out in a sweat." He then flipped open our box, revealing a perfect, stone-baked pepperoni pizza, with, call us crazy, onions and black olives.

"Yeah, well, olives are disgusting too," Cameron said before taking a big bite of his pizza.

"I think he's just marking his territory," Hank said casually, taking his own bite. He swallowed and then laughed. "The olives keep him from ours and the hot sauce keeps us from his." Hank gave him a quick wink. "It's a stalemate. Well played, young man."

"Busted," Cameron deadpanned.

I laughed, feeling my chest swell. Our family was smaller, and the void left by Margaret and Samantha had an impact, but I loved this dynamic too. It felt comfortable, natural just the same. I smiled at the men in my life.

Hank glanced at me. "You look tired," he said between chews. "How was your day?"

"Tired enough that we ended up with pizza for dinner on a Tuesday night," I replied with a nod. "It was a long day, but at least it wasn't as dramatic as yesterday."

"What happened yesterday?" Cameron asked, just as I'd hoped he would.

"Oh, well," I said, hiding my satisfaction, "I had some trouble with an upset client. Zelda was there when it happened, and she was great. We had a nice chat about the situation, and she really made me feel a lot better about the whole thing—"

"Wait, Zelda came by your office?" he asked, now completely focused on me.

"Yep. She came by to drop off some cream for my leg and some oranges she'd ordered from Florida—that was very sweet of her," I answered. "You know, she's really smart and I think she has a genuine knack for business."

"Yeah, well," Cameron said, "she's a lot smarter than me and way better with people." His words weren't as somber as I had anticipated, but he seemed to be doing better. He looked better too.

"So, how are things going with you guys?" I asked, trying to sound casual but also wanting to take advantage of his willingness to now, finally, talk about her.

"We're good," he said with a spark of excitement in his eyes. "We had a great talk last night. I guess you guys could tell I was pretty upset after she told me she didn't think we should be getting married."

"Yeah, we noticed," I replied almost immediately, "but we figured you just needed some space."

"I did," he said, looking up from his pizza. "When she told me, I thought it was just the beginning and she was going to break up with me when we got back. She kept saying that wasn't the case but...I dunno." He paused, momentarily mulling something over in his mind before continuing. "Anyway, we're still together and she still loves me. We're just not going to rush into anything right now."

"Sounds like a great idea to me," Hank said. "She seems like a wonderful girl."

"Thanks, Dad," Cameron said, sounding quite positive. "She really likes me and still wants to get married, just, not today."

"You know what?" I said, reaching across the table and taking his hand while Hank gave my leg another reassuring squeeze under the table. "I could totally see that happening."

Samantha's distorted voice screeched throughout the kitchen, her image moving haltingly on the screen. "*Hello?* Can you hear me?" she said.

"We can hear you," we said in unison as Cameron and Hank squeezed in beside me.

"I can hear you too!" Margaret shouted for the third time. Her phone bounced around while she followed someone to the door of her hotel room. "Thank you for your help. It was all so confusing," she said to whoever had been helping her.

Samantha's image flickered back to life, revealing her puzzled face. "Wait, what's confusing?"

"Zoom," Margaret shouted, apparently still unclear about how to position her phone and giving us all a close-up of her nose.

A few more minutes ticked by with our voices overlapping and images freezing, but eventually, the connections stabilized, and Margaret seemed to figure out how to position her phone properly.

"Okay, well, it seems like it's all working now—wait, let me move to another room," Samantha said as she took us on a virtual tour of the backpacker haven she was staying in. She led us through several half-lit, messy rooms, catching glimpses of a few diverse travelers all about her age playing card games, swapping stories, or strumming guitars on bright orange bean bag chairs. She finally settled on what appeared to be the top of a bunk bed and turned on the light beside her.

Margaret's voice boomed through the speaker. "Oh, there's that beautiful face," and then she bellowed, "and where's my Cameron?" Cameron leaned in from one side, and Hank from the other, as we tried to get all of us on screen at once. "Oh, there you boys are. Allison, scoot over. I can only see half of Henry's face and I want to see him when I tell you all my exciting news."

Oh boy, here it comes.

"What news?" Samantha asked just as Margaret's connection dropped out.

As we patiently waited for her to reconnect, Samantha kept us entertained. She cycled through a series of filters, transforming her appearance with bunny ears, floral crowns and more. Not to be outdone, Cameron joined in with his own mustache and googly eye filters. A few minutes later, Margaret finally reappeared, only this time with no audio.

"Wait, is she on mute?" Cameron said, turning to me and then looking back at the screen, which was now completely frozen.

I tried my best to maintain a smile as we struggled to find our rhythm with this conversation. Then, moments later, our screen unfroze, and there was Margaret clapping her hands together saying, "...so that's the plan."

Hank leaned in closer to the camera. "Wait, Mom. Can you start over? You were on mute, and our screen froze so we missed everything you said."

Margaret rolled her eyes and shouted even more loudly, "Can you hear me now?"

"Yes, we can hear you," we said together.

"Okay, well," she continued, her hands coming together in a joyful clap, "a space opened. I'm in!"

Hank crossed his arms in front of his chest. "So soon?" he marveled.

"Yeah, I thought someone practically had to die first," Cameron joked.

"Oh, no, Margaret, you didn't kill Bob, did you?" I said, giving Cameron a nudge.

"Very funny, Allison. The list wasn't *that* long," Margaret said, "and apparently there's a new residence opening down the street and the people that were ahead of me on this list decided to go there, so now I get first dibs on the one that just opened here. Isn't that wonderful?"

I could feel Hank tensing up beside me. He leaned in closer to the screen. "Shouldn't we talk about this a bit? What about your doctors, your friends, us..."

"Oh, Henry, don't you worry. I plan on traveling back and forth," she said confidently, "after all, we still have a business to look after, don't we, Allison?"

"Absolutely," I said, nodding and feeling relieved that she still intended to be involved in the business. I guess we'd have to figure out how and to what extent but most of what she did was over the phone anyway so I was sure we could make something work. For a second, I was tempted to change the subject and ask about Bob but with Hank already feeling tense, I decided to suppress the urge.

"I'm...I'm happy for you, Mom," Hank managed. "If you need anything...let us know."

"I will, and thank you, dear," she replied with a warm smile.

"Okay, guys, I gotta get to bed soon," Samantha said, letting out an audible yawn.

Taking his sister's cue, Cameron decided to call it a night as well. "I'm happy for you, Grandma. I'm going to go upstairs but we'll talk soon. *Bye...*"

Hank and I stayed on with Margaret a little longer. To his credit, Hank kept things positive and supportive. When it was time to say goodbye, he said, "We'll see you soon, Mom. Be safe, okay?"

"Yes, see you soon, Henry. And don't worry about me. I promise to keep my phone always charged and with me. Bye now!" she said, waving. She then pursed her lips as she attempted to find Zoom's leave button. "Oh, dear, how do I turn this thing off?" she grumbled to herself as her image froze once more.

When Hank stood up, readjusting his sweatpants higher on his waist, I gasped, quickly reaching out and gripping his arm. "*OH, MY GOD!*"

Hank's head whipped towards me. "What happened?" he exclaimed. He looked down at the screen and after Margaret's image came to life once again, he gasped. There, sprawled out on the other side of the bed with a playful grin on his face, was Bob.

"Oh, you little devil, you!" Margaret's laughter echoed through the speakers.

I leaped up from my chair and, with one hand, swiftly covered Hank's eyes to block the view. With the other hand, I snapped shut the laptop. Suddenly, I gripped his arm tightly again, caught between panic and agony. The pain was too much.

Hank sat on the edge of the bed, his warm hands gently massaging the back of my leg. "A week?" he said.

"That's what the physio said," I replied. "Apparently, I need to tame the pain, which means I'm supposed to rest up and lie on my back with a pillow under my legs for a week, if possible. At the very least, I'm supposed to limit walking to short distances, and avoid sitting or driving for prolonged periods." I turned my head toward him and moaned, "*And* I have to do *all* these stretches *three* times a day."

"Isn't there anything she can do?" he asked softly. "I mean, you've been dealing with this for a long time now."

"Well, she said that if reducing inflammation, stretching and strengthening doesn't work, we may have to see a doctor to consider possible surgery."

"Oh, Al."

All I could do was shrug helplessly. "She did say she doesn't think it will come to that and, honestly, it's partly my own fault. I've gained weight and haven't been getting any kind of exercise except for walking Bailey. And well, he's always so distracted so it's more of a stroll."

"So, does that mean you plan on following her instructions? Down and out for a week," he said.

Anxiety fluttered in my chest. "I don't know, Hank. I just don't think I can take a week off now," I said plaintively. "There's too much to do…Bea is useless and will be gone soon anyway. And with your mother staying in Florida, she really can't be much help until we figure how it's all going to work. So, that just leaves me."

Hank lay down beside me, trying to avoid disturbing the bed, and interlocked his fingers with mine. I felt his sadness. "I'm sorry she left you high and dry," he said. I watched him take a long, deep breath, his face a mask of somber contemplation.

"She's raised two families, Hank," I murmured softly. "I think she's earned enough badges to set her own course and live life on her terms, don't you?"

"Yeah, I do. I guess I never realized how much I was going to miss having her here, in the same house," he confessed.

Nodding, I caressed his hand, feeling the same way too.

27 – Cleaning Up and Clearing Out

After half a day of reclining halfway, I was agitated, in pain, uncomfortable, and unproductive. Papers and wrappers were strewn in every direction, and my laptop was threatening to roast me alive. My once neat notepad looked closer to a doodle pad at this point. My mind wandered too. I found myself contemplating whether the color on our bedroom walls was *blue gray* or a *gray blue* in the paint world. I'd chosen this color, be it blue or gray, years ago after we made the decision to paint over the fizzy peach color Margaret had surprised us with when we were away. It wasn't exactly a relaxing color. But then again, the color wasn't particularly soothing now either, not while I was busy turning myself into a pretzel in hopes of finding relief. I tried drafting an email but couldn't seem to manage anything that didn't sound like it was written by a petulant twelve-year-old. *Honestly, how could I be expected to function under these conditions?* I decided to lean into it.

Rubbing my hands over my face and surrendering to the inevitability of some impending business-related disaster, I decisively snapped shut my laptop and maneuvered myself, with my best approximation of grace, to lie on my side, facing the television. I used to fantasize about taking time on a workday to dive into a little simple escapism or indulge in mind numbing plot twists while life's everyday responsibilities faded into mere background noise. Still, I would have given anything to be out of this bed, back at work and, literally, taking care of business.

So, there I lay, a bundle of nerves surrounded by a mountain of pillows, wallowing in a cocktail of stress and a dash of self-pity, when I heard Hank, my knight in shining armor, ascending our creaky stairs.

Moments later, he inched open the bedroom door. "Hungry?" he asked.

My stomach rumbled. With a cautious shift, I carefully pulled myself into a sitting position. "Lunch time already?"

He handed me the tray, his warm fingers brushing mine, and then sat down on the edge of the bed. "If you feel up to it later, we can go for a two-block walk, and then I can drive you to the office to grab what you need," he suggested.

"Sure, but don't you have that conference call?" I savored a spoonful of soup, grateful that Hank had learned how to feed himself—and me— even if it was a simple lunch. Fueled by canned mushroom soup and a grilled cheese sandwich, I was ready to face the afternoon's trials.

"Rescheduled for this evening, so, if you want to get a *leg up*... Get it?" he laughed.

"Hah," I huffed dryly. "Fine. I'll do the short walk if you agree to tie Cameron's old sled to a rope and pull me back upstairs."

He chuckled, patting my shin as he stood. "Well, how about I just get your coat and boots out?"

"My hero," I called after him.

I couldn't believe my eyes when Hank and I first stepped into the office. It had undergone a complete transformation. Papers were neatly stacked, files were organized with military precision, and the usual cluttered desk surfaces were nearly unrecognizable. And there was Val, hair smartly tied back, dressed in skinny jeans and her favorite vintage inspired T-shirt. She had truly cleaned and restructured the entire space and was now in the midst of what appeared to be hanging an erasable scheduling board on the wall. Meanwhile, our bulky printer hummed in the back corner, spitting out sheets of paper that seemed to be part of presentation packages.

Val twisted her entire body. "You're here!" she said, her voice resonating with focus and resolve. "Mindful of the carpet, it's still damp," she cautioned us, pointing her finger toward the spot where Bea's tomato soup had been.

Stepping gingerly around the now spotless spot, I stopped and looked around as my watery eyes adjusted to the scene before me.

Val blew a stray piece of blonde hair back from her face, her lips curved into a smile. Clearly, she was in her element, and was a force to be reckoned with. "Hank called and said you were down and out, and we were both worried about you," she said.

"I wanted to make sure you could relax like you're supposed to," Hank said, casually leaning against the doorway.

I patted my hand over my heart, feeling a bit overwhelmed. "Thank you," was all I could manage. I turned back and looked at Val. Out of all my friends, who were more like acquaintances really, Val was the special one. My go-to person who, every single time, replenished my energy rather than draining my social battery like many others often did.

Val nodded towards Bea's desk with a look of mild horror. "That girl was an absolute mess—*oh*, speak of the devil." She snatched her phone off the shelf. "It's Bea finally calling me back. Brace yourselves, folks." Holding up her finger to us, Val dramatically stepped into my office to take the call. I turned my attention back to Bea's once-colorful domain. Gone were the photos, the vibrant explosion of trinkets, and random odds and ends, including her candy jars. And her bright plastic trays for paperwork sat neatly in a box, seemingly ready to be collected.

I was running my fingers over Bea's now dust-free desk when Hank's phone dinged.

As he started reading the message, a mischievously boyish grin appeared on his face. He looked up. "Um, Allie…"

"What? What happened? Tell me…"

"It's a confirmation code."

"A confirmation code? For what?"

"Italy. I got us tickets for May!"

"What? Really?!" I squeaked as a surge of excitement flooded through me.

Hank showed me his phone and pointed to the email he'd just received. "I did promise, didn't I?"

I leaned into him and put my head on his chest. "You certainly did," I said, closing my eyes and envisioning us sipping wine on some vineyard. "Oh my God, Italy?"

"Italy," he confirmed as he wrapped his arms around me and squeezed tight. *Italy, my dream vacation!*

Just then, something occurred to me. "Oh, Hank, that's amazing *but...*"

"*But?*" he said, his concerned expression remained in place.

A perpetual cloud of negativity and anxiety always seemed to surround me after big plans or decisions were made, such as traveling to Italy. I felt trapped in a cycle of *buts* and *excuses*. Each opportunity that arose was met with a mental list of reasons why it wouldn't work or why it was a bad idea. With reluctance and self-doubt pressing down on me, I cleared my throat. "How can I leave the business again so soon, especially if I'm trying to keep new clients happy?"

Hank leaned up against Bea's desk and, as he did, my eyes immediately landed on the bowl of oranges I'd set out on a small, nearby table. Courtesy of Zelda, they were such a cheerful burst of color and a spot of happiness.

"We'll figure it out. You've always wanted to do this, and I'm sorry it took this long," he said.

His words resonated in the air, but my attention was focused on the oranges. As his words slowly faded, my mind began to wander elsewhere. *What was it about those oranges?* Suddenly my mother's voice filled my head, drowning out Hank's talk about Italy completely. *Read the signs, Allie.*

The signs? Yes, the signs!

My mind tumbled through the possibilities. And then my heart skipped a beat when I realized the answer to my problems was staring me in the face. I was about to tell Hank what I had in mind when Val emerged from my office with a self-satisfied grin.

"*Ta-da!*" she exclaimed, practically bouncing on her toes. With her hands planted firmly on her hips, she proudly declared, "That went well, actually. Surprisingly well."

"Really? Was she upset?" I asked, feeling both relieved and horrible at the same time. Letting Bea go was necessary. The constant mishaps were becoming too costly. But Bea was practically family and having had Val do the deed probably seemed cold—but it was the best I could do, given the circumstances.

"Actually, I think she's even more relieved than you are, Allie," Val said, matter-of-factly. "Apparently the stress of the job and all the mistakes she's made has been affecting her health. She was even thinking of quitting but was too afraid to face you. I think she preferred that I was the one who dropped the ax."

I was about to respond when Hank's phone dinged again. "It's Sam," Hank said, reading the message. "Looks like Bea just messaged her. All good," he said, giving me a thumbs up and breaking into a smile, "and, she said she'd love to join us in Italy."

"Really?" I jumped up a bit. "Oh Hank, that would be amazing!" I said. Originally, I thought of this as a romantic getaway for just the two of us, but the second Hank mentioned Samantha, I knew what I really wanted was to be with my family. "I want Cam to come too!" I blurted out.

"Of course," Hank agreed immediately, "let's make it a family affair." Another smile gradually spread across my face, my eyes darting between Hank and Val.

"By the way," I announced, my voice brimming with newfound excitement and optimism, "I have the perfect solution now that Bea's gone."

28 – Are You There, Allie? It's Me, Margaret

Spring was in the air! It might have been a little later than usual, but it was *finally* here. As the sunlight filtered through my office window, casting a warm glow around the room, I felt a sense of confidence and determination, despite the lengthy list of tasks ahead of me.

Squinting at the whiteboard, my head nearly upside down, I finished off the last of my stretches. I marveled at the perfectly legible and logically organized list of tasks my new right hand and design assistant, Zelda, had laid out this morning. My once chaotic office was now an incredibly tight ship. Zelda had taken it upon herself to sync our schedules and made sure I had clear reminders, complete with color coded bullet points, for different tasks associated with client meetings, vendor meetings, staging days, and meetings with her.

Zelda poked her head into my office. "How's the stretching going?" Her cheerful demeanor immediately lifted my spirits. "Ready for lunch?" she asked.

I straightened up and smoothed my shirt. "All done," I said, grinning and feeling a sense of accomplishment. My leg was much better. Hank and Zelda had come up with a clever little reward system that had me sticking to a self-care routine. I was stretching, exercising, and eating better.

"Buddha Bowls with chicken?" she suggested.

"That'd be perfect," I replied gratefully, "but no onions, please." Those artfully arranged and balanced meal bowls seemed to be the go-to for every aspiring yogi these days. There was no denying their deliciousness. I returned to my desk and sank comfortably into my chair, watching Zelda's fingers dance across her phone screen with incredible speed and precision.

"You got it, boss," she replied with a playful wink and a mock salute.

And then, just like that, she was back at her desk taking an incoming call while pounding on her keyboard. Her ability to efficiently and effectively multi-task was quite a sight. To be honest, I couldn't have been prouder of my *future* daughter-in-law. *Yes, I had just casually referred to her as my daughter-in-law. Of course, the key word here is 'future'.*

Clearing the sudden lump from my throat, I settled back in my chair as a soft chime announced the receipt of yet another email. I straightened up when I saw who the sender was. It was Margaret. Her computer skills and comfort with technology had improved dramatically. Why hadn't she just called or scheduled a Zoom meeting? Shifting my hips slightly to ensure I maintained proper posture, and feeling both intrigued and a little apprehensive, I clicked on the email.

Dear Allison,

I anticipate a rather hectic day ahead of me, so I thought I would send you this update by email. Also, because it's not always easy telling you things on Zoom with Henry sitting right there next to you. We girls need our secrets, don't you think? 😌

So, the last time we talked, you asked about Bob. Well, he's certainly proven to be quite a character and while we have had some fun together, I think it's best that we just stick to being friends. He's fun to hang around with and he still makes me laugh, but truth be told, his bad breath and sloppiness makes anything more serious simply impossible. If you ever saw his condo at Whispering Palms, you'd know exactly what I mean. Plus, he has some serious health issues and I'm not looking to be anyone's nursemaid now. Fortunately for him, his latest girlfriend seems perfectly willing to take on the job. 😊

As for Bea, I had every confidence that you'd figure things out. I know I pushed you to give her a chance, but I completely understand why you had to let her go. So does Samantha. I hear the two of them will be doing some traveling together soon. 👍 ✈️

Now, about Zelda. I wanted to say that I owe you an apology. I know you were probably disappointed that I wasn't more helpful to you with 'Project Zelda', but that's because I was busy with another project—I guess you could call it 'Project Allie'. It wasn't anything formal and just kind of developed naturally. The more I got to know Zelda, the more I started to see how similar the two of you are. I thought you'd make a good team if you ever got to know each other. I tried to make sure that you got as many opportunities as possible to see that for yourself and I couldn't be more delighted with the outcome. It really warms my heart to see the two of you getting along so well. Cameron really is lucky to have both of you in his life. 😄

Now, if you don't mind, I'd like to share a little advice, from one seasoned old mother-in-law to her beloved daughter-in-law—because you'll eventually become a mother-in-law yourself. I know mothers-in-law have a reputation for being overprotective of their sons and mean and nasty towards their daughters-in-law. Of course, not all mothers-in-law are like that but I'm ashamed to admit that this was probably what your experience was like with me—just like mine was with my mother-in-law. I want you to know that I am sorry for that. These past five years living and working together have been wonderful. Who would have guessed I'd become a business owner at my age?! 😊

Anyway, here's my advice. First, don't think of yourself as losing a son. That leads to resentment and hostility. See yourself as gaining a daughter and always try to support her dreams. A little encouragement can go a long way. I'm proud of you and your dream. You've been so dedicated and have come so far. I hope you'll do even better now that you have Zelda's support and I hope you'll continue to love doing it. Some mornings, we all could use a little extra motivation to help us get out of bed. 🖤 🖤 🖤

Second, be honest, but not too honest. Honesty can help her grow but being too honest can hurt her feelings. Like when I didn't like that strange looking green polish you put on your toes. Instead of being critical, I could have complimented you about always taking the time to do them. Although, I do think you'd look better in those softer, more natural colors, don't you think? 🙁 *Just remember, in a world where you can be anything, be kind. Your mother told me about that one!* 😊

Third, even if you find that you just can't get along, don't be mean or try to undermine her. I'm genuinely sorry for all the cookbooks I've given you over the years. I should have given you better gifts. Everyone's got their own strengths and weaknesses. Not everyone loves to cook or even finds the slightest enjoyment in it. 👎 *Although, you are a much better cook than you used to be, so maybe they helped.* 👍 *Still, it's best to avoid giving your future daughter-in-law gifts like parenting magazines, gym memberships, and self-help books. If she needs help, she'll ask for it!* 🙏

Okay, that's about it for now. I've decided to come home this weekend. I need to take care of a few things to get ready for the big move down here. When I get back to Florida, I'm going to be staying with your mother until my place is ready. No reason to tell Henry about this though. I'll call him tonight and update him on my plans. Oh, and if you don't hear from me for a few days, don't worry. It just means I'm out enjoying the weather. 😎 😀

With all my love,

Margaret

P.S. Zelda's feedback about having you as her 'boss' has been glowing. It's good to know the business is in such good hands! 😎

I leaned back in my chair with a grin tugging at the corners of my mouth. I read her email a second time. I couldn't help but think about just how much Margaret, and our relationship, had changed over the years. And I'm not just talking about the fact that she'd clearly just fallen in love with emojis. Her message contained a wonderful mix of honesty and candidness, along with a couple of backhanded compliments thrown in for good measure. After all, she might be 'Florida Margaret' now, but she's still 'Margaret'.

Are you there, George? It's me, Allie.

I've come to the conclusion that life is funny. It seems like the more you try to control things, or people, the more miserable you end up. Life is unpredictable and control is an illusion. If I've learned anything over these last five years, it's how much better it is to just flow with the stream. I mean, if you'd told me a couple of months ago that Margaret would become such an independent, carefree person and she'd be moving to Florida at this stage of her life, I would have said you were crazy. And who would have thought that Zelda and I would have ended working together? Certainly not me, especially not after I went a little crazy after our first time meeting. It's funny, I think our family now has its very own Princess Zelda.

You know the saying, that some people can be like onions, with layers you need to peel back? I never quite understood that reference because no matter how many layers you peel, they still smell and taste like onions. Instead, I'd like to think that some people are more like an orange—you just need to peel the tough and bitter skin off to get to the sweet and juicy part inside.

Change is good, but no matter how much life changes, it's good to know that I'll always have you. Talk soon!

Love, Allie xoxo

ABOUT THE AUTHOR

Carolyn Clarke is founder and curator of HenLit Central, a blog focused on 'life and lit'. *And Now There's Zelda* is her second novel after *And Then There's Margaret* (2022). She has been an ESL teacher for over sixteen years and has co-authored several articles and resources with Cambridge University Press and MacMillan Education as well as her award-winning blog *ESL Made Easy*. She lives in Toronto, Canada with her partner, Tony, her two daughters and bulldog, Sophie.

Other Titles by Carolyn Clarke

"Fans of Marilyn Simon Rothstein will devour this one. A fun and relatable debut."
-ROCHELLE WEINSTEIN, *USA Today* and Amazon Bestselling author of *When We Let Go*

THE PERFECT LAUGH OUT LOUD DRAMEDY

AND THEN
THERE'S
MARGARET... A NOVEL

"You can love your
mother-in-law,
doesn't mean you have
to like her..."

CAROLYN CLARKE

NOTE FROM CAROLYN CLARKE

Word-of-mouth is crucial for any author to succeed. If you enjoyed *And Now There's Zelda*, please leave a review online—anywhere you are able. Even if it's just a sentence or two. It would make all the difference and would be very much appreciated.

Thanks!
Carolyn Clarke

We hope you enjoyed reading this title from:

BLACK❀ROSE
writing™

Subscribe to our mailing list – *The Rosevine* – and receive **FREE** books, daily deals, and stay current with news about upcoming releases and our hottest authors.
Scan the QR code below to sign up.

Already a subscriber? Please accept a sincere thank you for being a fan of Black Rose Writing authors.

View other Black Rose Writing titles at www.blackrosewriting.com/books and use promo code **PRINT** to receive a **20% discount** when purchasing.

Made in United States
Orlando, FL
11 July 2024

48855805R00150